Praise for Catherine Cavendish

'If there is a crown for queen of Gothic horror,
[Catherine Cavendish] should be wearing it.'
Modern Horrors

'Cavendish sets the scene exceptionally well and the book
is atmospheric and spooky throughout.'
The British Fantasy Society
on *The Haunting of Henderson Close*

'*The Haunting of Henderson Close* stands
shoulder to shoulder with the Gothic classics.'
Cedar Hollow Horror Reviews

'Cavendish draws from the best conventions of the genre
in this eerie gothic novel about a woman's sanity slowly
unraveling within the hallways of a mysterious mansion.'
Publishers Weekly on *The Garden of Bewitchment*

'Well-rooted in classic gothic traditions, the novel doesn't
furiously spill the blood like most modern horror, but
it maximizes its unique advantages. [...] An atmospheric
and gently scary tale that will appeal to horror fans and
Brontë enthusiasts alike.'
Booklist on *The Garden of Bewitchment*

'A brilliantly written, atmospheric and goosebumpy read.
You'll never look at a doll's house in the same way again!'
thebookwormery on *The Garden of Bewitchment*

'Cavendish breathes new life into familiar horror tropes in this spine-tingling tale of past and present colliding. [...] The story of female resilience at the heart of this well-constructed gothic tale is sure to please fans of women-driven horror.'
Publishers Weekly on *In Darkness, Shadows Breathe*

'A compelling, immersive, and intense time-slip horror novel with sympathetic characters that readers actively root for. The tale reads like *The Devil in. Silver* by Victor LaValle if it were written by Sarah Pinborough.'
Library Journal on *In Darkness, Shadows Breathe*

'An atmospheric read, packed with tension and chilling moments.'
On the Shelf Reviews on *In Darkness, Shadows Breathe*

'An engaging, multigenerational tale of dark magic and the occult.'
Booklist on *Dark Observation*

'If you enjoy gothic horror tales that will keep you on the edge of your seat, you're going to love this!'
Erica Robyn Reads on *The After-Death of Caroline Rand*

'*Those Who Dwell in Mordenhyrst Hall* is a very strong work of Gothic horror and may be Cavendish's best book so far.'
A Reviewer Darkly

'*Those Who Dwell in Mordenhyrst Hall* is a very good historical horror capturing the period and perspective on the classes, mixed in with some very satisfying scenes of horror. Highly enjoyable and well worth your time!'
Runalong the Shelves

CATHERINE CAVENDISH

THE STONES OF LANDANE

This is a **FLAME TREE PRESS** book

Text copyright © 2025 Catherine Cavendish

FLAME TREE PRESS
6 Melbray Mews, London, SW6 3NS, UK
flametreepress.com

US sales, distribution and warehouse:
Simon & Schuster
simonandschuster.biz

UK distribution and warehouse:
Hachette UK Distribution
hukdcustomerservice@hachette.co.uk

Publisher's Note: This is a work of fiction. Names, characters, places, and
incidents are a product of the author's imagination. Locales and public names
are sometimes used for atmospheric purposes. Any resemblance to actual
people, living or dead, or to businesses, companies, events, institutions, or
locales is completely coincidental.

Thanks to the Flame Tree Press team.

The cover is created by Flame Tree Studio with elements
courtesy of Shutterstock.com and: Aastels, Kseniya Ivashkevich, Vitaly
Kravchenko, zhuxiaophotography.
The font families used are Avenir and Bembo.

Flame Tree Press is an imprint of Flame Tree Publishing Ltd
flametreepublishing.com

A copy of the CIP data for this book is available from the British Library
and the Library of Congress.

PB ISBN: 978-1-78758-890-5
HB ISBN: 978-1-78758-891-2
ebook ISBN: 978-1-78758-892-9

Printed and bound in Great Britain by Clays Ltd, Elcograf S.p.A.

CATHERINE CAVENDISH

THE STONES
OF LANDANE

FLAME TREE PRESS
London & New York

For Colin

From our handfasting at the Ring of Brodgar to the
Barber Stone in Avebury, you have indulged my
never-diminishing obsession with standing stones.
Thank you for sharing the journey and my life.

CHAPTER ONE

Nadia

The (Almost) Present

I can't tell you the first time I laid eyes on the Neolithic circle of majestic standing stones that had graced the rural hamlet of Landane for millennia. It seemed I had always known them, those magnificent sarsens towering above my head. I nearly convinced myself that I had been created by them. That somehow, incredible and impossible as it might seem, they had given birth to me. How stupidly fanciful is that? Yet now, as I drive closer, I feel that old rush of excitement flowing through my veins as it has since…well, forever.

It's a feeling, a real sense of coming home. And I know that sounds crazy. Here we are in the south of England, yet I have lived all my life in the north, two hundred and fifty miles away. But much as I love the Pennines and their rugged beauty, I never felt I truly belonged there. Recently, I have come to realize that, only when I am in Landane, surrounded by those ancient stones, do I feel grounded, at home, where I belong. Even if it isn't always easy.

Safe? Is that the right word? Maybe not *safe* exactly but…protected, shielded from something I don't understand. Something I have never understood. It exists on the edge of my sight. I can't quite see it, but it's there. Like a fleeting shadow. When it happens, it's for a split second only. So fleeting that I am left unsure of whether it even happened. And it can occur at any time, without warning. Like that day at work….

I don't have a fancy job. I work as a sales assistant in a branch of a chain of high street pharmacies. One day, I was advising a customer on which type of moisturizer might suit her best when, out of the corner of my eye, it...whatever it was...flashed by. I let out a little cry. I didn't mean to. It just happened and it scared the wits out of the poor woman. Next thing, she summoned the manager, not to complain but to express her concern for my well-being. I was duly bundled off home for the remainder of the day and told to make sure I had a good rest, despite my protestations that I was perfectly all right. Evidently, my shocked face and the color draining out of my normally olive skin led him to think otherwise.

"You look like you've seen a ghost, Nadia," he said, so I suppose I must have. And he wasn't far off the truth anyway.

We have just whizzed past a road sign. Landane's only five miles away. Beside me, my partner, Jonathan, has fallen asleep. He did the lion's share of the driving this time. We've been together for over three years and even briefly considered marriage, but decided it wasn't for us. Likewise with children. I never felt maternal, and Jonathan's first marriage broke up because he had no desire to be a father. I have always believed that if the feeling's not there, you can't force it. Anyway, by the time I met him he had already had a vasectomy, so that was quite a relief.

Four miles now. My nerve endings are tingling. It's as if the stones are calling to me. They always have. It's been two years but I always knew I would return. They knew too. I only wish it wasn't under such sad circumstances but...well, I'm here now and this time feels different, as if something important is going to happen. No, important isn't a strong enough word. Life-changing. Monumental....

Jonathan stirs. He opens his eyes, yawns and stretches. "This looks familiar," he says. I wish he could sound more enthusiastic.

Both sides of the road are bordered by fertile hedges, resplendent in their bright green spring foliage. It's late April and the sun is shining.

It's late April and I'm coming home.

CHAPTER TWO

Jonathan

How We Began

When I first met Nadia Gale, it was as if I had known her all my life. You know that feeling you get when you find yourself so immersed in conversation that you lose all track of time? It was like that. It was odd too that we should meet at a party when neither of us could ever be described as a party animal. In my line of work, as a journalist, I have had to attend my fair share of them. Not as many these days since I went freelance and mostly work online, but back then I was a reporter working on the local rag and dreaming of better days, bigger fish.

I was fresh out of a marriage that should never have happened in the first place. A well-meaning friend had used all his powers of persuasion to nudge, cajole, persuade and then bulldoze me into accepting an invitation to his housewarming. I very nearly backed out at the last minute but gave myself a severe talking to and called a taxi before I could change my mind.

Ten minutes later, Jake introduced me to the most amazing woman in the room.

"This is Nadia. She lives next door."

I didn't hear what he said after that. I was captivated by her eyes. Okay, I know that sounds like the plot of a cheap romance novel, but this time, I swear it was true. She had these clear hazel eyes, fringed with dark lashes, and her hair hung glossy, shiny and black over her shoulders. When she smiled at me and ran her long, slender fingers through it, I had an almost irresistible urge to kiss her. Needless to say, I fought that urge, but it wasn't easy.

Armed with large glasses of an indeterminate red wine, we found a sofa sufficiently far away from the melee so that we could hear ourselves speak. The music wasn't too loud, the thirty or so other guests were far too wrapped up in themselves and each other to pay us any attention and we talked, listened, took sips of wine, then talked and listened all over again.

Over the course of around four hours, I discovered that she was single, thirty-three years old, born on Friday 13th November, had studied for a degree in history, but dropped out of university after two years. She was an only child and an 'anomaly' as she put it. Both parents were fair-haired, and light-skinned. She, on the other hand, had black hair and a Mediterranean skin tone. I got the distinct impression this had led to her feeling as if she didn't belong somehow.

Nadia had lived alone for the past thirteen years – a free and independent spirit, she told me, and I had no reason to doubt her. She was a sales assistant by day, advising women on makeup, perfume, and every cosmetic preparation on the market. The job was interesting, she said. She met a wide range of people. The pay covered her needs without a lot to spare, but from the way she spoke, I knew materialism wasn't her top priority. Neither was the latest scent by Yves Saint Laurent or Dior.

It was when she talked about her interests that those hazel eyes lit with such an intense fire, she drew me in and took me with her. As she spoke, I became entranced by her descriptions of circles of standing stones and the power they exuded. Power, it seemed, she could somehow tap into. As I write this now, I can see how crazy that makes me sound. Any geologist would have a field day with me. Those massive blocks of stone, each one weighing goodness alone knows how many tons, dragged into position by a labor force numbering in the dozens, if not more, for some purpose long since forgotten. How could they possess supernatural powers or the ability to transmit forces drawn from…who knows where?

But Nadia was sure. She was so certain. More than that, she offered to take me to the place where she had first 'realized' their unique and special power.

Landane.

I had heard of it, of course. There are so many stone circles and the like dotted around the landscape of the British Isles, but only a few have earned the status of household names. Stonehenge, the Ring of Brodgar and Callanish in Scotland. And Landane.

We would go there, she said. She would show me 'her' stones.

It was around then that Jake appeared with a bottle of red wine in hand.

"Well, you two seem to be getting on like a house on fire," he said. "Have a top-up."

It was as if he had broken a trance. The room had gone quiet. The music played softly in the background – an old Captain and Tennille song, 'Do That to Me One More Time'. All the other guests had departed and a swift glance at my watch showed me why. It was one-thirty in the morning.

I declined his offer of a drink. "I have to get back home. Work tomorrow and a lunchtime deadline. Not all of us get the weekends off, you know." I thanked him and his partner, Mario, for a lovely evening and left with Nadia.

I don't remember either of us suggesting she come home with me that night but we both seemed to know she would.

We fitted together perfectly, as if we had known each other for years. As that spring became summer, she mentioned Landane again and again but my work was relentless then. Truth be told, I didn't exactly need too many excuses to get out of a trip wandering around standing stones. The thought didn't appeal to me in the slightest, but the months went by and a year after we met, I simply ran out of excuses. The decision was made. We would spend a few days in Landane staying at the local pub, The White Hart. Nadia made the reservations before I had time to change my mind. I heard her on the phone, talking to the landlord as if speaking to an old friend. She told me she had lost track of how many times she had stayed there, but this would be the first time she had ever taken anyone with her.

The booking was made for July. When we set off bright and early in my car, the weather was warm, sunny and perfect. I squeezed her hand and moved a stray lock of hair out of her eyes. She smiled at me, caught my hand in hers and kissed it. "You're going to love Landane," she said in her soft voice. "And Landane is going to love you."

★　　★　　★

Approaching Landane for the first time is an unforgettable experience, even to a total philistine like me. Coming off the motorway onto a single carriageway main road, you wend your way around sharp bends, fields of wheat and barley on either side, interspersed with cattle grazing in green pastures. Trees, hedgerows, and the occasional parking place for weary drivers to stretch their legs for a few minutes all add to the pleasant, timeless rural landscape. Breaks in the tree cover allow for views stretching for miles over gently rolling green hills.

And then you see it.

Landane Mound is an impressive man-made structure resembling a conical hill and is some four thousand years old. It somehow manages to blend in completely with its surroundings, yet still retain an air of having been plonked down there by some alien race in ancient times. I really shouldn't have read Erich von Däniken quite so avidly all those years ago.

"Pull over. Pull over!" In the time we had been together I had never heard Nadia so excited. "There's a small car park. There!"

I saw it and just had time to signal and move over, earning myself a loud honking of another driver's horn accompanied by some furious and highly explicit hand gestures. I had no sympathy for him. After all, he shouldn't have been so close up behind me in the first place. I gesticulated back, using a gesture I had picked up on holiday in Italy.

Nadia laughed.

I switched off the engine and we climbed out of the car. We were alone, the only sound to disturb the peace being the occasional vehicle passing us on the road. As we negotiated our way along a narrow stony path taking us closer to the mound, I began to get a much better appreciation of the scale of the structure.

"There used to be a moat all around it but that dried up when they altered the course of the river," Nadia said. "The ground is marshy though, so we need to keep to the path."

I let her lead. The closer we got, the more I felt something I had never experienced. It was as if I was being drawn in by a magnet. A gentle breeze blew, but suddenly I found it hard to breathe. I bent double, gasping, trying to fill my lungs and failing. Panic rose inside me. I was suffocating for lack of oxygen and yet it was all around me. Fresh, clean, sweet country air, but it seemed I could get none of it.

Nadia put her arm around me. "Don't worry. It'll soon pass. It's always this way at first. Next time you won't feel it."

The sensation was so unpleasant, I wondered if there ever would be a next time, but I hadn't enough air left in my lungs to voice this.

"Oh, poor Jonathan," she said, cradling my head.

Darkness, like a fuzzy black veil, descended on me. A loud buzzing as from a hive full of bees echoed through my head.

Nadia kissed me full on the lips, and suddenly I could breathe again. She broke away so I could cough and splutter the air back into my straining body. The buzzing stopped. I blinked in the sunlight and there, only for a second, I swear I saw her in a different light. Not as I knew her, but as she might have looked many lifetimes ago, back when Landane Mound was being built, swathed in animal furs, her arms raised to the sun, her face shining with reflected light. And then the vision was gone.

"Jonathan? Are you all right now?"

I couldn't speak. I put my arms around her and held her to me so tightly I felt her flinch. I lessened my grip and she pulled away. Her expression was concern mixed with surprise, maybe a little shock.

"Perhaps I was wrong to bring you here," she said. "I thought...."

This place means so much to me, I hoped we could share it and you would grow to love it as much as I do, but maybe that's not possible."

"No, you weren't wrong. I don't know what that was, but it's passed now. I'm fine and Landane Mound is magnificent. We'll come back tomorrow, but let's get checked in at The White Hart and have something to eat. I'm probably just tired from the driving."

"That's my fault. We should have switched over when we stopped at the service station. I'll drive us the rest of the way – not that it's far. Only a mile and we're there. Back when it was constructed, Landane Mound was probably some kind of beacon guiding people to the stone circle. It would have really stood out in this flat landscape. Of course, it would have been as white as the Cliffs of Dover back then. Its outer construction is all chalk. Over the centuries grass has grown over it, but it must have been quite something. You wouldn't miss it."

"I doubt you could miss it now," I said, looking back over my shoulder as we started back to the car.

She had been right to change the subject. Concentrating on her words and the information she gave helped take my mind off the peculiar experience that had so affected me.

Nadia smiled and we were back on track. I had scared her. Hell, I'd scared myself. I gave an involuntary shudder and hoped she hadn't noticed.

★   ★   ★

The proprietor of The White Hart greeted her with a hug. "Hello, Nadia. So lovely to see you again."

"Hello, Ken. Good to see you again too. This is Jonathan, my boyfriend. It's his first time in Landane."

"Well, I sincerely hope it won't be your last. Welcome to The White Hart, Jonathan." The middle-aged man with a broad grin shook my hand and steered us to the bar, where he took down a twinlock file and proceeded to handle our registration the old-fashioned way. "My accountant says I have to start getting all this on the computer but I keep putting it off. Hopefully my son will sort it out for me when he gets back from university next month. He's promised to get me set up with something called Excel? Is that right?"

I nodded. "It's a standard spreadsheet program. You'll soon get the hang of it."

Ken shook his head. "I doubt that. I really do. At Easter he tried to get me using something called Access. He kept rattling on about relational databases and how it was going to make my life much more straightforward. By the time he'd finished I felt like I'd gone six rounds with Mike Tyson."

"I'm not surprised," I said. "Anyway, you don't need that. Any accountant will be more than happy if you submit your accounts on an Excel spreadsheet."

Ken gave a wry smile and nodded at Nadia. "Does any of it make sense to you?"

Nadia laughed. "Not really. But then I don't run my own business."

"Neither do I…yet," I said. "But it's good to try and keep up with technology if you can. Within reason anyway."

"I'll take your word for it." Ken handed me a pen and I duly signed on the dotted line. He then took the ledger and slid it under the bar. I swapped the pen for the room key and Nadia led the way upstairs.

The White Hart was exactly what you would expect from a mostly fifteenth- and sixteenth-century amalgam of a village inn. Low ceilings and original exposed timbers, with an array of small bars leading from one to another before rambling off around corners. A narrow, carpeted staircase took us to the upper floor, where uneven floors creaked when you so much as looked at them and protested when you put your foot down.

Our room smelled pleasantly fresh and well aired. The ceiling was lower up here than downstairs and the first thing I did on crossing the threshold was bash my head on the timber doorframe. My exclamation of "Fucking hell, that bloody hurt" received scant sympathy.

"That's what you get for being six-foot-two," Nadia said. "People were shorter back when this was built."

I grimaced and rubbed my sore head. After that I took to stooping, with my shoes off.

Everything about the room was in keeping with its age except the modern duvet that topped the oak four-poster bed. The windows were small with chintzy curtains, a little twee for my taste, but they suited the general ambience. Nadia opened a door to reveal a closet with plenty of hangers.

The second door led to the bathroom. It creaked and groaned like an old man with constipation. "We'd better keep that open at night or we'll wake each other up if we need the loo," I said. I peered around the door. An old-fashioned bath with clawed feet promised a wallow after a day's walking. The shower was in the corner of the room and seemed out of place as it was unashamedly modern, but at least Ken was doing his best to cater for changing tastes. An array of white fluffy towels adorned the towel rail that was heated without burning your hand.

"I think I'm going to like it here," I said, circling Nadia's waist with my hands.

She nestled into me and before long we had christened the room in our own special, intimate way.

★   ★   ★

Not every pub can boast a view of the remains of an ancient stone circle, but then not many pubs have one at the bottom of their garden. It was Monday and the sun was dipping down, ready for its final descent into sunset on a wonderfully balmy summer night. We were alone, mellow from the effects of a bottle of Merlot and a couple of brandies, and replete from a delicious homemade fish pie. A whole choir of songbirds twittered happily and I recognized the distinctive trill of a blackbird, but the identities of the others were a happy mystery.

"It's so peaceful here," I said, "I can see why you keep coming back."

Nadia took a sip of wine. "It *is* peaceful, but that's not why I keep coming back. I have to."

"You *have* to?"

"I know. I sound crazy, don't I? But it's true. I keep being drawn back here as if Landane's a kind of magnet. I've thought many times about moving here permanently. Maybe I should. What do you think? Could you be happy living here?"

I didn't see that one coming and my face must have registered the surprise I was feeling because she turned away from me.

I covered her hand with mine. "I'm sorry, Nadia. You startled me. I had no idea you felt like that. Are you serious?"

She looked back at me, a lock of hair falling over her face as it so often did. She nodded. "I am, but…sadly I don't see how to make it work, financially. I mean, look at this place." She waved her free hand expansively. "There aren't exactly hundreds of jobs going. It's a tiny hamlet in a rural community and I know nothing whatsoever about any aspect of farming or anything else, for that matter. There's one shop, this pub and that's it."

"Maybe Ken needs an extra pair of hands."

"The White Hart is strictly a family business. His wife, Jackie, does the cooking, his older son and daughter are the waiters and bar staff, and everyone mucks in with the guest rooms. And before you suggest the shop, I asked. It's been in the same family for generations. In fact, they can trace their ancestry back to the eighteenth century when some property speculator called Robinson started felling and breaking up the stones in the circle for building material. The shop and the cottages along the main street were all built by him. Mr. Merrick, who owns the shop, told me that his umpteenth great grandfather was one of the laborers Robinson brought in to do the felling. Living here is just a dream of mine. One day maybe, but I can't see how it would ever work. So, until then I keep coming back as often as I can. To go a whole year is possibly the longest gap I can remember since my early twenties. If you hadn't agreed to come when you did…." She let her words hang there for a few seconds.

Would she simply have come down here by herself? Possibly. But that hadn't happened. We were here now.

"Anyway, as I say, living here is a pipe dream."

I can't say it wasn't a relief. Much as I liked the place, and loved Nadia, I had no inclination to swap my town life for a rural idyll that would see me bored out of my brain within six months. Less even. What would that do to our relationship?

Nadia drained her glass and jumped up. She grabbed my hand. "Come on. Everyone will have gone home now. It's the perfect time for me to introduce you to the stones."

Her enthusiasm was infectious, much as I was perfectly content at that moment to relax for the rest of the evening. I held her hand, marveling as always at the touch of her smooth, warm skin. We half-ran to the stile that took us into the field where the stones of Landane ruled supreme.

Nadia was right. An hour earlier, there had been tourists by every megalith, some hugging them, touching them, trying to tune into the magnetic energy they believed was contained within them, most taking photos of themselves standing in front of this stone or that one as people must have done since photography was first invented.

"I'm going to take you to my favorite stone," Nadia said. "There's a legend about it. I'll tell you when we get there."

I lengthened my stride to keep up with her. She had changed from being a mature, sensible thirty-four-year-old woman into a sixteen-year-old girl in a matter of a few minutes. I wasn't sure I welcomed the transformation. It made me feel far older than the couple of years that separated us.

We passed one stone after the other. I couldn't see much difference between them. Each was at least twelve feet tall, broad, and didn't look as if they had been chiseled in any way. How on earth the prehistoric builders had transported them there, let alone stood them up on end and lowered them into their prepared foundations, I had no idea. And why do it in the first place? Religion? Maybe. That was the popular theory anyway. It certainly seemed to work for Stonehenge.

"You must look at that one, Jonathan. If you stand where I am now, and especially with the light fading as it is, it looks just like a hooded monk."

I duly stood right next to her and peered at the megalith. It took a moment but then I saw what she saw. A stone monk, head bowed and concealed under a hood. The resemblance was uncanny. I shivered.

"You're not cold, are you?" she asked. "It's still quite warm. We can go back if you want."

But she didn't want to, so I shook my head. "It's not that. You're right. It looks a lot like a hooded monk."

"Imagine if he came to life. Imagine if he moved. Right *now*."

I nearly jumped out of my skin. "My God, Nadia, warn me when you're going to do that, will you? You scared the life out of me."

She laughed like a schoolgirl. "Warn you? Where would be the fun in that? Oh, your face. It's a picture!" The giggling seemed unstoppable. It unnerved me. Coming from her it didn't feel right.

"Nadia, please." I put a restraining hand on her shoulder. She shrugged it off like a petulant child. I froze for a second. This was a Nadia I had never met before. I almost felt as if I was in the company of a stranger, not the woman I hoped to spend the rest of my life with.

"Come and meet *my* stone." She skipped. Yes, *skipped* to the next sarsen. I followed her, relieved that at least that insane laughter had ceased.

Her stone was different. It was as big as its neighbors on either side but instead of being basically straight and lozenge-shaped, one side was slanted so that it resembled one half of a diamond.

"Jonathan, meet the surgeon's stone. Surgeon's stone, meet Jonathan." That irritating tinkle of laughter punctuated her introduction.

"Nadia. Please."

"Say hello to the stone, Jonathan."

"Hello, stone."

"That's better. The stone says 'hello' back."

I stared at her. Was she simply playing a juvenile game with me? The trouble was that when she had instructed me to greet the stone, her expression had been deadly serious. Maybe I simply didn't know her as well as I thought I did. Fifteen months was hardly a lifetime of getting to know each other.

Nadia seemed to be studying my expression for some reason. I didn't know why, and it made me uncomfortable. All around us, the light was fading, and it was so quiet. Impossibly quiet. Then I realized. The birds had stopped singing. It felt unnatural. As if something was waiting to happen. Whether Nadia sensed it too, I couldn't guess. Her expression didn't change. Her eyes never wavered from mine until she spoke.

"See these holes?" She indicated some small, perfectly round indentations in the stone.

"Yes," I said.

"The stone made them. If you put your finger in, you'll feel something. Try it."

I moved up close to the stone until I almost touched it. A strange sensation of being too close to some source of power came over me. Unpleasant. It made the hairs on my arms prickle.

"Now put your forefinger in the hole there."

I backed away. "Maybe tomorrow. It's almost dark now, Nadia. Let's call it a day."

"No. It has to be in the evening or at night. After sunset and before dawn. The energy is different."

Against my better judgment, I stuck my finger in the hole. At first there was nothing. Then a strange tickling started on my fingertip and spread rapidly up to the knuckle. I withdrew my finger and stared at it, expecting to see some insect wriggling away. But there was nothing. Nadia was doubled up with laughter.

"My stone likes you," she said.

I stared at her incredulously. "What did you say?"

"I said my stone likes you. Look, you have to see this."

Nadia pressed her body against the stone. Almost as if she was caressing her lover and so intense that I felt a wave of ridiculous jealousy. She nuzzled the stone and then spread the fingers of her right hand over three of the small holes. "Watch carefully," she said.

I stared as her fingers seemed to elongate then retract twice. It had to be a trick of the murky dusk because, for a second, I was sure her whole hand became transparent. I could see the stone through it.

"Stop it, Nadia. Stop it *now!*" I grabbed her and an electric shock shot through my body, flinging me back onto the ground.

I lay there stunned. Nadia's face looked down at me. She had detached herself from the stone and was now kneeling beside me. "Jonathan, are you all right?"

I sat up and let her help me stand. My legs buckled under me.

"We'll go back. I'll help you," she said.

"What the hell was all that about?" My voice was as unsteady as I was. I concentrated hard on keeping upright, but it took every bit of effort I possessed to stop me from collapsing under the weight of my own body.

"It's magnetic energy. The stones generate it somehow, but it only happens after sunset, and I don't think it affects everyone the same way. I seem to be particularly sensitive for some reason. I've no idea why."

Finally, my legs obeyed me and I stood straight and firm again. "Remind me again why it is you love it here so much?"

My weak attempt at humor apparently resonated with her. When she laughed this time, it was the usual Nadia laugh, not that odd parody of a child from a few minutes earlier. Thankfully, that had departed, leaving my girlfriend back in charge. Silently I thanked whatever deity might be listening and took a deep, calming breath.

★   ★   ★

"You look like you've had a nasty shock," Ken said, taking in my disheveled appearance. "Have a seat. I'll bring you a brandy."

He shot a questioning glance at Nadia, but as she had her back to me, I couldn't see her reaction.

"I'll have one too please," she said, and two large Courvoisiers arrived moments later.

"So, what have you two been up to then?" Ken asked.

"We went to the stones," Nadia said. "And you're right, Jonathan did have a bit of a shock."

"Of course. It's your first time," Ken said. "Nothing ever prepares you for it."

"So, you've experienced it too?" I said.

"Oh, aye. It's a sort of rite of passage around here. Of course, it's mostly a local tradition the tourists don't know about, but Nadia here discovered it by accident and now she's shown you."

I took a swig of the drink. It burned and then warmed me. A pleasant glow spread through my veins. "Does that make me part of some exclusive club or society then?"

Ken smiled. "No, nothing like that. It simply means you've done something our ancestors have done for centuries. That's all. Nature's strange and wonderful, isn't it?"

"In this case, I think it's rather more strange than wonderful."

Ken nodded, smiled and went back behind the bar to serve a customer who had just wandered in.

"Sorry," Nadia said. "That was unforgiveable of me. I should have warned you not to touch me when I'm up close and personal with the stones, especially *that* stone."

"Why that one particularly?"

She took another swig and shrugged. "I don't know. I was…drawn to it is probably the best way I can describe it. It sounds crazy but it's as if the stone chose me."

"What do you feel when you're close to it like that?"

"I feel safe. At home. It's where I belong. The only place I belong."

The loneliness of her words hit me like a punch to the stomach. Her right hand lay limply on the table. I clasped it and drew it to my lips. Her skin tasted salty where it had touched the stone. "You've got *me* now, Nadia. You're safe. You belong."

She smiled. But there were tears in her eyes.

CHAPTER THREE

I woke suddenly. The room was shrouded in darkness and I wanted to simply go back to sleep, but increasing pressure in my bladder dictated otherwise. If I switched on the bedside lamp, I risked waking Nadia, who was sleeping soundly. A sliver of moonlight cast a silvery glow diagonally across the carpet, so I slid out of bed and aimed for it. Fortunately, there was nothing in my way. Equally fortunately, there was no one to see a six-foot-two, naked, thirty-six-year-old man staggering around in the dark as I felt my way to the bathroom. There it was clear I would have to risk the creaking hinges. No way would I manage to relieve myself without some illumination.

As gently as I could, I pushed the door closed. The hinges protested and I heard Nadia stir. I waited, doing my best to ignore the increasing urgency of my full bladder. Silence. I pushed again and the door closed with a slight click. I flicked the switch and the bright light made me blink.

In a few seconds, I was washing my hands and caught a glimpse of myself in the mirror. Behind me seemed strangely dark. I looked down to turn off the taps and reached for a towel from the rail on the wall next to me. I almost dropped it. Someone had moved close up behind me. Warm hands slid around my waist. I glanced up at the mirror. Everything behind me was cast in shadow and I could see no one else there. But my reflection was out of sync. I moved and a split second later my reflection moved. I must have been in a state of fugue between sleep and wakefulness and my brain was playing tricks on me. I blinked and looked once more into the mirror, where everything had returned to normal as if I had imagined it all. The darkness had vanished and I could see the shower behind me where it had been lost in a gray murk. More than that, I no longer felt the arms around my waist.

Fearful that it would all change back again, I switched off the light and opened the door, but I had forgotten the hinges and they gave a loud creak. Nadia's bedside lamp switched on and she hoisted herself up, peering at me through sleep-filled eyes. "Are you okay, Jonathan?"

"Sorry. I forgot the damned door. Go back to sleep. Everything's fine."

Maybe my voice betrayed me because she hesitated before fatigue won out and she lay back down, asleep before I made it back into bed. Her lamp was still on. I left it that way.

★   ★   ★

"You look so tired," Nadia said as we made our way along a path that stretched for nearly a mile from where we had parked the car. We were bound for an ancient burial site – a chambered tomb where, a century earlier, the remains of more than forty people had been found.

"I didn't sleep too well," I said. "Weird dreams."

"My lamp was on when I got up," Nadia said. "I vaguely remember you coming out of the bathroom."

"You were so sleepy I thought I'd just leave it. I'd already disturbed you, so I thought it would only make it worse if I started scrambling around."

Nadia smiled.

"Come on then," I said, "tell me about this place."

"Okay then. Here's the history bit. Moreton Landane is a Neolithic chambered tomb built around five and a half thousand years ago. It seems to have been a place where the dead would have been venerated but was probably only in use for around a thousand years before they sealed it up. The odd thing is the archeologists only found partial remains. It's likely that there were a number of stages in the burial process and that the barrows were an important part of the ritual."

"If they only found partial remains, which bits were missing?"

"It varied. There weren't enough skulls for a start. In some cases, there were leg bones but no arm bones. Ribs were missing on some but not others. It could be that when a person died, their body was exposed to the elements. A sky burial, like they did in Tibet and elsewhere, where the body is left to decompose in the open air, usually on a hill. It would explain the missing bones because they could have been carried off by scavenging birds or animals."

Nadia stopped. We had reached our destination. Ahead of us, three massive sarsen stones, that could have easily enhanced the stone circle at Landane, towered above us.

"This way," Nadia said. She weaved around the first stone and I followed her, my feet scrunching the gravel-strewn path as we negotiated two more stones that acted as sentinels either side of the narrow entrance.

The contrast of warm, bright sunshine outside with the cool, sepulchral darkness within was striking. Around us on three sides were walls constructed of expertly matched, weighty stones laid as if the tomb had only been constructed yesterday. "This is one hell of a restoration job," I said.

"Oh, there's been no restoration. They built it this way. These people were master stonemasons. Look up at the ceiling."

I did so. All I could do was marvel. "How the hell did they get those stones up there and position them like that? Each one must weigh tons." My voice echoed. With no one else around, the place was eerily quiet. The stones provided wonderful insulation so that no external sound penetrated. Here was a place of tranquility. I lowered my voice. "I don't know how they could do it. They only had primitive tools like deer antlers, flints and stone axes to work with."

"They knew what they were doing, and it was important to them."

I noticed Nadia was whispering too. Moreton Landane exerted a strong influence even after all these centuries. I wandered a little ahead of her, stepping into semicircular chambers, noting the shelves built into the walls. I felt Nadia at my elbow. "Is that where they put the bones?" I asked.

Her voice came from outside the chamber. "Sorry? I didn't catch that."

I gave a jump as Nadia entered.

"I could have sworn you were just here. Standing next to me."

She shook her head. "No, I was out in the main passageway."

"But...." It was no good. I had imagined it. This was a spooky place, so no wonder my imagination was fired up. "I asked whether these shelves were where they put the bones."

"Yes. I believe so. A lot of them anyway. Skulls mostly, I think."

"And to this day we don't really know why they did any of this."

Nadia shook her head. "There are lots of theories but, as there are no written records, I don't suppose we'll ever know for sure."

"Do you have any theories?"

Nadia laughed, the sound echoing and bouncing off the walls. "Plenty, like everyone else," she said at last. "I don't subscribe to the human sacrifice theory, nor do I think that it had anything to do with aliens from outer space. Personally, I believe that Moreton Landane, like others around the country, was a place of the Noble Dead. Tribal leaders, shamen, that sort of thing; people who were venerated, maybe even worshiped in life. When they died, their spirits lived on, and the general population would gather at Landane for rituals and Moreton Landane was part of that. Maybe at Landane they worshiped life and here they celebrated the dead."

"Or the other way round."

"I doubt it. There are no burials at Landane. Well, only one. I never did tell you the legend of the surgeon, did I? The surgeon's stone was lying where it had fallen – or had been deliberately toppled in an earlier century – when archeologists excavated early in the last century. When they lifted it, they found the skeleton of a man who had various tools with him in what had obviously been some kind of leather bag attached to his waist. From these they determined he was probably an itinerant surgeon who had come along to Landane to see if anyone needed a tooth pulled or a boil lanced back in the fourteenth century and had become involved with a stone felling. You know, like that Robinson man who built the cottages and the shop two or three hundred years later. Unfortunately for him, though, the stone must have toppled and landed on him, so they left him there, buried under it."

"Some gravestone."

Nadia nodded. "When they found him, they gave him a proper burial, but you can see a plaster cast of him in the museum. It's pretty lifelike."

We moved out of the chamber and farther along until we came to a dead end. "There's more of this surely, isn't there?" I asked.

"Much more, but it's never been excavated. You can see from the outside that the barrow continues, but so much has collapsed that it would take a great deal of money and time to excavate thoroughly. Plus, this is actually on private land. There's a public right of way that we came up, but the barrow itself belongs to the local farmer. Maybe he doesn't want a posse of archeologists and enthusiastic students, not to mention a load of New Age hippies, trampling around his meadows."

It was so dark at that end of the barrow I could barely make out the two small chambers on either side of the passageway. Then there was a sudden burst of light.

"Good job one of us thought ahead," Nadia said, and waved her flashlight around.

Out of nowhere, a face gleamed a ghostly greenish white. I gasped, "What the hell?"

"What's the matter, Jonathan?"

My mouth had dried up and I couldn't speak. I pointed at the apparition, but even as I did so, it faded and a second later was no longer to be seen. I moved my dry tongue around my mouth in an attempt to stimulate some saliva. Finally, I could speak. "Didn't you see that? You must have seen that."

"What?"

"On the wall. Some kind of…. Nadia, I don't know what it was, but there was something there. I swear it. It was a figure…like a photographic negative. You've seen pictures of the Turin Shroud?

Like that." I shuddered. "Come on, let's get out of here. This place is getting to me."

She stepped aside to let me pass, her face expressionless. I couldn't get out fast enough. My heart beat so fast I thought it would explode any second. Once outside, I swerved around the stones and sat down heavily on the grass verge.

Nadia joined me and squatted down. "Whatever's wrong?"

I tried to explain but out there in the open air with the warm sun, gentle breeze and soft smell of wildflowers, my story seemed as ridiculous as it must sound. She heard me out and at least she didn't tell me I was stupid.

"It's a strange place and it's your first time in there. It's easy to see things, especially with me switching the flashlight on without warning. I didn't see anything out of the ordinary, but then I didn't have a disturbed night. Come on, let's go back to Landane and get a coffee."

"Good idea. Maybe it'll flush the cobwebs out of my brain." At least, once I had put into words what I had seen, I had more perspective. It had been an illusion; my brain playing tricks on me. I could smile now. And my heart had stopped racing. As for my imagination? I would have to keep it in check.

★   ★   ★

Back at The White Hart we went up to our room to take off our boots and don some lighter footwear. An afternoon mooching around the museum seemed in order and would give me more of a handle on the surrounding area and its vast history.

I was in the bathroom, combing my hair, when Nadia sidled in, naked. She stood right behind me, and I closed my eyes to savor her nearness. I felt her hands slide gently around my waist...as my world went black.

CHAPTER FOUR

"There's nothing wrong, honestly, Nadia." I could tell she didn't believe me. It was hard to sound convincing when my insides felt as if they were being wrenched apart. I kept telling myself it wasn't her fault I had had that waking dream or whatever it was in the bathroom. When I regained consciousness and staggered out of there, my watch showed barely a minute had elapsed. She was standing, fully dressed, hair neatly groomed, staring out of the window. She heard my gasps for breath and spun round, her face registering the shock my odd appearance must have caused her. As she couldn't be in two places at once, it couldn't have been her in the bathroom. Hell, I couldn't even bring myself to tell her about my peculiar experience. Whenever I tried, the words would not come. Or those I could think of uttering made no sense. In fact, precious little of anything had made sense since we had set foot in Landane. Three more days and then we could return to civilization. Would we make it?

"As long as you're sure," she said, stroking my cheek. "You're so pale. You look as if you saw a ghost in there." I squeezed her hand and kissed her fingers, savoring her warmth. A stupid illusion, a mind game of my brain's creation. A little worrying because this wasn't a condition I was used to and it seemed to be happening too frequently right now, but this, Nadia's concern, the love I read in her eyes, the warmth of her skin and the soft touch of her caress...this was the Nadia I knew. At that moment, everything fell back into perspective. I had been letting the unique atmosphere of Landane get to me. I had to make that stop.

We made our way up the main street to the museum. A few tourists spilled out onto the road. A car passed traveling too fast and honked its horn at a couple of elderly women who had strayed into its path. Their angry and shocked expressions no doubt concealed their inner fear that they could have just been mowed down by a speeding BMW.

"It's always a Beamer, isn't it?" Nadia said. "I've often wondered, is it the car that makes the person like that or is it simply the type of person who's attracted to that type of car?"

"They're not all like that. I had a BMW once. Never knowingly ran down any old ladies. Or young ones, come to that. I did have an altercation with a squirrel once. He got away."

It was good to laugh together again and we made the rest of the way to the museum hand in hand.

Landane Museum was one of those traditional places. Small, compact and utterly dedicated to one subject – the archeology and history of its local community and landscape. Not that there was any shortage of material, although, as so often happens, most of the best stuff had been hived off by the British Museum or the main county one. The plaster skeleton of the surgeon was impressive. I honestly wouldn't have known it wasn't real, except the 'bones' were exceedingly white. It lay, curled in fetal position as if it had died in tranquil sleep, apart from its smashed skull. Death, I guessed, must have been instantaneous. The last thing the poor man must have seen was a massive sarsen toppling down on him. The last thing he heard? Screams from his compatriots and probably himself.

"Come and have a look at Sir Charles," Nadia said, indicating a life-size portrait of a man dressed for a dig in the early nineteen hundreds. Tweed three-piece suit, sturdy shoes and a safari fedora hat adorned a middle-aged man with a luxuriant beard, holding a drinking vessel I now knew to be called a beaker – much beloved of the early Bronze Age settlers who came to the area around four and a half thousand years ago.

"He looks like he means business," I said and bent down to read the inscription. "Charles Scott 1858–1932." I straightened. "Archeologist I presume?"

"Very much so," Nadia said. "He's the one who excavated Landane properly for the first time. He used careful scientific methods and recorded everything properly. He also caused the fallen stones like the surgeon's stone to be re-erected and set in concrete."

"He was the one who discovered that poor bugger who got squashed to death?"

"That's him. He was an interesting character from what I've read. Part scientist, part believer in the occult. Sadly, this combination seems to have led to a lot of his stuffy academic colleagues at Cambridge University doubting his archeological findings and conclusions. He came from a wealthy family but ended up leaving the university, spending all his money on his digs, here and in Egypt, and dying in relative poverty."

"I'm guessing he never had his Howard Carter moment then?"

"No. No Tutankhamun for him, I'm afraid. I've always thought it was a real shame he never achieved the recognition he deserved."

"Maybe he should have kept his beliefs to himself."

"Maybe. But why should he?"

"Different age. Different beliefs. People wouldn't care so much now. In fact, they would probably love him all the more, but even so, I doubt he would be taken all that seriously by the more traditional academics."

"I wish I'd met him." Nadia's voice held a wistfulness in it that made me look at her. She seemed lost in her own world.

I touched her arm. "Hey?"

She looked at me and smiled. "Ignore me, I was miles away, wondering what it was like back then. Sometimes the past can be so real, can't it? I mean, you feel you could almost reach out your hand and touch it and bring it all back again. Haven't you ever wanted to do that?"

"Live in the past?" I shook my head. "Can't say I have. It wasn't all better back then. They didn't have antibiotics or a fraction of the medical treatments we have now, and that's before we get started on technology."

Nadia's expression was curious. She looked as if she was about to disagree but thought better of it. "Come on, you've had enough history lessons for one day. Let's go back outside and wander around the stones for a while."

We circumnavigated the entire circle while other tourists, a few dogs, and a small party of chanting men and women, who looked as if they had stepped straight out of 1967, wandered around. The chanters danced and skipped, their faces painted in rainbow colors.

"Whatever they're on, I think I need some," I said, laughing as a girl who looked to be in her late teens suddenly thrust a handful of short, deep-red blossoms into my hand. Her expression struck me as odd. She seemed to recognize me at first but then frowned, stared, and looked as if she didn't believe quite what she was seeing. There was a strange otherworldly sense about her – about the whole group in fact – as if they shouldn't be there. The girl glanced quickly at Nadia and then turned away before skipping back to join her friends. Confused by the gift and her strange behavior, I watched her go before examining the flowers. They resembled a cross between a small rose and a carnation, but my knowledge of flowers had never been more extensive than that.

Nadia held out her hand. "Give them to me," she said.

I hesitated. "What was all that about? What sort of flowers are they?"

"Begonias. They're a pot plant. Not meant to be picked."

"But why would a total stranger give me begonias?" I stared over at the group who had moved across to the far side of the circle and were dancing around the stone that looked like a hooded monk. The girl kept glancing over, but as soon as she caught my eye she turned away. There were other people nearby who paid no attention whatsoever to them. The whole scene felt wrong, although I couldn't explain it.

"She's just high," Nadia said. "Ignore her. Give me the flowers, Jonathan. Please."

Her tone was sharp. Unnecessarily so. "What's the problem?" I asked, trying to make light of it. "You're not jealous because she picked me, are you?"

"I'm not jealous. I'm just not a big fan of begonias, that's all. What are you going to do with them anyway? They don't have proper stems, so you can't put them in a vase of water. They'll be dead by the end of the day."

I sighed and handed them over. She immediately flung them away from her and the petals separated and fluttered in the breeze. I looked over at the girl. She was watching, too far away for me to make out the detail of her expression, but something inside me knew she disapproved. Perhaps she was even saddened.

Nadia wiped her hands on a tissue. The smile that appeared on her face seemed forced. "Come on, let's carry on. They've gone now." Whether she meant the begonias or the hippies, I don't know, but when I looked again, there was no sign of the chanting group. Nor was there any sign of the begonia petals.

As we approached each stone, Nadia stopped and touched it, almost reverentially. I watched her and touched some of the stones myself. I could feel no sensation such as I had the previous evening, but Nadia had said the energy only worked after sunset.

Finally, we came round to the surgeon's stone. Nadia's stone. It felt colder than the others, but that was surely my imagination playing yet more tricks, or maybe the sun hadn't warmed it as much. Nadia went round to the opposite side of it, out of sight. I looked around the field at the stones, still searching for any sign of the hippy troupe. They had spent a few minutes at the next stone along, so I left Nadia to go and check it, but there was nothing. No dropped flowers. I walked all around the stone. When I got to the other side, I looked over at the surgeon's stone expecting to see Nadia there, leaning against it, bathed in afternoon sunlight, but there was no one there. She must have gone round to the other side and was probably wondering where I had disappeared to. I went round to the front but she wasn't there either. Then, suddenly she was.

"You startled me," I said. "I couldn't see you."

"I didn't mean to. I was with my stone. You wandered off."

"Yes, but I…. It doesn't matter." It was starting to feel as if the day was slipping away from me. I suddenly felt exhausted, as if I'd run a mental marathon. "Do you mind if I go back for an hour or two? I'm not feeling too good. Need to have a lie down."

She frowned. "You're not sickening for something are you?" She reached up and laid the flat of her hand against my forehead. "You don't seem to be running a temperature."

"No, I don't think so. I'm suddenly incredibly tired. As if I'm going to fall asleep at any moment."

"Do you want me to come with you?"

"No need. You stay and enjoy yourself soaking up all the atmosphere and I'll see you back there in a couple of hours." I kissed her on the lips and she responded warmly. She squeezed my arm, and I kissed the top of her head. A surge of love for her poured through my veins. Nothing else mattered but how we felt for each other. I reasoned I had been working hard for months without a break. I was exhausted, that was all. Exhaustion messes with your head. Everyone knows that. My brain was telling me to sleep and recharge my depleted batteries. Who was I to argue with it?

★　　★　　★

I slipped under the cool duvet, grateful for the clean smell of newly laundered bed linen and for the tranquility of the room. I felt cocooned in a soft caress and sleep came quickly and deeply.

The dream was vivid. I stood by the surgeon's stone but the circle was different. It was complete. Every stone was a sarsen, every one upright, and there were no concrete markers indicating the position of missing megaliths. This is how Landane must have been long ago. I rotated three hundred and sixty degrees, taking in the landscape as I did so. There were no houses, no road. The church had disappeared, as had The White Hart. In the distance, the sound of chanting wafted toward me on the breeze. The grass beneath my feet was much longer than it had been and some distance away, cattle grazed. At least, they resembled cattle, but much bigger, with massive horns. Surely these must be aurochs. I had heard of them and seen images of them. Prehistoric man drew cave paintings of them. They had been extinct for hundreds of years, yet my sleeping brain had no problem with them being here in my dream. To my left, in the distance lay a field of pale golden corn. I had no idea what it might be. Wheat? Barley? Rye perhaps?

The sound of chanting grew louder. I jumped as a large flock of crows suddenly took off from a small grove of trees and flew noisily overhead, cawing and circling me. What was the proper collective noun for a load of crows? Oh yes, a murder. A murder of crows. How appropriate. They worked together, didn't they? Right then I could imagine the ones circling me swooping as one, without warning, claws and sharp beaks at the ready, rending, tearing....

The chanting grew and grew; a deep monotone, repeated again and again. Approaching. Closer, ever closer. Any second now and I would see whatever or whoever was making the noise that filled my brain and made me clamp my hands to my ears. I yelled at it to stop.

Something shook me.

"Jonathan, wake up. You're having a bad dream."

The dream didn't want to let me go. It clung on, trying to suck me back in. I could smell the fresh air of another world, another time. Nadia was shaking me but I could feel the soft breeze ruffling my hair, stroking my cheek, and I couldn't let it go. Above all I could hear that chanting. There must be hundreds of them. Men, women.... No, the sound was male, deep, like monks praying. Louder. Louder....

"Jonathan. *Please!*"

With a huge effort I snapped myself awake. Nadia's eyes were wide, scared. I had never seen her like that. I sat up and rubbed my eyes.

"That must have been one hell of a nightmare," Nadia said.

"It was. I was out there. I'm sure it was Landane, but it was different. It looked as it must have around the time the stones were erected and there was this chanting. I couldn't see anyone but I knew there must be hordes of them coming to the circle. Another minute or two and they would have been there. They would have seen me. I would have seen them. I...." I shook myself. Nadia's expression had turned from fear to confusion. She was looking at me as if she were seeing a stranger.

I must pull myself together. "I'll get up now. What time is it anyway?" I pushed the covers off me and Nadia moved aside to let me up.

"Just after six."

"That's why I'm starting to feel hungry. What did you get up to when I left you?"

"Oh, just wandered around for a while. I do that here. I don't need to do much of anything really when I'm in Landane. Simply being here's enough."

I opened the wardrobe and selected a blue shirt. My mouth tasted stale, so I made for the bathroom and brushed my teeth while Nadia opened the curtains. When I came back, she was staring out of the window, engrossed in her own thoughts as she was doing so often in Landane. At that moment, I even developed a private name for it. Her 'Landane Look'.

Now it was my turn to slide my arms around her waist; no imaginary encounter this time. She caught hold of my hands and snuggled into my arms. "Do you think it's possible that when we sleep, we can transport ourselves to other places and other times?" she asked.

"Why do you ask? Because of my dream?"

"Maybe, a little perhaps, but I've often wondered. I have such vivid dreams sometimes. Some keep recurring. I dream I'm here, standing in the center of the circle, but all the stones are in place. I can smell the dew on the grass. There are cattle grazing in the fields, but they're huge compared with ours. Here and there are wooden huts where all the people live. I see someone coming towards me. He's an old man and he uses a stick for support. It's an old tree branch but it does the job. He's dressed in white and his hair and beard are also white, long and flowing. He stares at me, his gaze never leaving my face, until he's no more than three feet away. He doesn't speak. He points to the stone. My stone. The surgeon's stone. He points at it and then at me. I can tell he wants me to approach the stone, so I do. I get right up to it so I can feel it against my cheek. The man places his hands on my shoulders. Then there's a really odd sensation as if I'm speeding through a dark tunnel." She paused.

Her words rang far too true for comfort. Everything she had described about the landscape was exactly what I had seen, yet this was the first time we had ever spoken about this.

"What happens next?" I asked.

She disentangled herself from me. "I don't know. I always wake up then and wish I hadn't. I feel a profound sense of having lost something important. Something I will never get back. Weird, isn't it?" She gave a light laugh. It sounded forced.

★   ★   ★

Once again, the restaurant was quiet. Only two other tables were occupied – both with couples staying there. Ken served us another excellent meal. A simple but delicious homemade cottage pie prepared and cooked by Jackie. Nadia and I made short work of it. We topped it off with cheese and biscuits and lingered over coffee and cognac. The others left and, as the bar was also quiet, Ken came over to chat with us.

"How do you like Landane, then?" he asked me.

"It's quite…I mean it's full of history and quite extraordinary. How on earth did they do it?"

"How indeed. I've heard all sorts of theories. Some of those stones weigh fifty tons and all they had were primitive tools and sheer brute force. Some say they used pulleys and ropes. They've experimented and they managed to erect a stone that way, but it's anyone's guess really. One guest a few years ago said he was certain the stones were placed here at the behest of the devil who bewitched the locals and gave them superhuman strength so it only took six of them to erect each stone."

"Had he been indulging in a little too much of this?" I indicated the brandy glass.

Ken laughed. "He may well have. But not just then. It was breakfast and he was, or certainly appeared to be, completely sober. His wife was with him and she was just as convinced as he was."

"How did you keep a straight face?" I asked.

"Practice. Years of it. I hear all sorts in this job." He smiled across at Nadia who was listening to every word with total concentration.

She cleared her throat. "Don't you think there could be something in what he said?" she asked. "Oh, I don't mean literally. But isn't it possible there were forces at work then that we don't understand?"

Ken hesitated before he replied. I wondered if he was unsure whether she was joking or not. To me, she seemed deadly serious and it bothered me. At home, Nadia had never come across as the fanciful type. No, she had her feet firmly on the ground, maybe a little too much so. I had suggested she lighten up a bit sometimes. Her intensity could be a little off-putting on occasions. But here in Landane, she took on a different persona. Here she seemed capable of believing almost anything, however incredible.

Finally, Ken seemed to have sorted out what to say. "I hadn't considered it, but I suppose you could be right. We know so little about the people of that time. They seem to have built these stone circles on sites where the Earth's magnetism is greater, or at least, that's what I've been told. Without technology to guide them, they must have been more in tune with natural forces than we are because we certainly can't detect changes in the Earth's magnetic field without instruments to measure it."

"And why build the things in the first place?" I asked. "And not only here. There's Orkney, Cumbria. Stonehenge of course. Loads of them dotted around the landscape, and not merely in this country. All over the world at around the same time, massive stone structures were being erected while their builders made do with wooden huts."

"They had a greater purpose," Nadia said, her eyes half closed. "The gods must be appeased or the harvest wouldn't come, the seeds wouldn't germinate. The cycle of the year would be broken. It happened once and mustn't happen again." She suddenly slumped forward.

I cried out. "Oh my God, Nadia!"

Both Ken and I leapt out of our seats and, one on either side of her, gently lifted her head. Her eyelids fluttered, then opened. She appeared to be having trouble focusing on either of us. She raised her hand to her face and her movements were uncertain, uncoordinated.

I took hold of her hand, shocked at how cold it was. "Nadia. Can you see me? Can you hear me?"

It was as if I had flicked a switch. She smiled. "I'm sorry about that, I don't know what happened there. It was like everything cut out for a second, but I'm fine now."

"I'll get you a glass of water." Ken didn't wait for a response.

"Are you sure you're all right?" I asked. Her hand grew warm again – in stark contrast to the cold, lifeless appendage I had held a few moments earlier.

Ken returned with a tumbler of water which Nadia accepted gratefully. She drank half of it in one go before placing her glass down on a coaster. "I must have been dehydrated," she said. "That can do strange things to you, can't it?"

I nodded. Ken said nothing. He knew as well as I that she had consumed half a bottle of chilled Chablis, plus a cognac and most of an Americano over dinner. Whatever had caused her momentary loss of consciousness, it certainly wasn't dehydration.

"Maybe we should take a trip to the hospital and get you checked out," I said, receiving a nod of agreement from the landlord.

"No, no, that's quite unnecessary. I'm perfectly fine now. I've had that glass of water and that's all that's needed."

"Has this happened before?" I asked.

"No. And I doubt it will happen again either."

"All the same—"

"I won't hear of it. Now what were we discussing before my moment of drama?"

"Just speculating on how and why the ancients constructed stone circles all over the place," I said. "You wondered if there might be some kind of supernatural force at work."

"Did I? Really?" Her expression couldn't have been more incredulous. "No wonder I passed out." She stood. "I'll be back in a second. Just need to go to the ladies'."

I watched her go. She walked steadily with no hint of hesitation until she rounded the bar and was out of sight. Ken immediately leaned forward. "She's not telling you the truth. About her blackout. It *has* happened before. I know because it happened here. Last time she was here, the year before and I don't know how many times. I even managed to persuade her to go to hospital on the last occasion. I took her there myself. They ran blood pressure tests, an ECG. You name it, they did it. They kept her in overnight. Nothing. They could find no cause at all."

"Has she had an MRI?"

"You'd have to ask her that. I don't know but it would be the logical next step, wouldn't it?"

I nodded but caught sight of Nadia returning and shifted in my seat as a signal to Ken. He latched on immediately. "I was telling Jonathan, you must spend some time at Landane Mound. It's fascinating."

"We can't climb up it anymore, though," Nadia said. "It's too unsafe."

"Yes, it's a shame, that. When I was a boy, we used to regularly have races to the top. It's an amazing view from there. You can see right over to the hills. I used to imagine what it would have been like when people gathered for festivals and so on. Must have been quite a sight." Ken glanced at his watch and grimaced. "Ah well." He stood. "Best get on. Preparation and paperwork calls."

"Thanks for another splendid meal, Ken," Nadia said, smiling.

"My pleasure."

As soon as he was out of earshot, I spoke. "That wasn't the first episode, was it?"

The smile melted in an instant. "What do you mean?"

"Your blackout. It's happened before. More than once here, let alone how many times elsewhere."

Her lip curled. "Ken."

"He's concerned about you. So am I. As soon as we get back home, you're going to the doctor and getting a referral to a consultant. I'm coming with you to make sure you don't back out of it."

"I'm not a child, Jonathan. Don't treat me like one." Her voice was rising.

"Then do as I say. Be sensible. There has to be a reason for these episodes and we need to get to the bottom of it and get something done. Now."

I will never forget the look she gave me at that moment. The woman in front of me had Nadia's face, her eyes, her hair. To everyone else she was Nadia Gale, but if she had introduced herself as her identical twin, or even someone bearing an uncanny resemblance to her but otherwise not related, I would have believed her. I can't explain it. Maybe it was something deep within those hazel eyes, but whoever stared at me, barely blinking, wasn't Nadia.

"I'm going to bed, Jonathan. I'm tired."

Any other day I would have said I was going with her, but that evening? With that woman who had once again become a stranger? No.

"That's probably best. After your experiences, you need a good night's rest."

She inclined her head slightly, a pale imitation of a nod. I watched her leave. She moved steadily, purposefully, and then she was out of sight. I sank down into the chair and finished off my brandy.

The bar was busier now, a mix of locals and tourists alike. Ken acknowledged me as I approached.

"I'll have a bottle of Bud, please," I said. He handed one over and I took it to a table by the window where I sat, stared outside at nothing in particular and let my mind wander. My thoughts were random, confused. I couldn't make out what was going on with Nadia. She denied the blackout had ever happened before, but Ken knew different. I had to find out more.

My chance came when a party of six left the bar and for once Ken had no one to serve. I motioned him over. Whatever he had to say I didn't want the world listening in and the table I was at was in a small recess. Quite private should anyone enter, or Nadia decide to come back down.

"Nadia's gone to bed then?" Ken asked, sitting down where he could keep an eye on any customers requiring his attention.

"Yes. She felt tired. You said earlier that she's had these blackouts before."

"She certainly has. Most peculiar. Did you ask her about the MRI? Whether she'd had one or not?"

"I haven't had a chance yet, but what I need to know is how long they've been going on."

"Well, I can only speak about what's happened here, but I would say the first one was maybe five, six years ago now. I wondered then if she suffered from epilepsy. Not the full-blown fitting kind but the milder version, where a person blanks out for a few seconds."

"You mean petit mal?"

"Do I? I'll take your word for it."

"But that's been ruled out, has it?"

"I believe so. I'm pretty sure I asked her about that, and she said she didn't have it. You could always ask her yourself to be certain."

"I'll do that tomorrow when she's had a chance to have a good sleep. Did she ever bring anyone else with her when she came down here?"

Ken shook his head. "You're the first. She never socialized either. Oh, she was friendly to me and my wife and always polite to everyone, but apart from that she kept herself to herself and spent almost all her time up at the stones. Some nights she didn't get back until after midnight and once or twice she didn't sleep here at all, so where she went I have no idea. I've never quite been able to fathom her out. Nice woman though."

"Thanks, Ken."

"You'll have to excuse me. There's a couple of thirsty people at the bar."

He left me to my thoughts and the remains of my beer. I made short work of the Bud, but my thoughts remained as tangled as a plate of spaghetti carbonara.

Nadia was sleeping peacefully when I tiptoed into the room trying to remember where the creaky floorboards were so I could avoid them. Inevitably, I caught a couple of them and she stirred. I hesitated but, within seconds, the gentle purring of her breathing told me she was once again sleeping.

I undressed and slipped straight into bed, hoping my dentist would forgive the lapse in dental hygiene for one night.

Sleep wouldn't come. I lay for ages, staring straight up at the ceiling. The moon's silver light filtered in between the gaps in the curtains providing just enough light to cast an eerie, unwelcome glow. It wouldn't take much to imagine shapes moving around the room when all that was happening involved clouds passing briefly over.

Eventually I must have drifted off, because I awoke with a start. Next to me, the bed was empty. The curtains were drawn right back, the small windows were wide open and there was Nadia in her long, white nightdress, standing statue-like and facing out. The breeze ruffled her hair. The moon's glow created a halo around her.

"Nadia?"

She either didn't hear or chose to ignore me. I flicked on my bedside lamp, got out of bed and went over to her. "Nadia. Please, come back to bed." I tried to pull her toward me but she resisted. She turned to look at me and her eyes were blank.

"I can see shapes…moving toward the circle."

Her voice seemed to come from far away. An echo. Once again, she resumed her gaze, transfixed by something I peered at but could not see. We had a clear view of part of the stone circle in daylight, including the surgeon's stone, but in this dim pre-dawn haze, everything appeared shrouded in mist.

"I can't see anything. Nadia, come back to bed. Please." I tugged her arm harder than I would normally have dreamt of doing but still I couldn't move her. It was like some force within her was rooting her to the spot.

"I see them…" she said. "I must go to them."

Now she moved. She shrugged me off and started to walk toward the door.

"No, Nadia. You can't go out there. Not at this time. Not dressed like that."

Nothing. It was as if I wasn't even there. But no way was she getting out of that door. I sprang in front of her, blocking her way. She tried to dodge around me, but I caught hold of her. Her whole body went rigid as every muscle tensed. Even her breathing stopped.

"Nadia. Nadia. Wake up!"

She gasped, her muscles went slack and she fell against me. I steered her back onto the bed and she lay down, allowing me to lift her legs and help her settle into a comfortable position. She closed her eyes as I covered her with the duvet.

I shivered in the unexpected iciness of the room. Closing the windows stopped a breeze that had suddenly whipped up. As I did so, I caught sight of a movement outside. In the distance, something or someone was walking. As I watched, it became clear that there was more than one person. Shadowy figures, dozens of them or maybe more, were trooping across the field away from me. I had no clear idea where they were coming from or where they were making for, but I stood and watched until the last of them disappeared into the gloom.

I couldn't tell whether they were male, female, old or young, but one thing I felt sure of, whoever they were, they didn't belong in the twenty-first century.

CHAPTER FIVE

"Good morning, sleepyhead." Nadia smiled down at me. The old Nadia.

I pulled her to me. "I'm so glad you're back," I said as I kissed her hair.

"Don't be silly. I haven't been anywhere."

"Oh, believe me, you have. Don't you remember any of it? Last night? You were standing by the window talking about shapes moving towards the stones. You even had me going for a while. I thought I was seeing things as well."

Nadia frowned. "It must be all this fresh country air. It's making you hallucinate. It's going to be a lovely day. Let's go to Landane Mound."

At least we would be away from the circle for once.

"Good idea. Shame we can't climb up it."

She leaned toward me and winked. "But we can. I know a way. Ken showed me once. He made me promise I would never tell."

"You've broken your promise. You told me."

"Ah, but I haven't told you where it is. When we get there, I shall blindfold you until we are safely inside and then you won't know, will you?"

I laughed, then caught her expression. "Are you serious?"

"Deadly. It's important that only a few of us are in on it or the same things could happen as happened with the traditional route – the whole thing collapses in on itself and endangers the integrity of the whole structure."

"You sound like you've been reading an architectural handbook."

She laughed. "No, that's what Ken told me."

"He also told me you've been having those blackouts for at least five or six years. Why haven't you had them investigated?"

"But I have. In the local hospital here and then an MRI back at home. I knew they wouldn't find anything and they didn't. No sign of stroke, epilepsy, tumor, aneurysm or any other nastiness. I'm perfectly healthy. It was one of those things, that's all."

"'One of those things' that keeps on happening. That isn't normal, Nadia. Does it happen elsewhere, or only here?"

She shrugged. "Maybe only here. I don't know. I am unaware of anything happening at all."

"It certainly hasn't happened since we've been living together, unless anything went on at work."

Nadia shook her head.

"So that leaves Landane as the common denominator. The only question we now have is, why?"

"Look, this isn't getting us anywhere. I'm not worried and it's my body so if there was anything to concern myself with, I would be concerned, wouldn't I? But I'm not. Now, please, Jonathan. Let's not spoil a perfect day by getting into an argument about some silly fainting spell."

"And what about the middle of the night when you were standing at that window seeing shapes moving around?"

"I don't know what you're talking about. Maybe I was sleepwalking. I was very tired last night. Look, I'm going to put my boots on. The ground can be really muddy and marshy by the mound."

All right, she would have her way. For now. But I was determined to get to the bottom of this one way or another.

★　　★　　★

Nadia was right. I was glad of my sturdy hiking boots as we squelched our way across the marshy terrain. Every footstep saw peat-colored water squeeze out of the grass as we sank a good inch or more. It was like wading through porridge.

"Are you okay with this?" I called to her. She was a good three or four yards ahead of me and didn't seem to get as bogged down as I did.

I was breathing hard and wishing I had used that gym membership I bought on a whim as part of a failed attempt at getting fit. So much for New Year's resolutions!

"I'm fine," she called back to me. "Keep up. You're falling behind."

"I'm trying not to fall down let alone fall behind."

"We'll have to stop soon and I'll put the blindfold on you."

"If I promise I won't tell anyone, even if they put the thumbscrews on me, can we skip that part? I really need to see where I'm putting my feet."

"No, you don't. I shall be your eyes."

My breath was coming hard when she stopped in her tracks and turned to face me, clearly amused by my exertions.

I caught up and she waved a silk scarf at me. "It's time," she said, a broad smile lighting up her face.

Against my better judgment, I let her tie the material round me. I even bent down so she could reach easier. The scarf pinched a little but was otherwise a snug fit.

"Can you see anything at all?" she asked.

"Nothing. Not even a speck of light."

"That's good. Can't have you peeping and me breaking my promise. Now all you have to do is take my hand and do exactly what I say."

I could have protested. I could have ripped the scarf off and refused to play her game, but this meant a lot to her. I didn't want to upset her unnecessarily. After all, what did a few minutes' nonsense matter?

She gripped my hand and steered me forward. A faint whooshing sound and a sudden blast of earth-scented cold air hit my face. I coughed. The sounds of the open air faded as I moved forward. The ground seemed hard and compressed but fairly even. I put out my free hand and it touched a wall of stone. Either she didn't notice or didn't mind because she said nothing as I carried on steadying myself by sliding my hand along that bumpy wall. It reminded me of the walls of the long barrow. I was aware of being drawn in farther and farther.

"Are we inside the mound now?" I asked.

"I couldn't possibly tell you where we are, but it's not far now." There was a trill to her voice that told me she was enjoying herself. This was Nadia in her Landane element. I felt an uneasy chill. I wasn't really claustrophobic but some situations made me incredibly uneasy. Being underground was one of them. I found that out quite by accident on a vacation in Malta when a much-anticipated trip to a prehistoric burial site in underground caves called the Hypogeum led me to break out in a cold sweat. Right now that feeling was welling up in me. Much longer and I would have to turn back just as I did on that occasion. I would deal with the humiliation later, as I had then.

She must have sensed my unease. Her voice grew softer, almost a purr. "We're only a few steps away. Then you'll be out in the open air again."

I concentrated on breathing. The air became fresher and the atmosphere around me lightened. My free hand felt nothing. The wall had ended or receded somehow. Never had birdsong sounded so welcome. I could have kissed that blackbird.

Nadia removed the scarf and I blinked. I looked around me. We were standing at the top of the mound. For as far as I could see, the rolling green pastures and low hills stretched out below and before me. The breeze whipped up the short grass beneath our feet. For the first time, the full extent of Moreton Landane long barrow was revealed. Goodness alone knew how many unexcavated bodies remained buried under its surface.

"But this is crazy," I said. "We've climbed all the way up here. What? A hundred and thirty feet?"

Nadia nodded. "I believe so. Thereabouts."

"I was walking on the flat all the time. I haven't climbed."

"It's a very gentle incline," Nadia said. "And you were blindfolded, don't forget."

How could I? "Even still...."

"But we're here, aren't we?" She spread her arms wide. "What other explanation could there possibly be?"

Put like that, she was right. At any rate, the view was spectacular.

We stood in silence, drinking it all in, until I spoke. On a sudden impulse, I put my arm around her and she didn't resist. "Tell me, what's your theory about why this place was built? Only as a gigantic marker post? Or is it something more?"

"I've always thought it was part of the ritual of the life cycle of Landane. As I said when we were over there." She pointed at the long barrow. "I believe the stones represent the life-giving force, and here and Moreton Landane are at the other end of the spectrum. If you look at how high this is.... Well, it's easily the highest summit around here. It certainly would have stood out, especially when it was coated in brilliant white chalk, but I think it was much more than that. They built the tallest structure they could. Then, when their great leaders died, they would bring them up here and leave them for the sky and its messengers, the birds, to take. Whatever was left, maybe the following year, they would bury in Moreton Landane for the earth to reclaim."

Her voice was mesmerizing; it had taken on a lilt I had never heard from her before. It was as if she had acquired a new accent – slightly singsong in a Welsh way but with an intonation and cadence all its own. When she finished speaking, I found myself wanting more. Instead, she shifted position and moved closer to the edge of the mound to look over.

"Be careful," I said. "I shouldn't think the ground is too stable up here."

"It isn't," she said. "But it won't harm me. I know the right places to walk."

Her confidence didn't make me any more inclined to get any closer to the precipice. When she turned round and made her way back to me, my relief was such I let out a breath I hadn't realized I was holding.

"We should get back now," she said. "I have to go back to the stones."

"*Have* to?"

"Yes. It's all right. I can't explain and you wouldn't understand anyway. Please humor me. It's something I have to do."

"You're worrying me now."

She gave a light laugh and kissed my nose. "You worry far too much. I'm fine. Really."

If only I could believe that.

"Sorry, but the scarf has to go on again."

"I guessed as much."

This time I concentrated on my angle of descent...except I couldn't discern one. As far as I was concerned, I was walking on a mostly level surface. I guessed it was composed of compacted mud. Once again, I had the sickening feeling of being hemmed in, of the walls closing around me. I told myself I was imagining things and that, anyway, it would all be over in a few minutes.

And then everything changed. I was suddenly out in the open. But not at Landane Mound.

I stood in the center of the stone circle and the hippy troupe danced around me. Beyond them, the landscape was shrouded in a silvery mist that didn't seem natural. It glittered in such a way as to suggest someone had actually sprinkled some sort of sparkling dust on it. I no longer wore the scarf and when I looked down at my legs, I didn't recognize the trousers I was wearing. They were deep burgundy in color, old-fashioned bell-bottoms from the sixties. My arms were bare and tanned, as was my naked upper torso. The girl with the begonias laughed. She caught hold of my hand as she danced to some tune one of the others was playing on a flute. I resisted her efforts to get me to join in with her and she let go of my hand, continuing her gyrations alone.

Her long flaxen hair blew wildly around her. Just like the clouds, her face was adorned with glitter. Her eyes were heavily made up in the style of Julie Driscoll, whose picture I had seen in a book about icons of the sixties and for some reason it had stuck with me. Something about her eyes, the expression maybe. This girl could have been channeling her. Of course, the rest of her, especially the long blonde hair, was far different. Her dress was flowing, wildly dyed in swirls of pink, green, yellow, red and orange. As I watched her sway and swirl to the music, she looked so authentic, it was hard to believe she could actually be a millennial.

"Come on," she said, "dance with me." She was nothing if not persistent.

"I'm sorry, I don't know who you are," I said, wishing I didn't sound so pathetic.

She stopped whirling. The smile died on her face. Her expression changed from a sort of ethereal dreaminess to one of total confusion as she looked from me to the scene around her. "I don't know who I am either. Not anymore." Her friends also stopped dancing and the flautist ceased his folky tune.

A man with as much hair as anyone could reasonably expect to grow in a lifetime, plus matching beard, closed in on me. He peered into my eyes as if trying to inspect my brain. He seemed out of it. High on something. He slurred his words when he spoke.

"Hey, man, where have you been? We've all been looking for you. Have you been tripping out somewhere? Shelly's been worried sick." He waved vaguely in the direction of the girl.

"I haven't the faintest idea what you're talking about," I said. A wild idea flashed into my head. "What date is this?"

"You serious?" the hirsute one asked.

"Oh, believe me, I'm as serious as it gets."

"July 15th."

"And the year?"

"It's 1967. But you know that, right? Man, you're just winding us up." He looked at the others. Some sniggered. Others looked baffled. Shelly looked as if she would dissolve into tears at any moment.

"What if I were to tell you that this is 2023?" I asked.

More sniggers except for Shelly. She made a choking sound. Her bearded friend put his arm protectively around her. "You're upsetting her and you're not making any sense."

"Nor does any of this."

Shelly made a half step toward me but her friend pulled her back.

"Leave him, Shell. He's not one of us anymore. *They've* got him now. I said it would happen. I could see it. You know I have the gift."

"I gave him the flowers, Davy."

"He didn't get it. He doesn't understand that language. He's not with us. Come on, let's go."

The group turned their backs to me. Shelly reluctantly. She kept squirming to turn around, but Davy wouldn't let her. He held her in a firm grip he wasn't going to relinquish anytime soon.

From somewhere in the distance, a pure, clear voice rang out, singing a cappella:

"Fear her now, fear the queen,

As in her stone she reigns supreme...."

★   ★   ★

"Jonathan. *Jonathan.*" I opened my eyes to see Nadia staring down at me.

"Thank goodness. I wondered what had happened. I couldn't wake you."

There was grass beneath my head and, as I sat up, I half-expected to find myself back on top of Landane Mound but, instead, I was lying on the wide verge next to the car. Ahead, towering above, was the structure I had somehow ascended and descended.

"I had the strangest dream," I said. "But more important, how did I get here? I was in the mound with you and then I was in the stone circle with the hippies.... I haven't a clue what's going on here."

"I reckon it's the fresh air. You're not used to it after all the city smut." Nadia laughed. I wished I could laugh with her, but those people had been real. That was no dream. I had to face facts. At least as I knew them, however impossible they might seem to any sane person.

Nadia had taken me via a secret route, to the top of Landane Mound. So far so, almost, normal, but when we had returned, something incredible had happened. Incredible and seriously disturbing. The hippies. Maybe they were a reenactment group and I had been caught up in one of their games. I wanted to believe this more than anything. The only problem was that none of it added up.

"What time is it?"

Nadia glanced at her watch. "Ten past three."

"How long was I out?"

"I was dozing too. I'm guessing around twenty minutes or so. You were making some strange noises, as if you were talking to someone but really quickly. If I could have recorded it and then played it back at a slower speed, I might have been able to tell you what you said. Or it could have been total gobbledygook. Who knows with dreams?"

"If it *was* a dream."

I helped her up and wondered why she avoided my eyes.

CHAPTER SIX

I was caught in that half-world where sleep is still claiming you but your conscious mind is pushing you towards wakefulness. It's a time when your body doesn't do what you want. I instructed my arms to move and they stayed stubbornly where they were. I was flat on my back, they stuck rigidly to my sides. If I had been standing, I would have been at full attention. I willed my legs to move, my feet to twitch, my toes to give the merest hint of a wiggle, but nothing.

Around me, shapes whirled in an amorphous mass, but I knew that, somewhere, Nadia was among them. Ask me how I knew that and I haven't a clue. Indistinct figures moved around the bed, chanting softly. The smell of patchouli wafted over to me. Heady, strong, evoking the era of peace, love and flower power when transcendental meditation was all the rage. Way before my time. My mother had been a practitioner when she was a student at Oxford. That was back in the days when someone had managed to plant a cannabis seedling in a sheltered corner of the garden of one of the college deans. I thought about it now. She told me the plant had flourished in its privileged surroundings. It produced a very pretty flower as if trying to outdo the long-established and abundant hollyhocks and delphiniums. I suppose my strange 'encounter' with the hippies must have led to this. My brain was fixating itself on 1967 for some reason I could not for one moment fathom.

A minute must have gone by, but I still couldn't move. Sleep paralysis normally only lasted for a split second and the longer this went on, the more panic began to form into a tight ball in my stomach. The shapes changed, swirled like dervishes, misty gray, no longer smelling of patchouli but of lavender overlaid with another, sweeter scent. Roses maybe. I drifted. The panic waned. My eyes closed although I had no sense of having caused them to do so. A feeling of weightlessness took hold of my body and I felt myself floating up and off the bed. A cool breeze fanned my cheeks and I opened my eyes.

The sky was a mass of stars, twinkling high above me, yet they seemed to be closer than they should be. There were more of them than I could normally see. I tried to move and this time I could. Except I moved independently of my body. I lifted an arm only to find I could see straight through it. When I looked down there was my actual, physical arm, pressed against my side. I turned round and craned my neck to see the rest of me, lying, eyes closed, apparently asleep. I stood and found I could do so with ease, but I was standing on nothing, although I was directly above my chest.

I couldn't see below me. Everything beneath resembled a white cloud. Not just below either. For as far as I could see on every side, nothing existed apart from this white world. Except above me. There the myriad stars twinkled silver against a dark blue, velvet sky. I felt the breeze but not the cold, or warmth. I should have been scared but I had no sensation of emotion at all. Only a feeling that everything was as it should be, as it had always been and as it would always be. I could explain none of it, yet it made perfect sense. My mind accepted the seemingly impossible. I knew I was moving, but there was no sensation of motion and I certainly wasn't propelling myself in any way. Something was moving me. Why didn't that scare me? For some inexplicable reason it didn't. I knew it would stop sometime, when the time was right, or when it had achieved its purpose. Until then it didn't matter. I waited. Time must have passed. It always did, so it must be doing so now. I had no idea if it was day or night or some kind of twilight world where there was no conception of such a phenomenon.

I grew sleepy and lay down. To lie on something which resembles nothing is a strange and surreal experience. I tried to recall the times Mum had spoken of her misspent youth as a student. By all accounts not a great deal of studying went on, or at best it was squeezed in between parties and drunken, trippy nights. When, at the end, she had been lying in that hospice bed, doped up to the eyeballs with morphine and whatever else they could find to stave off the pain, her mind wandered back to the late sixties. At times she thought I was her friend, Mike Chandler. Mike was my godfather and had been openly gay when it was a dangerous thing to be. Mum talked to me, calling me Mike, confiding the latest gossip and exploits from other friends of theirs. In her mind she was a young, carefree girl again and she sounded it. Her voice was pitched higher and she giggled a lot. That's when I found out about the cannabis plant, the acid trips, the free love. That was the most embarrassing part. No one should ever hear about their parents' sex life and here she was going into graphic detail. I played along with her, trying to say as little as possible while remembering Mike's many flamboyant traits, his flowery language and extravagant gestures. The way he sat, double-crossing his legs – quite an awkward thing to do and not a little uncomfortable when you're the wrong side of thirty and a stranger to the gym.

She had me bring her patchouli oil and roses. She gave me a white rose from a bouquet of flowers someone had sent her and told me, "Give it to Laurence. You owe him after your indiscretions last weekend." I had no idea what Mike had allegedly been up to, but a large, awkwardly delivered wink from Mum, whose face was by now half-paralyzed from the ministrokes she had been having, told me it had almost certainly involved sex.

On one occasion, Mum told me about an acid trip she had experienced when she felt she had been floating on air. She too had seen the stars brighter than usual. She had lain on a cloud....

*   *   *

The sun streamed through the window. Nadia was up, a beaming smile on her face. "Come on. Time to get showered and dressed. It's nearly ten-thirty."

I rubbed my eyes and swung my legs out of bed. All that had been another dream? Apparently, because this was undoubtedly reality.

"Did I move around a lot in the night?" I asked as I pulled on my bathrobe.

"I don't think so. I slept right through until about half an hour ago, so I really don't know. I took my shower but I left the bathroom door open so it wouldn't squeak and wake you up."

"Thanks. I had some weird dreams. So vivid, I was sure it was actually happening to me."

"What was?"

"It's muddled, but at one point I was floating out there somewhere," I pointed out of the window. "At least, I presume that's where I was because all I could see was the night sky and loads of stars. Everything else was a white sort of blanket or cloud, and I was outside my body. It reminded me of something my mother told me about her misspent student days tripping on acid."

Nadia looked away. "I've had out-of-body dreams. I think everyone does at some time or another."

"Probably. I'll get my shower."

When I emerged, washed, shaved, teeth brushed and hair wet, she was drinking coffee.

"Want one?" she asked. "We missed breakfast."

"Yes. Thanks."

She poured hot water onto some instant coffee, added one sachet of sugar and a capsule of milk and set it down ready for me as I dressed.

"What do you suggest for today?" I asked.

"We could go into Charnford. It's a lovely city. Beautiful cathedral and lots of winding medieval streets. Bookshops galore so you'll be in your element."

"Sounds good to me. I'd like to get a book about local traditions and folklore of this area. Strikes me there should be shedloads of legends."

"Oh, there are. Believe me. You don't know the half of it."

★   ★   ★

The only problem with charming, medieval cities and towns in England is that the streets were never constructed with motorized transport in mind. This, coupled with the now common practice of deterring as many cars as possible from gaining access to – or parking in – the center, and you have a recipe for a hell of a lot of driving around, searching for somewhere to leave your four-wheeled pride and joy in safety, without incurring a hefty parking fine or wheel clamp. The residential streets proved impossible with their parking zones and double yellow lines. Finally, we managed to bag one of the last two spaces in the one and only multistory car park around a quarter of a mile from the cathedral. It took us fifteen minutes to drive from Landane and thirty to locate that precious bay.

I duly forked out the required fifteen quid for the privilege, muttering, "Bloody exorbitant. Fucking profiteers," under my breath and stuck the small ticket on the inside of my windscreen.

"Lead on," I said.

Nadia smiled and took my hand. "We'll catch the bus next time. That's what I usually do."

I refrained from demanding why she hadn't suggested that in the first place as I remembered I had once held forth on why I hated taking buses. Without experiencing what the situation was like in Charnford for myself, I would have no doubt insisted we take the car. In future I would learn to embrace my inner bus lover. It must be lying there dormant somewhere.

We emerged from the gloom of the brutish early sixties architecture of the car park into another gloriously sunny day. As we passed a general store, I caught sight of a tabloid headline proclaiming it to be the hottest, driest July on record. I certainly wouldn't argue with them.

Nadia led us straight to the cathedral. Built of sandstone, it commanded its landscape, as do all great cathedrals. A massive single spire reached hundreds of feet high.

"Three hundred and seventy-five to be exact," Nadia said. "Give or take an inch or two. They started to build it in the thirteenth century and it took around two hundred years before it was finished. Now there's always scaffolding up somewhere or another. Yes, there it is. They're doing the roof above the east window."

The scaffolding almost obliterated what was clearly a magnificent stained-glass construction.

Nadia sighed. "It's such a glorious sight when the sun streams through, but with all that tarpaulin and the scaffolding I don't think we're going to get a lot of that today. Shame, but that's what it is with ancient buildings."

"Let's go in and see what we can anyway. Then, I propose you take me to the best bookshop."

"You're on."

Inside was peaceful, tranquil, and, despite the number of people milling around, a respectful hush was being maintained. Sadly, as Nadia had feared, the east window was revealing little of what it was capable of in normal, unshrouded circumstances, and an enquiry of one of the volunteers at the information point as to how long the work would take resulted in a vague, "About two years, maybe three. It's hard to say. They keep hitting new problems."

We conveyed our thanks and moved away, stopping at the more elaborate tombs and reading epitaphs. Some contained the mortal remains of dignitaries hailing from Landane. Most, though, were Charnford's great and good.

"The crypt's really interesting," Nadia said. "The Anstruther Mausoleum especially. It's locked so you can't go in there, but through the wrought-iron gates you can see some magnificent tombs. Come on, I'll show you."

She took me down a flight of stone steps that led under the cathedral and into a world of the dead. A central corridor had sets of double wrought-iron gates leading off to left and right. Each supported a nameplate.

"Here it is."

She pointed to a brass plaque on which was written one word. Anstruther.

"You'll need to put on the flashlight on your phone to get a better idea. In fact, if we use both of ours, we'll light things up even better."

We duly did so and were rewarded by the sight of magnificent marble sarcophagi in shades of rose red, white, gray and black. Ornately carved, each was topped with an effigy of the deceased.

"One of the guides told me that the first Anstruther was buried here in 1685. His name was Thomas and he became mayor of Charnford, but his family hailed from Landane. The latest and probably last was Olivia, who died in 1928. Apparently, there were no more Anstruthers by then. The line has died out completely."

We moved our flashlights around. A sudden movement out of the corner of my eye made me jump.

"What's the matter?" Nadia asked.

"I thought I saw something move."

"A mouse probably. They're bound to have them here, although I believe there are two cathedral cats who do a good job of keeping them under control."

I didn't tell her that what I saw couldn't have been a mouse. Not unless cathedral mice had developed the ability to stand on two legs and wear a funeral shroud.

★   ★   ★

"The best bookshops are all clustered in this one little road," Nadia said after we had walked about a hundred yards from the cathedral along a narrow medieval street. "It's a good job it's pedestrianized because people have a habit of wandering all over the place reading their latest purchase."

"Everyone does that with their phones anyway."

"True. Look, this is the one. Lockhart and Sweeney. Supposedly the oldest bookshop in Charnford. If they don't have books on local folklore, no one will."

The shop front was small, quaint and filled with new and secondhand hardbacks. Inside was like the TARDIS – far bigger than you could have imagined from outside. Walls of books stretched seemingly forever. The helpful shopkeeper steered us to a well-stocked Witchcraft, Legends, Superstitions and Folklore section and handed me an old, leather-bound volume.

"I'm sure you'll find plenty on these shelves, but this is a good place to start. It's the story of the Anstruthers of Landane. Of course, it's been out of print for years, but this is a copy in excellent condition."

I thanked him and took the weighty book from him. Nearby was a small table with two chairs and I sat, ready to peruse its pages while Nadia carried on down to the fiction section.

A quick scan of the contents informed me that this well-born family used to own Landane Manor and at least one of the last females took a keen interest in local archeology. There were photographs clustered throughout the book. I switched to them, flicking through until I came across one that zapped the breath out of me.

It showed a woman in late Victorian dress standing next to the surgeon's stone. Her long, dark hair was secured behind her head and, unusually for the time, she wasn't wearing a hat. Her clear eyes shone out at me.

I read the caption. 'Olivia Anstruther and an unidentified man in the stone circle at Landane'. Next to her, a man I gauged to be in his twenties, with longish hair resting on top of his collar, also dressed in late Victorian style, held a spade. I stared at it, willing it to change, but it didn't.

"Nadia. Come here. I need to show you something."

She was there within seconds. "What is it? You sound…Jonathan, are you all right? You've gone so pale."

I pointed at the photograph. "Look at this. Tell me what you see."

She looked, and then she stared. "It says it's Olivia Anstruther and… it can't be."

"You're seeing what I'm seeing, aren't you?"

"Right now, I don't believe *anything* I'm seeing."

"I know. It can't be true, but it is."

"He's the image of you."

"No, not the image of me. He *is* me. And she is…she's you, Nadia. Only that's not possible because look when that photograph was taken."

She glanced down at the caption. "It says 1900."

CHAPTER SEVEN

Olivia

1900

"Olivia. *Olivia!*" Marina Anstruther normally refrained from raising her voice. Her mother had always insisted it wasn't ladylike, and that she would never bag herself a suitable husband if she went around yelling like a fishwife.

Finally, the young woman raised her eyes to address her mother. "Yes, Mama?"

"What do you spend all those hours mooching over? Always in a daydream. Off in your own little world. I was talking about the invitation from the Muncasters. Such a good family, with an impeccable history. Mrs. Muncaster was telling me that their eldest son, Giles, has taken quite a shine to you. What do you think about that? You could do a lot worse."

"That's...that's...very flattering, I'm sure."

"Flattering? Flattering? Is that all you can say?"

"I don't know what else you would have me say, Mama. If indeed he has taken a shine to me as you put it, I'm afraid that his feelings are not reciprocated. In fact, if you must know, I find him an insufferable, snobbish prig."

Marina Anstruther stared at her as if she were wondering if she had dreamed that and how those words could come out of the mouth of the daughter she had spent the last twenty-one years raising to be a lady. "Sometimes I simply don't understand you, my girl. Time is not on your side, you know. Most of your contemporaries are planning their weddings if they're not already married. If you don't get a move on, you'll be left on the shelf. An old maid everyone pities."

"I don't see what's wrong with being a single woman. There are things I want to do. I have no desire to be tied down with babies yet. If at all."

That was too much. Her mother leapt to her feet. "I don't know how you can say such things. Being married and having children is what we women were born to do. It is your duty to provide the next generation. How would it be if all women felt like you? The whole human race would die out."

"Then perhaps it is fortunate that they don't all feel like me. But I want to make something of myself. See the world. Discover wonderful things."

"Not more of this archeology nonsense. Leave that to the men. Ladies do not go about scrabbling in the dirt. It is quite unthinkable. Remember what your father said. He told you, in no uncertain terms, that he would not pay for you to go to Mesopotamia or anywhere else for that matter, just so you could be up to your knees in sand and eaten alive by mosquitos."

"Then it's probably as well that we live here in Landane, isn't it? There's plenty to discover right here on our doorstep. The experts reckon there's a whole stone circle – and a big one at that – right here in the village. I intend to help prove that one way or another."

"And who, pray, is going to finance that little jaunt?"

"Oh, don't worry. I shan't be asking Papa. There are some clever people at Cambridge University who are in the process of getting together a team and raising the money from wealthy benefactors. I intend to apply to join them."

"I absolutely forbid it, as will your father."

"Mama, as you pointed out, I am an adult. I'm twenty-one and can make my own decisions as to the conduct of my life. I don't need your permission and, as I knew you wouldn't give it anyway, I'm not asking for it."

Marina Anstruther felt her head swim. Maybe her corsets were laced too tightly today. Her personal maid had certainly given the ribbons an extra hard yank that morning and breathing had been rather more restricted than usual. She sank back down in her chair, wincing as the whalebone stays dug into her ribs.

"Get out of my sight, Olivia. I have had quite enough of you this morning. Perhaps you will come to your senses when you've had chance to reflect on how much you have upset me."

Olivia nodded, stood, said nothing and left the room, her long skirt swishing as she moved.

★   ★   ★

With her bedroom door closed firmly behind her, Olivia let out a deep breath and crossed the floor to the window seat. From there she could see across the manicured lawn and tidy flower borders, over the brick wall and into the garden of the rectory. Here a myriad of tall flowers bloomed in the July sunshine. She caught sight of a movement and her heart gave a little lurch as the tall figure of the rector's eldest son, Grant, came into view, striding down the path, pausing every now and then to examine a rose, or deadhead one, before putting the faded bloom into a basket, destined for the compost heap. If she waved at him, would he see her? But that would be very forward of her and Mama would not approve. But then Mama made it abundantly clear that she disapproved of pretty much everything Olivia did, thought or said, so what did it matter? She raised her arm.

He was too far away and looking in the wrong direction. She would have to engineer another chance encounter. It was a beautiful day. What would be more natural than for her to take a little walk? And if that little walk happened to take her past the rectory, and Grant happened to be deadheading the flowers in the front garden, well, that was a happy coincidence, wasn't it?

Olivia quickly grabbed her summer straw hat with the wide brim. Adorned with a broad white ribbon sprigged with tiny rosebuds, it went well with her floral-patterned dress. Her white shoes were impractical for anything other than a short stroll, but no matter. She wasn't planning on a three-mile hike. She checked her appearance in the mirror, pinched her cheeks to give them a flattering rosy hue and took one final glance out of the window. He was still there, but in the process of making his way back toward the house. At the end of the path a gate led to the front garden. Olivia paused long enough to see him take that route before she bounded out of her room and down the stairs, almost knocking over the parlormaid.

"Sorry, Daisy," she called behind her. Then she was out of the front door and through the gate. She forced herself to breathe normally, and to take leisurely, ladylike steps.

The lane twisted round to the right, leading to the center of the village. Only a few more yards and she would see him. And there he was, snipping a brightly colored pink rose. He didn't see her at first. She would have to attract his attention and make it seem natural. She paused by his front gate.

"Good morning, Mr. Ford." Why had her voice risen an octave?

He stopped, pruning shears in hand. A smile lit up his tanned face and he tipped his cap. "Good morning, Miss Anstruther. Beautiful day, isn't it?"

"It is indeed. I think I should have brought my parasol."

"Perhaps best to stay in the shade as much as possible."

"Indeed. Your roses are looking particularly lovely this year. Are you doing anything different with them? A new fertilizer perhaps?"

"No, we don't really go in for a lot of fussing in the garden. I keep it tidy, and deadheading ensures we have blooms all through summer."

"That's what our gardener says...." Her voice faltered. How crass of her to mention a gardener. It merely served to emphasize the class division between them. The rector couldn't possibly afford gardeners and servants, apart from a maid-of-all-work who must be hard-pressed to cover all the tasks a team of servants would have previously taken care of. With the exception of that one girl, the Fords had to do for themselves. It couldn't help that they had such a big garden and that the house was large enough for a family of ten. As it was, there was

Mr. and Mrs. Ford, their sons Grant and Maxwell, and their youngest, a daughter, Cynthia.

Grant smiled. "You're welcome to have a look at the garden if you would like. Maybe you can give me a few hints. Your gardener probably knows far more about these things than I do and maybe he passed some more helpful hints on to you."

Olivia smiled, nodded and opened the gate.

Grant led her along, pointing out the different flowers. "Those tall ones are hollyhocks and delphiniums. Really traditional English country garden flowers, and over there." He pointed to a bed of bright green-leaved bushes with long stems of blueish-purple flowers. "That's lavender. Every year when they finish flowering, it's Cynthia's job to trim off all the dead flowers and dry them. A few years ago, it was my task, then it was Maxwell's and now it's hers. Poor girl's drawn the short straw. I don't see Ma having any more children so she's stuck with it until she leaves home or Dad gets another living somewhere. Ma makes lavender bags to put in our clothes drawers and wardrobes. They keep moths and other nasties at bay and smell lovely too."

"Flowers have meanings too, don't they?" Olivia asked. "I mean rosemary is for remembrance, daisy is innocence, forget-me-not is exactly what it says. I don't know them all."

His smile crinkled the corners of his eyes. Olivia felt a rush of heat and hoped it wasn't reflected in the color of her cheeks. She concentrated on his words, but then he had such a pleasant voice, a slight local accent, not too pronounced, issued in a warm baritone that belied his years. He couldn't be more than twenty-two or twenty-three, but he sounded so much more mature. Her attraction toward him was getting out of hand. She really must get a grip on herself. She must concentrate on *what* he was saying, not merely on *how* he was saying it.

"Ma used to tell us all about them. She has a book on the language of flowers. I remember hollyhocks are for ambition, delphiniums mean cheerfulness, red chrysanthemums say 'I love you'...."

Olivia felt her cheeks burn. Now, she couldn't look him in the eyes for fear of betraying her true feelings for him. They had stopped on the path. From under lowered lashes, she caught sight of him staring off into the distance, clearly feeling as awkward as she did. It was a relief when he broke the silence.

"Begonias," he said, pointing to the borders on either side, resplendent in showy red, orange and yellow blooms, each one attached to a small plant with dark green leaves. "Begonias can mean beware. So, if anyone ever gives you a bunch of begonias, be wary."

Olivia crouched down and gently took one of the flowers in her hand, taking care not to dislodge it. "They would have a difficult job, I fear. The stems are too short. You couldn't put these in a vase of water."

Grant laughed. "No, they're for looking at, not for picking. Come on, let me show you the back garden. You can see this from your house, I believe."

"I always admire it from my bedroom window."

"Yes, I've seen you sometimes." He opened the gate, before standing aside to let her through.

Instantly, the sweet heady aroma of honeysuckle greeted her. Fronds of it had been trained all around the trellis work surrounding the gate, and the display of pale yellow and white flowers was providing a happy hunting ground for a dozen or so industrious bees.

Olivia inhaled deeply before moving on to discover more heavenly scents. Roses of every color grew in profusion.

"You know that each color of rose has its own symbolism too, don't you?" Grant asked.

"I know that you should never give a sick person red roses and white roses together, but on their own white roses mean purity and innocence. Red roses mean love...." There was that word again. First Grant and his chrysanthemums and now her with red roses. Olivia's cheeks burned. He couldn't fail to see the blush spreading across her cheeks.

He snipped off a long-stemmed yellow rose. It was yet to fully emerge from its bud. A perfect bloom. He handed it to her. "For friendship and new beginnings," he said, and their eyes met. Olivia took it from him and it was only then that she noticed she had forgotten to put on her gloves. Yet another *faux pas* that would earn her mother's displeasure and one more ticking off to add to the bulging collection. Well, what she didn't know wouldn't harm her.

"Grant?"

He and Olivia turned. Mrs. Ford stopped in her bustling trot toward them. "Oh, Miss Anstruther. I didn't realize it was you. The hat...." She indicated how Olivia's millinery had concealed her profile.

"Good morning, Mrs. Ford. I trust you are well."

"Very well, thank you. Grant, your father would appreciate your help in the study. He's struggling a little with his sermon and he says your advice is better than any dictionary."

"Of course, Ma. Miss Anstruther, thank you for calling round. I hope you enjoyed the garden."

"I did indeed." She addressed his mother. "I was telling Mr. Ford how delightful it is. He is very knowledgeable about the language of flowers. I found it most enlightening."

His mother gave a half-smile. "Yes, well, Grant has always had a way with words. I'll show you out while he goes to help his father."

Grant tipped his cap once more. "Good morning, Miss Anstruther. I trust you will enjoy the rest of your walk."

"Thank you, Mr. Ford."

His mother and Olivia strolled down the path while Grant sped on ahead. Evidently his father didn't like to be kept waiting. Certainly, Reverend Ford, standing tall in his pulpit, surveying his congregation every Sunday morning, could look stern and forbidding, especially when he chose temptation and sins of the flesh as the topic for his sermon.

At her front gate, Mrs. Ford hesitated. She seemed to want to say something, but was unsure of how to put it into words.

"Goodbye, Mrs. Ford. I so enjoyed my tour of your lovely garden. It was most kind of your son to show me—"

"Miss Anstruther. I hope you will forgive me for being blunt, but I don't think it would be a good idea for you and my son to pursue any kind of...friendship."

"I'm not sure I know to what you are referring, Mrs. Ford."

"Oh, I think you do. I can see there's an attraction between the two of you and it would only result in heartbreak. We're from different worlds, you see. Society would not permit.... Your parents, Miss Anstruther. They simply wouldn't stand for it."

Olivia wished she had some witty, intelligent riposte to offer but nothing came to mind. Besides, Mrs. Ford was right. Her mother would have a fit if she had seen her and Grant talking together, alone, even if it was in the open air in broad daylight. Her reputation. That was what mattered. If the merest hint of scandal were to emerge, her prospects of securing that good marriage her mother was always harping on about would be severely compromised. Olivia pursed her lips. It was anger that flamed her cheeks this time. Mrs. Ford was right, of course. She had feelings for Grant. If she were only of his social class, they could have a chance at happiness together but, as it was....

"Thank you, Mrs. Ford. I shall of course take heed of your words. Good day."

The older woman nodded, her expression more than tinged with sadness. She had not enjoyed saying those words to her, that much was plain to see.

Olivia moved off, back in the direction of home, her heart heavy.

By the time she had reached the sanctuary of her room, her anger had fueled determination. This was 1900, the beginning of a new century. The old queen was not in good health. Soon there would be a new monarch on the throne. It would be a period of momentous change. Most people had only ever known a time when Queen Victoria, in her perpetual widow's mourning, had ruled with her lack of humor, emphasis on the status quo and everyone knowing, and keeping to, their place in society. The future king was a very different character. By all accounts he enjoyed life, mixed with people from many classes and embraced all things new. This was the start of a new world and Olivia intended to play her part. Women might not have the vote yet, but one day they would – and *then* watch them flourish. Mrs. Emmeline Pankhurst had already formed the Women's Franchise League, fighting for the right of women to vote in local elections. Olivia knew her mother found the idea quite shocking. "Politics is for men. It is far too grubby for women to dabble in," she said on more than one occasion, to her father's approval. Olivia said nothing, but silently seethed. One day she would join the Women's Franchise League, but right now she had other things on her mind.

Archeology and Grant Ford for a start.

⋆　　⋆　　⋆

The following afternoon, she found Grant in the large field in the center of the village. She watched him pacing between massive fallen stones. Each time he did so, he wrote something down in a small notebook with a pencil he tucked behind his ear.

"Hello, Mr. Ford," she said.

He looked up from his notebook. "Miss Anstruther." He tipped his cap to her and smiled.

"I think you should call me Olivia. After all, we're much the same age and it seems silly to be so formal."

"Very well, Olivia. You shall call me Grant."

"I shall be happy to, Grant. What are you doing?"

"I'm helping with the early stages of the excavation that will be starting here in a couple of days. Professor Scott has asked me to take some measurements. He's in charge of the whole operation. He did some work on Stonehenge and he's also worked on digs in Scotland and Egypt. He has some fascinating theories."

"Does he think we have another Stonehenge here, then?"

"Oh no, much better than that. He feels Landane was possibly the most important site in England in its time."

"And when was that?"

"About five thousand years ago. Maybe more."

"Was it built by druids? I read somewhere that they built Stonehenge."

"That's an old theory. No, the druids couldn't possibly have built it. They only date from around three hundred BC – only two thousand years ago, give or take a few hundred. The people who built Stonehenge, the monuments in Scotland and elsewhere, and here, were long before that. The druids just adopted the circles and standing stones for their own practices."

"May I help? I haven't much to do and this sounds so interesting. I'm fascinated by archeology and I know so little."

Grant paused. "Why not? The more the merrier. Take my notebook and you can start by writing down the measurements I give you. It will save me having to stop all the time."

The next twenty minutes were spent dodging curious sheep, trying not to step on their droppings, and recording distances between the visible stones. When they had circumnavigated the field, they sat on a fallen stone to examine the results.

"It's exactly as the professor thought," Grant said. "The distance between some of the stones is almost identical and then there's a large gap until the next one, before the pattern emerges again."

"So, there are missing stones."

"Probably, but equally they may be buried. A few hundred years ago, the church decreed that these stone circles were heathen and the work of the devil. They had to be destroyed. As a result, gangs of local people and those drafted in from elsewhere began the work of toppling the stones into massive pits and covering them over. Some were broken up and burned. The type of stone is sarsen and, with the repeated application of fire and water, it'll break sufficiently that it can be used as building material. That's why you see so much of it worked into the cottages and even the church."

"I thought they quarried it specially to build the village."

"If you look at some of the stones in the church walls you can still see the scorch marks."

"What does the professor intend to do?"

"Resurrect and reconstruct the entire stone circle. Of course, he's meeting some strong opposition. Mainly from people like my father. Even in this day and age, with all the advances in science, superstition still prevails. Dad won't see it. To him the stones are evil and the only way to cleanse them is to destroy them."

"Then why are they built into the church? Surely that means evil has been invited into a holy place."

"That's an excellent point, Olivia. But my father believes that because they're incorporated into the fabric of the building, the evil has been cleansed. Nullified even. Convenient logic, wouldn't you say?"

"It's not my place to criticize the rector," Olivia said.

"Oh, don't hesitate on my account. I criticize him often. He asks for my help with his sermons, but only so that I can correct his grammar or suggest a more suitable noun or verb to get his point across. The minute I dare to suggest that some of the content is outdated or inappropriate, there's one hell of a row. I apologize for my language."

"No need. I have the same problem at home. It's my mother mainly, though. She's the one charged with my upbringing, so she has the privilege of telling me I don't know what I'm talking about and that the old ways are the best. Even when, clearly, they're not."

"Ah well, I suppose it's their generation. I mean, look at the example they've had. The Widow of Windsor's hardly a barrel of laughs, is she?" Grant winked at her and Olivia burst out laughing. Yet another loss of control that would have had her mother reaching for the smelling salts. The thought of that caused her to laugh even harder. Grant joined her.

He was easy to be with and Olivia found herself genuinely interested in what he was telling her about the professor's work and the importance of the stones of Landane. The fact that they also seemed to share many of the same opinions was refreshing too. Time sped past until the church clock struck five. Olivia leapt to her feet.

"I must go, I promised I would be back half an hour ago. Mama will kill me. She has two of her old biddies coming to tea."

Grant stood. "Until the next time, Olivia. I can't remember when I last had such an enjoyable conversation."

"I shall look forward to it."

"I'll be here tomorrow if you should happen to be free."

Olivia nodded. "Now, I must dash."

★   ★   ★

Her mother's thunderous look said more than any words could have conveyed.

The two old ladies – Miss Fortescue and Miss Monkton, spinsters of the parish – set down their teacups and waited for the inevitable argument. They seemed more than a little aggrieved when it did not materialize. But then, Mrs. Anstruther was always the soul of propriety. In company, a look would suffice. Once the ladies had been safely dispatched, replete with Earl Grey, cucumber sandwiches and Victoria sponge cake, then the ax would fall.

An hour of inane and tedious conversation about needlework, flower arrangements and the autumn church fete, and Olivia felt she wanted to scream. Is this what her mother wanted for her? Granted, these two women were unmarried, but a life composed of afternoon teas, village fetes and good works, interspersed by pregnancies, was hardly the future Olivia wanted for herself. As Miss Fortescue droned on about dahlias, Olivia made a decision. Tomorrow she would ask Grant how she might join the dig at Landane.

CHAPTER EIGHT

"Well now, Miss Anstruther, you seem to be settling in splendidly." Professor Charles Scott was a hearty man in his forties, who sported a bushy mane of red hair liberally streaked with gray. His generous beard and eccentric moustache added to an appearance that was topped off with a ruddy complexion and generous proportions encased in a tweed suit with a loud check. His pipe was rarely out of either his mouth or his hand and, while he must have spent many an hour on his knees in the mud and dirt, these days he had others to do that for him. Olivia reckoned that if he even managed to kneel now it would take at least two sturdy men to haul him to his feet. But his blue eyes were kind and intelligent and there had been no protest from him when she had lodged her request to join in.

"Young Grant here tells me you have made some finds already."

"Yes, sir. Some old coins I believe." Olivia handed the professor a small box containing some badly corroded discs.

"Coins are such handy things to find. They give us reliable dates. Provided we can still read 'em of course." He guffawed. Olivia smiled. "Well done, young lady. Keep up the good work. Interesting you should choose this stone. It's my favorite too. We'll raise this one first, I think. I have a feeling what we find underneath it will be worth the effort." Professor Scott turned to go. "Oh, by the way. There's a young chap around here somewhere. He's taking photographs for the local newspaper. I'll send him over. Not every time we have a young lady on a dig. I understand your father is quite a bigwig around here."

"He's a High Court judge, sir."

"And what does he think about his daughter getting her hands dirty?"

"He doesn't know."

Professor Scott nodded. "Guessed as much. Oh well, he soon will, eh? He soon will."

At that moment the promised photographer arrived and before she could think through the consequences, Olivia was being posed alongside Grant who was asked to stand with his shovel poised as if about to dig a hole. It was all over in a few minutes, despite the need to stand perfectly still while a bee decided to pay her a little too detailed an inspection.

"Thank you, Miss Anstruther," said the photographer, collapsing his tripod and hoisting it and the camera over his shoulder. "It will be in Friday's edition."

"He didn't take your name," Olivia said to Grant, who shrugged.

★ ★ ★

Percival Anstruther jabbed his finger at the front page of the *Charnford Gazette* while Olivia sat quietly at the dining table awaiting the inevitable explosion.

His cold eyes bored into her. "When did you propose to inform us of this?"

"I knew you wouldn't approve so—"

"You knew I wouldn't approve so you went ahead and brazenly defied your position in society. Scrabbling about in the mud. Young ladies of a certain position do not indulge in such filthy practices."

"It's called archeology, Papa. Professor Scott is an academic at Cambridge University."

"And presumably doesn't get his hands dirty. He has minions to do that for him and you apparently have elected to become one of them."

"It's better than staying here festering away at one tea party after another."

Across from her, Marina Anstruther took a sharp intake of breath.

Her father slammed his fist down on the table, setting plates, cups and saucers rattling. "Apologize to your mother immediately."

"For what? I haven't said anything out of place."

Olivia had never seen her father's face turn quite that shade of purple before. He stood, throwing his chair backward so hard it toppled over. "You know perfectly well that your mother is a charming hostess. Apologize for your appalling disrespect *immediately*."

"Very well. If I have offended you, Mama, I apologize. But I don't see anything wrong in participating in an important piece of historical research. Lots of young women do these days. Some even set up their own expeditions. Why, Marcia Conway is in Arabia at the moment—"

"Marcia Conway has been educated for such a life. You have not. Her personal reputation is not all that it could be either. Not by a long way. I have heard her morals leave quite a lot to be desired. People talk, Olivia. Important people. People who can make or break your reputation and your standing in society. That woman is most certainly best staying out of this country. She would never be accepted in smart circles should she return, and I am not risking that fate descending on you. You will stop all this nonsense forthwith *and* you will cease to associate with Grant Ford. Both his father and I believe your friendship is inappropriate and could have serious consequences."

Olivia could no longer contain the swell of anger rising inside her. "By that I assume you mean it would spoil your chances of marrying me off to some well-connected numbskull. I'm telling you, Papa. I won't have it. I'm an adult with my own mind and I will not be treated like a child or sold off to the highest bidder."

For Olivia, the shocked silence that followed was punctuated only by her thudding heartbeat. Her mother looked as if she would dissolve into tears or faint. Maybe both. Her father stared at her as if he was seeing a stranger. An unwelcome one at that.

"Get out of my sight," he said at last. "Go to your room and stay there until your mother and I have decided what to do with you."

Olivia pushed her chair back and, without a word, left the room. She raced up to her bedroom and shut the door.

Then the tears came. It seemed they would never stop, but by the time they had she had resolved to leave that house as soon as she could and never return. As to where she would go, she hadn't a clue, but she was determined to carry on with the dig. The stone she was working on drew her to it. She couldn't stop now.

And then there was Grant. Olivia dried her eyes, pocketed her handkerchief and went over to the small writing desk by the window. She sat, opened the top drawer, withdrew a pristine sheet of notepaper, unscrewed her fountain pen and began to write. When she had finished the half-dozen sentences, she selected a matching envelope, folded the paper and inserted it before sealing the envelope. Then she rang for the maid.

The fresh-faced parlormaid appeared within a couple of minutes.

"Ah. Daisy. I'm so glad it's you. Your sister is the maid at the rectory, isn't she?"

"Yes, Miss."

"I need you to do me a big favor and I must ask that you keep this between ourselves. On no account are my parents to hear of it."

Daisy bit her lip.

"Please, Daisy, I really need you to do this. You're the only one who can help me."

Maybe it was the chance to have a bit of an adventure, to be a tad daring for once in her young life, but Daisy stopped gnawing her lip and smiled. "All right, Miss. What do you need me to do?"

Olivia restrained the impulse to hug the girl and, instead, handed her the envelope. "As you'll see, it's addressed to Mr. Grant Ford. Only he is to see this, apart from your sister of course. Please make sure she understands that. Mr. and Mrs. Ford would not approve of me corresponding with their son. It is all quite harmless but they wouldn't see it like that. Do you understand?"

"I think so, Miss."

"Very well. Could you deliver it today please? Now if possible. It's really important and time is of the essence."

"Of course, Miss. I think I can get out now. I'll only need a few minutes. Cook's having her afternoon lie down and it's Mr. Dunwoody's afternoon off."

Olivia had forgotten their butler took Friday afternoons off. She thanked whatever deity might be listening and Daisy departed. She returned around twenty minutes later.

"I delivered the note, Miss. My sister says to tell you that Mr. Grant is at the dig but will be home for his tea at about five o'clock. She will see he gets it as soon as he returns. If there is any reply, we'll get it to you."

"Thank you, Daisy. That's very kind of you both."

"I'm to ask you to come down to the drawing room, Miss. Mr. and Mrs. Anstruther wish to see you. They don't look too happy."

"They're not. Thank you. I'll come now."

Olivia inhaled deeply a few times. She drew a modicum of comfort from the action.

Her father looked up when she entered. Her mother stared straight ahead without acknowledging her presence. Olivia stood in the center of the hearthrug, her hands clasped in front of her. She felt as if she was in her father's court, awaiting sentence.

Her father cleared his throat. "Olivia. I can only assume you were momentarily out of your mind earlier. Your mother has explained how such things can happen to a young woman at certain times of the month."

Olivia resisted the urge to protest. Besides, her period wasn't due for another couple of weeks yet – and her mother knew it.

"As a result, I am willing to overlook your uncharacteristic outburst on condition that you never repeat it. In future I shall not be so lenient. For now, you will desist from scrubbing around on your hands and knees at this…whatever you call it, and you will not make any attempt to see Grant Ford. Naturally, owing to the nature of his father's position in the village, this will not always be possible, but on no account are the two of you ever to be alone together, either indoors or out. Do I make myself perfectly clear?"

"Yes, Papa."

"Very well. We shall say no more about it. Now go. I have matters to discuss with your mother."

Olivia nodded and left. As she shut the door, she leaned heavily against it, willing her heart to slow down. She had never expected to be let off so lightly, but there still remained the unresolved issues of how she would continue with the dig and, of course, Grant.

★   ★   ★

The following morning, Saturday, Daisy came in to draw back her curtains at eight-thirty as usual. She handed her a slightly crumpled envelope from her pocket. "Lily dropped it off earlier," she said. "It's from Mr. Grant."

Olivia sat up in bed and ripped open the envelope.

'My dear Olivia. I am so sorry to hear of the problems you are encountering, but I may have a solution. I shall speak with Professor Scott tomorrow (Saturday) and see if he can intervene. Maybe he has some ideas. I know he values your contribution to the work. I shall hope to see you there as soon as you are able. With best wishes, Grant.'

"Is there a reply, Miss?"

"Just a verbal one this time. Tell him 'thank you' from me."

"Very well, Miss. Lily's popping back here in half an hour or so. She went on some errands in the village."

Olivia dressed and went over to the window. Grant was deadheading some more roses. The mere sight of him sent her heart racing. He looked up as if he sensed her watching him and glanced over in her direction. She waved. Did he see her? At first she thought not, but then he raised his hand and gave his cap an almost imperceptible touch. Anyone seeing the gesture would simply think he was adjusting it, but Olivia knew better. She knew he had been instructed to discontinue any personal contact with her. His father would have issued much the same instructions as her own, but that wouldn't stop them having feelings for each other. Even if the future did seem hopeless.

Suddenly the new century seemed as old and staid as the previous one. The world might be on the cusp of new beginnings but for Olivia it seemed Landane was stuck firmly in the past. Surely a very different past from the one lived by the builders of its stone circle.

★   ★   ★

"Professor Scott, what a lovely surprise." Olivia greeted the man who was dressed in his habitual tweeds. He seemed perfectly at home in their drawing room while her mother poured tea and Daisy handed round the perfectly triangular bite-size sandwiches.

Her father set down his teacup and saucer. "The professor asked to see us regarding your work on the stone circle. Naturally he appreciates my position regarding the nature of your participation there, but I believe we have reached an acceptable compromise, wouldn't you agree, Professor?"

Professor Scott paused in the act of taking a bite of cucumber sandwich. "Oh, undoubtedly, undoubtedly." Out of sight of her parents, he winked at Olivia.

She had to cough to cover an irresistible urge to laugh. Her mother gave her a suspicious look.

Her father continued. "I have agreed that you should be allowed to continue as an unofficial student of the professor's. You can follow him around, take notes, that sort of thing. But, on no account are you to undertake any digging or manual labor of any kind. Do you understand?"

"Yes, Papa."

"The professor has agreed to see to it that you obey my instructions and, so long as you do, then you may continue to attend the excavations."

A great weight slid off Olivia's shoulders and she could have danced around the room but, instead, she kept her voice under control. "When may I start, Professor?"

"Not tomorrow, obviously, as it's Sunday. But how about first thing on Monday morning. Say, eight-thirty? We're concentrating on that stone you took such a shine to. There have been more finds. Those coins you found are almost certainly fourteenth century, and young Grant discovered the remains of a leather purse. It wasn't much more than a stain on the ground but it was probably where the coins were concealed. He also dug up a couple of tools. One looks like a heavily corroded pair of iron scissors and the other resembles a lance. They are the sort of tools an itinerant surgeon might have carried around with them around the time the coins were minted. I strongly believe there is more to come. Maybe much more. It will be handy to have you there sketching and noting down all the finds and their measurements. We'll take photographs of course but notes are so much more important as a record of our excavation."

"That sounds fascinating. I shall look forward to Monday."

"Then that's all settled. Now, if I could avail myself of a slice of that delicious-looking cake, I shall be delighted."

When it came time for him to leave, Olivia saw him to the door.

"I can't thank you enough, Professor."

"Think nothing of it, my dear. When Grant told me of your... difficulties, I had to step in. You see, there's something about your relationship with the stones here. I don't think you realize it yourself, but you may do. In the future."

"I'm sorry. I don't...."

"As I surmised. No matter. All will become clear, I'm sure. It did the last time. Well, to be truthful I have only ever witnessed it once before."

"I'm really confused now."

"Don't be. All will be as it should be. Trust the stones. They hold power. Power our ancient ancestors understood far better than we do. We've lost the ability, you see. We think we know so much when actually we don't know anything, and we've forgotten the little we did. Those ancient people knew. Yes, they knew all right. Well goodbye, my dear. Until Monday."

Olivia was left holding the open door, baffled by the professor's words yet, deep within her, something stirred. A long-buried memory? Maybe. All she knew was Monday couldn't come soon enough.

CHAPTER NINE

Olivia....

Olivia straightened up from where she had been bending down, using the huge fallen stone to steady herself. She shielded her eyes against the sun. Had the voice been audible or was it in her head? It was strange because she had heard it but couldn't even hazard a guess as to the direction of sound. More than that, surely if it had been audible, the two people nearest to her would have registered it as well. Grant was closest. He was using a trowel to dig around the stone.

"Did you hear that?" Olivia asked. Grant stopped troweling and looked up at her.

"Hear what?"

"Someone called my name."

"Just now?"

Olivia nodded.

Grant shrugged. "I didn't hear anything."

"Neither did I," the bespectacled student she knew as Christopher said.

"Never mind. I must have imagined it."

The two men resumed their work, but Olivia continued to look around her, searching the landscape for a sign of anyone, but increasingly sure the sound she had heard came from inside her head.

Then it happened again. Louder.

Olivia....

There could be no doubt this time. The voice was inside her head. In front of her, the air shimmered. "This isn't right."

"What isn't?" Grant set down his trowel and wiped his hands on his corduroy trousers. "What's the matter, Olivia? You're as white as a sheet."

"I don't know. I keep hearing a voice."

Christopher also stopped. Both men stared at Olivia. "I'm sorry. Maybe it's the heat."

"It *is* a little warm," Grant said. "Perhaps you need to get indoors, out of the sun."

"Yes. You're right. I'll...."

The girl appeared as if from nowhere. She was tall, slim, with waist-length blonde hair and large blue eyes that held a question in them. Her lips moved. "When am I?"

Before Olivia could respond, the girl vanished. A loud buzzing filled Olivia's head and she staggered forward. Grant caught her. Professor Scott's voice boomed out across the field.

"Is she all right?"

Olivia felt herself losing consciousness. She felt Grant's arms around her, breaking her fall.

When she came to, it was in the relative cool of the finds tent. Professor Scott and Grant looked down at her as she lay on a camp bed. Her head thumped painfully.

"May I have a glass of water, please?" Her voice wavered and she fought to control it.

Grant produced a cool, refreshing glass of water and she drank it down.

"Take it steady, young lady," the professor said. "You don't want your stomach to reject it. I think the combination of a hot day and lack of liquid refreshment have proved an unholy combination. No more work for you until at least tomorrow."

That wouldn't do at all. Olivia struggled to sit, angry at limbs that would not function at her command. What was the matter with her? "I shall be fine in a few minutes, Professor, and we're at such an important juncture. We raise the stone tomorrow."

"And you will see it. Rest assured, Olivia. You will see that stone re-erected where it stood all those centuries ago and there'll be no toppling it this time. It'll be firmly set in concrete."

"Did you see her? Did either of you see her?"

"See who, my dear?" Professor Scott's expression worried Olivia. If he thought she had lost her reason, there would be no more dig for her, under any circumstances.

"Oh, it's nothing. Sorry, it was just before I fainted, everything went a bit peculiar. As you say, I should have been drinking more water, but I was too absorbed in what we were unearthing. I should have been more careful. I will in future." She hoped she had sounded convincing. At least the frown that had crept onto the professor's craggy face had dissipated.

He patted her hand. "That's quite all right. When you feel up to it, get yourself off home or, better still, let young Grant walk with you."

Olivia smiled and nodded. Professor Scott left them.

"You know I can't walk you home alone, don't you?" Grant said.

Olivia nodded. "Too many prying eyes and ears around. In a village you have no privacy and someone would be bound to tell my father, or yours. Papa wouldn't accept any excuse. Even if I had a broken leg and you were the only person left in the village, the sight of us walking together, unchaperoned, would be quite enough for him to forbid me from ever joining this dig again, and it's getting so exciting now. Those finds today. Amazing."

"My money's on us finding a body. Well, what's left of one anyway. There's too much there. Finding that shoe today sealed it for me. I reckon that by this time tomorrow we'll know whose foot it belonged to."

A shiver traveled up Olivia's spine. She swung her legs off the camp bed and Grant helped her stand. Thankfully her head didn't swim but, out of the corner of her eye, she caught a movement. A slender figure of a girl with flowing hair flitted across the entrance to the tent. She moved far too quickly for a normal person and with a strange jerky movement. No point in asking Grant if he had seen her. He had his back to the entrance. But, somehow, Olivia doubted he would have even if he had been standing right in front of her.

Her solitary walk back home was spent in deep thought. Either she was going mad or that girl existed. If she did, who was she? What was she doing there? And why was it that only she, Olivia, was able to see her? Then there was the strange question she had asked. "When am I?" Who asks that? *Where* maybe, but *when*?

She was almost at her gate. But the girl was standing in front of her, barring her way. Olivia gasped. "Who are you?"

The girl blinked. "Who am I?"

"Yes. I want to know who you are and why you are here."

"Here? What is here?"

"Here is a village called Landane. Now please answer my questions."

The girl smiled but the smile ended at the corner of her lips. Her eyes continued to stare straight at Olivia as if they were staring into her. Maybe even through her. The sensation was unpleasant, like a violation of her body. Olivia wanted to cover herself even though she was fully dressed. The girl looked to be in her teens and as Olivia watched, transfixed, she faded before disappearing. As the last of her vanished, a cold breath of wind whipped her hair and a soft, feminine voice murmured the opening lines of a gentle song:

"Fear her now, fear the queen,

As in her stone she reigns supreme...."

CHAPTER TEN

"My dear Olivia, you have joined us at the precise moment of discovery." Professor Scott took Olivia's hand and led her forward to where a team of strong men equipped with cables, pulleys, tractors and an array of mechanical equipment stood ready.

At a signal from the professor, a traction engine, powered by steam, roared into life, providing an almost deafening cacophony, and a choking mix of oil and smoke filled the air. The cables pulled taut around the stone and slowly the massive sarsen began to shift. Inch by inch it rose as the men worked on it, repositioning cables where necessary, adding more where needed. Olivia watched fascinated while, beneath her feet, the ground rumbled. She glanced at Grant and caught his eye. "Can you feel that?" she mouthed. He nodded.

With agonizing slowness, the stone elevated. The hole had been prepared for it, to precise measurements that Olivia herself had recorded at Professor Scott's dictation. All they could do now was pray the calculations were correct. If so, the stone would drop neatly into the hole which would then be filled with concrete.

Grant moved closer to the stone. He leaned forward and pointed. Gesticulating wildly, he raced over to Olivia and the professor.

"It's there. The body. It's *there*."

The professor clapped him on the back. Olivia kissed his cheek before she realized what she was doing. All three of them laughed.

The rumbling grew louder.

An earsplitting crack rent the air.

The engine cut out and men scattered in all directions as cables snapped around the stone.

"Get out of there," the professor yelled.

One of the cables snapped off, whipping round and round, like a furious serpent. It missed one of the men by inches. He let out a cry and threw himself on the ground. The cable came to rest next to him. The other men crowded round him.

"Is he all right?" the professor called.

"Seems to be," one of the men said. "He's more shocked than anything, I think. That was a close one."

"How could that happen, Professor?" Olivia asked. "Weren't the cables secure enough?"

The man who had just spoken protested. "I'll have none of that talk. I checked those cables myself. They were perfectly secure."

"Hey, Fred," one of his team said. "You're not going to believe this. Look at this cable."

The man joined him. Olivia, Grant and the professor moved closer. One of the men held up the heavy-duty steel cable. It was frayed as if it had been shredded.

"Faulty, do you think?" Professor Scott's tone indicated he didn't see that as a likely explanation.

The foreman shook his head and took the cable from his mate. "I don't understand it. I've been working with these for twenty years or more. Never had one do this on me. Never had one break, let alone disintegrate like this."

"Then, what—" He didn't have time to finish his question. The subterranean rumbling started up again, louder, fiercer. The ground shook. Flocks of birds took off, crows cawing loudly.

"It's an earthquake," someone shouted.

Grant pointed. "The stone. Look at it."

The stone tilted as if it weighed a fraction of its estimated thirteen tons.

"How can it do that?" Olivia asked the professor.

He shook his head. "I truly don't know."

"It's as if someone, or something, is balancing it, but nothing could possess that degree of strength, could it?"

"Not that I'm aware of. Certainly nothing we have here."

"It's not natural." The man who had so nearly been killed pointed at the stone with a shaking hand. "The devil's at work there. My mother told me and her mother told her. There's evil there. Pure evil. We should never have messed with it. Nothing good is going to come of this."

Two of his friends held him back or he would have attacked the professor. His eyes were wild, insane. The sight of them chilled Olivia's blood.

Professor Scott stood his ground. He appeared deep in thought, almost oblivious to the threat posed by the hysterical man. He merely nodded when the foreman assured him they would get the man home safely.

Olivia switched her attention back to the stone. It had come to rest at a crazy angle, partially in the hole. Another few inches maybe and it would have dropped right in.

A sudden movement sent her pulse through the roof. Emerging from the back of the stone came the now-familiar figure of the ethereal young girl. The girl who couldn't exist but somehow did.

Without taking her eyes off her, Olivia called to Grant. "Tell me you can see her. By the stone."

He looked. "Yes. I see her."

The girl leaned against the ancient sarsen, stretching her arms upward. She never took her eyes off them.

Olivia shouted over to the professor. "Can you see her? That girl?"

"What girl?"

"By the stone."

"There's no one by the stone, Olivia."

The ground lurched once more. Olivia almost overbalanced. Grant and the professor stumbled to one side along with the remaining members of the team of laborers.

"She's fading," Grant said as he staggered closer to Olivia on the still-shifting ground.

"It's as if she's melting into the stone."

"I see it. Yes. And the stone's moving. But she couldn't possibly...."

Silently, the stone slid into place, erect once again. The rumbling stopped and the ground settled. The girl had vanished.

"Fill the hole," the professor ordered.

The laborers exchanged worried glances but did as he instructed.

Professor Scott gestured to Olivia and Grant. "Come along, you two. While they're doing that, let's have a look at that body."

Olivia stared up at the stone, now perfectly upright in its new home. "It can't topple onto us, can it?"

"No, my dear," the professor said. "No need to worry about that. That stone is there to stay and when the men have finished mixing and applying that concrete, nothing will shift it. Now then, let's meet the person who owned those artifacts."

The skeleton lay on its side, curled in a fetal position. The skull was hopelessly fractured and most of the visible bones were badly crushed.

"I suppose you can't have thirteen tons of solid stone fall on you and not end up in this state," Grant said.

"I suppose not." The professor looked thoughtful.

"Is something wrong?" Olivia asked.

"It's probably nothing, but.... It seems rather odd that he should fall and land in this position. I would have expected him to have fallen forward or backward, but this is almost as if he lay down to sleep and the stone fell and hit him."

"Maybe that's what did happen," Grant said. "Perhaps he was having an afternoon nap or something.... No, that doesn't sound terribly plausible, does it?"

Olivia thought for a moment. "Even if he had no home, this wouldn't be a good place to sleep at night. There wouldn't have been any shelter and, in any case, they were working on that stone. It was bound to be unsafe."

Professor Scott tapped his teeth with a pencil. "I suspect we'll never know the answer to this particular riddle, but we must document everything before we give this chap a decent Christian burial as I'm sure he would have wished."

"I can have a word with my father," Grant said. "I'm sure he would be happy to oblige."

"Excellent, my boy, excellent. Well, to work, Olivia. Get your pencil and notebook out. I'll send the photographer chappy along. I suspect the press will be here before long, swarming around like mosquitos."

Olivia smiled. During the short time she had known him, she had developed not only a respect for the professor's knowledge but also a genuine warmth toward him. There was nothing stuffy about him, unlike her father with whom she had always enjoyed an uneasy, awkward relationship, and Mama who never seemed to let anyone in. She was such a closed person. Olivia felt *she* didn't even know who she really was. Had they ever exchanged a joke, or a laugh? As a child, her nanny had provided the only real affection she had known. Olivia had wept for days when she had said her goodbyes. The parting had come suddenly for her, although, looking back, she suspected that Nanny Morgan had known for some considerable time that her days were numbered. Olivia had outgrown the need for a nanny so that was that. Her contract would be terminated and Nanny Morgan would have to move on to her next charge. From then, until the age of sixteen, Olivia would have a governess to teach her the skills she would need to be a fine lady one day and run her own house as her mother ran hers.

Nanny had cried too. Mama had expressed her disgust. "Such lack of self-discipline. In front of the child as well."

Olivia had grown accustomed to being referred to in the third person even when she was present, as she had been on that occasion when Mama had been hosting one of her afternoon teas. With the governess not yet installed, although imminently expected, she had been allowed to attend the tea as long as she played quietly with her favorite doll in a corner of the room and did not make a nuisance of herself. Olivia would never have dreamed of disobeying. At eight years old, she knew that children should be seen and not heard.

Now, as she sketched the ruined skeleton in front of her, Olivia glanced occasionally at the professor as he supervised the men filling the hole around the stone. What sort of father would Professor Scott have made? Maybe he had children of his own. If so, they were lucky to have such an approachable parent.

"Olivia."

Olivia jumped. "Oh, Grant. You startled me. I was miles away."

"Centuries maybe?" He indicated the skeleton. "I wanted to talk to you about that…whatever it was we both saw. Apparition, I suppose. Did we see the same thing? I saw a young woman – well, a girl really – with long blonde hair, wearing some sort of gown. Not fancy, more like a nightdress, I suppose."

"Yes, that's what I saw. I've seen her before, a couple of times. Once at least, I'm fairly sure she spoke to me. Only to call my name, but no one else heard her. Even you. Then another time she asked me the oddest question. She said, 'When am I?' So strange."

"Strange indeed. I'm pretty sure I've never seen her before today and yet I dreamt about her last night. It was the oddest dream. I was here in this field, the moon was full and it was so quiet. Too quiet really, as if someone had turned the sound off. I know that doesn't make sense, but it was a dream after all. Anyway, suddenly, I could hear again and the noise was like people marching. The ground was thudding under my feet. Not like today but thudding as if thousands of people were on the move. Then I saw her. She was standing right by this stone, and it was erect as it is now. Then, just as we saw today, she leaned into it and disappeared. That's when I woke up."

A thought struck Olivia. A bizarre idea, but as everything seemed pretty bizarre now, what was the harm in mentioning it? "Are you sure it *was* a dream? What if that actually happened? Something's been bothering me about all of this – apart from her, I mean – but I think it may all be tied in. Earlier, we were being thrown around by the most violent earth tremors. We're here in the middle of the field in the center of the village. Did you see anyone come out of their houses to investigate?"

Grant shook his head. "Now you come to mention it, that *is* odd.

Those tremors were surely strong enough to knock glassware off shelves and cause all sorts of damage, but no one seems to have been aware of it."

They both looked past the field and onto the street, maybe a hundred yards away. People were going about their everyday business. A normal weekday. Nothing untoward.

Olivia continued. "Where's the panic? I mean it's over now, but surely, after something like that, people would still be reacting, dealing with the damage, something."

"They never felt a thing." Professor Scott had come up behind them. "It's all right. I've seen this sort of thing before. Years ago, when I was on a dig in Egypt. Of course, there they put it down to the wrath of the ancient gods reacting to the violation of one of their sacred places. Utter rot of course, but I never did discover how it was possible that an earthquake could be confined to such a small place. Usually, tremors are felt for miles around."

"What's your theory, Professor?" Grant asked.

"Over the years I've had many. For a time, I half believed the local people, but my logical side and all my training wouldn't allow it. These days, I put it down to Earth's natural forces of which we are all too painfully ignorant. Even that's too much for some of my colleagues. They prefer everything neatly tied up with brown paper and string." He smiled. "They think I'm a bit dotty. Spent too much time under the hot sun. They may indeed have a point."

"I've completed my sketch, Professor," Olivia said, handing him her notebook. "You said our poor man here was a sort of traveling surgeon, wasn't he?"

"Almost certainly, given the tools he carried around with him. That's a fine sketch, my dear. Such a shame we'll never know the poor chap's name, however he got here."

Now seemed as good a time as any to probe a little deeper. "Professor, have you ever seen anything you couldn't explain?" Olivia heard Grant inhale deeply. "Here, I mean. Any...I suppose, ghostly figure or something of that kind."

"Are you asking me if I believe in ghosts?"

"I suppose I am."

"I keep an open mind, with a healthy dose of skepticism thrown in for good measure. In my experience, most strange occurrences can be explained by natural phenomena. Having said that, I've had experiences which defied logic, at least as far as I was concerned but, again, I must stress our knowledge of what the Earth is capable of is in its infancy."

"The reason I'm asking is because both Grant and I have seen the same thing. Right here by this stone. A young woman, only she wasn't real. Not in the sense we are. She seems to have been some kind of apparition and she disappeared into this very stone."

The professor stared at them. He appeared about to speak when a shout rang out from across the field.

"Professor Scott!"

"Oh good grief, here they come." The professor seemed to paste a smile onto his face as a man in a brown suit ran toward him, followed by a smaller man wielding a heavy camera and tripod. Half a dozen others followed, some armed with cameras, some without.

"Here we have the gentlemen of the press," the professor said just before the first of them arrived, panting heavily.

Olivia and Grant stepped aside. The pressmen clearly weren't the slightest bit interested in them. Grant moved over to the next fallen stone which served as a convenient place to sit. Olivia joined him. Maybe propriety dictated that she shouldn't sit so close to him, but her aching feet overruled such a consideration. When she sat, they were no more than six inches apart.

"Olivia," he said, and she studied his face. She took in the deep brown eyes, hair that curled slightly around his ears and that he wore longer than was the fashion so that it rested on his collar. It looked as if it would be soft to the touch and Olivia longed to do just that.

"There's no one watching us," he said softly and, when he took her hand in his, she didn't pull back. She focused on his face. How it would feel to caress his cheek. To kiss…. His lips would taste slightly salty. How she knew that and why it would be, she had no idea, only a certainty that it would be so. He wouldn't taste or smell of tobacco, though. She had never seen him smoke and that was unusual. Even her father enjoyed a cigar after dinner, and she had certainly seen him smoke cigarettes during the day.

Grant had awakened something in her. Something that had lain dormant all her life and maybe even before that. She wanted to taste those lips so much it hurt. She sensed they were of a mind on that but, even though no one appeared to be taking the slightest bit of notice of them, it would only take one pair of prying eyes....

"We can't...." Tears welled up in Olivia's eyes. She looked away.

Grant squeezed her hand. "We'll find a way. I'm in love with you, Olivia. Don't ask me when it began, I have no idea. If I think about it, it seems I have always been in love with you, ever since we first came to Landane and we were both no more than children. I don't intend to lose you."

She hadn't expected him to say that but as soon as the words were out, she allowed herself to feel what had lain so long suppressed. "I love you too, Grant. But I don't know how we'll ever be together. My father...."

"And mine, but this is 1900; their world is passing. It's our turn now. The future is ours and we can't let their old ways deny us the happiness we deserve. I don't care how long it takes; I'm not giving you up."

Minutes later, the newspapermen started drifting away. Cameras were packed up. Reporters replaced notepads and pencils in pockets. Two of the professor's postgraduate students embarked on the painstaking work of transferring the surgeon's remains to boxes to be reassembled back at the university.

The professor relit his pipe and took a few puffs. "We'll be able to learn all sorts of valuable information about that poor chap once we get him back. Then we can arrange his burial. If you could speak to the rector, Grant, I would be most grateful. I think it most fitting he should find his final resting place here in Landane. In the churchyard maybe?"

"I'll let you know what he says tomorrow, sir. I'm sure he'll be amenable."

The professor looked from one to the other. "I don't think there's any need to detain you further today. My students know what to do and they'll be busy for a few hours yet. Tomorrow, I have work for you to do on that very stone." He pointed to where they were sitting. "A most interesting one I feel. Yes indeed. Well, good afternoon to you both."

"Good afternoon, Professor," they chorused, and he returned to his students.

Olivia stared up at the stone that had until recently hidden the body of the surgeon. "I think it should be called the surgeon's stone. The poor man may not have kept his name after death, but at least he will always be commemorated for his profession."

"Did we really see a ghost?"

"Yes, Grant, I'm sure we did. I shall go to my grave believing it, and there's a reason we saw it. I can only pray it's a good one."

CHAPTER ELEVEN

Olivia blinked hard. There was no moon and she shivered in the cold night air. Clad only in her cotton nightdress, her breath misted as she exhaled. In a moment she would wake up, turn over and go back to sleep. Except that the moments were adding up. Everything seemed too real for sleep. She hugged herself. She must find out where she was.

The moon emerged from its cloud blanket, casting sufficient silvery light to enable her to make out the field. By her side, the majestic, newly named surgeon's stone stood tall and proud. How she had managed to get herself there she had no idea, but all that mattered now was getting home safely before she ended up with pneumonia. She took a tentative step forward, and the voice called to her.

"Olivia."

It wasn't in her head. It was all around her. A low hum made the earth tremble beneath her bare feet.

"Olivia."

She spun around. Whoever it was must be right behind her, but she saw no one. Then the stone began to give off a gentle glow. The sound was coming from it. That was what was making the ground rumble. Had it caused the tremors they had experienced earlier?

"Hello, Olivia."

The girl stood maybe three feet away, her hair gently blowing around her shoulders. She stretched out her arms to her sides and gradually brought her hands together in front of her. Olivia was bathed in a warm cocoon of light. She wasn't cold anymore. There was no fear or concern as to what was happening to her. This was what it felt like to be protected and it felt good, so good she never wanted it to end.

"Come with me."

The girl was as real as she was, her hand warm as it clasped hers. Olivia went willingly. In front of them, the stone shimmered. No longer solid sarsen, it formed an entrance, then surrounded them as they crossed over.

Olivia felt she was gliding on air. There seemed nothing solid for her to put her feet on, until the ground beneath her shimmered and she stared down at a sea of pure iridescent blue glass with a sheen so high she felt sure they would slip, but she proceeded, sure-footed, one foot in front of the other. Beside her, the girl did the same. Together they passed through hallways of glittering, magnificent crystal. Stalactites hung down from the ceiling way above their heads, forming incredible and impossible shapes, twisted and transparent in places. There was no sound. Total, reverent silence. The place was like an enormous temple.

Salty but fresh air filled Olivia's lungs as, with each breath, she felt her spirit lighten. If only Grant could be here with her. At the thought of him, sadness invaded her peace. She pushed the unwelcome emotion aside. The girl stopped moving. Olivia also stopped. "Where are we?" she asked.

The girl raised her eyes to Olivia and smiled. "Where you are meant to be."

She vanished. Olivia was alone. In front of her, an archway promised more wonders. From where she stood, the path stretched out before her, darker now but still smooth and glassy. Ahead, the walls had gone from white crystal to gleaming black jet, sprinkled with what looked like gold dust.

Am I meant to go on, or wait here?

"Olivia." This time the voice came from farther away, somewhere along the path.

She stepped forward tentatively, still wary of the impossible floor, but kept moving until she was nearly at the entrance to the new hall.

"Olivia! Don't go in there!"

"Grant?"

Olivia realized she was standing on a bridge of some kind. A bridge between two worlds. Behind her, she could just make out Grant. He was exactly where she had stood only moments earlier. She could go back to him. Maybe this was where they were meant to be together.

"Olivia." The now-familiar female voice called to her from the unknown with a hypnotic, irresistible quality that was almost impossible to resist, but to follow it would take her away from Grant. Unless he came with her.

"Grant, come across. It's this way. This is where we're supposed to go."

"No, Olivia. It's an illusion. It's a trick. Come back. Come back before it's too late."

★　★　★

Olivia sat up. It took a moment to realize where she was. In her own bed. She got up and padded to the window. Outside, the moon was behind a cloud but she could see across to the rectory. Light shone through an upstairs window. Maybe Grant or his parents. She stood and watched until the light was extinguished, her thoughts jumbled. The dream had been so real, she half-expected to find that her soles were dirty, but, lifting one foot and then the other revealed that they were perfectly clean.

Back in bed, she pulled the covers over her and lay down. Tomorrow she would talk to Grant about her experience. They both knew there was something peculiar about that stone and, by association, probably the entire stone circle. Could this be another manifestation of it?

★　★　★

Grant ran his hands through his hair. "We had the same dream."

"But that's impossible." Olivia clenched her hands in her lap as the two of them sat on a fallen stone early the next morning. The professor hadn't yet arrived, and they were alone.

"Nevertheless, what you described is what I saw, except I saw it through my eyes. I followed the girl into the stone and went through the same crystal chambers. I stood at the entrance and called to you. She told me to call you back. She said your life was in danger if you went any further into the Black Chamber. That's what she called it. Then she disappeared and all I knew was I had to get you back. Then I woke up. I lit my lamp and sat for ages, trying to work it all out in my head."

"I think I saw your light. I stood looking across from my window until you extinguished it. What does it all mean?"

"I haven't a clue. I thought of asking my father, but I'm not sure how he would take it. He's not altogether thrilled at me working here. It's only because he respects the professor that he's willing to take a chance. If I start coming up with stuff like this, he's likely to start thinking there are evil forces at work and then.... Well, let's say he won't be satisfied until every last stone is broken up and carted away."

"Maybe he's right and that's exactly what should be done."

"Olivia, no, not you too."

"I'm sorry, that was a stupid thing to say. Forgive me."

Grant smiled. "Of course. It's a lot to take in. Maybe the professor has some answers."

"He seems ambivalent on the subject of ghosts. Although he did say to me that he believed there were things beyond what we know to be true. I was reminded of that quotation from *Hamlet* – 'There are more things in heaven and earth...' – that one. But even if he retains at least a partially open mind, entering solid standing stones is a big step beyond that."

"As you say though, he has had some odd experiences."

"But he puts them down to things we don't understand about the Earth's magnetic forces and a knowledge our ancestors possessed which we have now lost."

"If not him and not my father.... Then who can help us?"

"There you are." Professor Scott stood in front of them, grinning broadly. "Nice to see you're both up and ready to go again. I spent an interesting night at The White Hart. Needless to say, as we anticipated, no one felt a thing when we were being tossed around like ships on a rough sea. I was treated to a few strange looks, I can tell you." He laughed. "Then the damnedest thing happened when I'd gone to bed. One of my female students who is also staying there started screaming and crying, running out of her room, down the stairs and into the bar where the rest of us found her cowering behind a chair in the corner by the fire. She swore she had seen some man, dressed in the sort of apparel we associate with ancient times. He stared straight at her, pointed out of the window in this direction and then promptly vanished. What do you make of that? Naturally, all the poor girl wanted to do was pack her bags and go home. One of the other female students agreed to stay with her for the rest of the night and the landlord took her to Charnford Railway Station first thing. I assumed at first she had merely experienced a nightmare, but she is normally such a practical, down-to-earth kind of girl that to see her in such a state of distress has left me somewhat flummoxed."

"Do you think she saw a ghost?" Grant said.

Professor Scott drew a sharp intake of breath. "I won't dismiss the notion out of hand, but I didn't see anything myself and neither did any of the other guests. The landlord and his wife swore nothing like that had ever been seen during their thirty years there. That leaves my original conclusion as the most likely, however out of character it may appear to be. The girl must have had an unusually vivid dream that woke her up and stayed with her into wakefulness. It's not uncommon, you know. Now," he clapped his hands. "Let's get to work. I understand rain is forecast for later this afternoon, so time is of the essence."

Grant and Olivia exchanged glances. Grant raised his eyebrows but said nothing. He didn't need to. Olivia knew he shared her view that the student had indeed seen what she thought she had seen. For some reason, probably linked to their work on the stones, they had stirred something up in Landane. Something ancient and mysterious. Now, though, was not the time to try to win the professor over to their way of thinking. It was time to go to work. Olivia flicked through her notebook until she arrived at a fresh page. She took out her pencil from her skirt pocket as the three of them walked the few steps to the stone designated to be the next to be excavated and restored to its rightful position.

Professor Scott issued instructions to some of his students. Grant picked up a shovel.

Olivia needed to share her thoughts. "Have you noticed which student is missing?"

Grant nodded. "Diana. She was working on the surgeon's stone."

"There don't seem to be as many other workers here as usual. I'm sure there are at least two missing."

"And guess which two? They were also working on the surgeon's stone."

"I wonder what happened to them? And what about the other laborers who supplied the extra manpower and the equipment to move the stone? I wonder if they're all right."

A sudden yell from the professor interrupted them. "Oh, for heaven's sake. That's exactly what I don't need."

"What is it, Professor?" Grant asked.

"Two more of my men have left the dig without any warning. One of them informed Jack here at eight o'clock this morning that he and his mate wouldn't be coming back. They said they couldn't in all conscience continue to work on such an evil project. So now I'm three down and the clock is ticking."

His face was growing so red, Olivia feared for his heart.

"Then we'll all have to work that bit harder to make up for it. Maybe some more men will come along," she said.

"With respect, Miss, I don't think that's likely." The hapless messenger, Jack, twisted his cap in his hands. "You didn't see the state Billy was in. Shaking all over, he was. He said Denis was even worse and couldn't even speak he was so scared. Now I've known both of them all my life and they're not cowards. Nor are they the superstitious or fanciful types. Far from it, but Billy said, after what he'd seen in his own home, with his own eyes, last night, he wouldn't be setting foot in Landane ever again. He and Denis both. They've packed up their things and gone to a boarding house in Charnford until they can get themselves sorted out. Their wives and children are staying with relatives. Billy told me to get out too."

"Did you see anything strange last night?" Olivia asked.

"Yes...no...I don't know. It was too dark and I'd had a couple of drinks and it was only there for a minute, or maybe less."

"What was?" the professor demanded.

"This man. I think it was a man. He was wearing peculiar clothes and his hair was long, so was his beard. He was standing by that stone we put up yesterday. I was taking a shortcut across the field you see, back from The White Hart. It shook me up a bit seeing him there like that. Then I thought maybe he was a tramp, but the clothes he'd got on didn't seem right. They were like animal skins sewn together, but really rough. I stopped, stared at him, and then he disappeared. Almost as if the stone itself...." The man caught sight of the professor's skeptical gaze and stopped speaking. He cast his eyes downward.

"As you said," Professor Scott said, "you had been drinking."

"Yes, sir."

"Back to work, everyone. Let's hear no more of this alcohol-fueled nonsense."

Olivia touched the man's arm. "If it's any consolation, Jack, I believe you and so does Grant."

Jack looked up. "Thank you, Miss."

★   ★   ★

The congregation drew 'Guide Me, Oh Thou Great Redeemer' to a halt, closely pursued by the organist, and there then ensued a few seconds of shuffling and swishing of long skirts and nauseating wafts of mothballs as they settled themselves back down on the hard and unforgiving pews.

Reverend Ford ascended the steps of his pulpit, set his sermon book down, opened it at the appropriate page and gripped the stone balustrade with both hands. He surveyed his audience over his pince-nez.

Olivia, seated next to her mother, gave a light cough into her gloved hand. What was it about the rector that always made her feel guilty of something? Of course, this particular Sunday, she quite possibly was. Guilty of the sin of defying her parents. She had no intention of not seeing Grant on her own. They would just have to be careful, that was all. At least they could legitimately work together.

"'For we wrestle not against flesh and blood, but against principalities, against powers, against the rulers of the darkness of this world, against spiritual wickedness in high places.' Ephesians Chapter Six, verse twelve." The rector paused, waiting for his words to take effect while he scanned the congregation with his stern gaze.

The sonorous voice boomed out, echoing off the stone walls. "How preoccupied we can be, in our day-to-day lives, with the mundane things of life. We fail to see what is in front of our very eyes as we busy ourselves with our daily tasks. We fail to read the warning signs that all is not right among us. In our own village – this rural haven that is Landane – evil forces are at work."

Mutterings and shuffling greeted this.

"Oh yes, my children. We must be vigilant, for in our midst, there are forces at work. Primeval forces of darkness. I know for I have seen them." The rector raised his arm in a tight fist.

Someone gave a little cry as the rector's voice rose and flecks of foam appeared at the corners of his mouth. Next to her, Olivia's mother made a disapproving tutting sound. "Whatever is the matter with him?" she said, half to herself.

Reverend Ford lowered his arm. He wiped his mouth with a white handkerchief. Olivia stared at him. For one second he had seemed to be taken over by something. The congregation gradually fell silent but it was an apprehensive silence. Olivia stole quick glances around her. Others were doing the same. Reverend Ford could be something of a thunderer, but this outburst was uncharacteristic even for him.

He adjusted his spectacles and once again gripped the pulpit. "Within this village, thousands of years ago, our pagan ancestors constructed a circle of stones for the purpose of worshiping their false gods. Now, it seems, this circle is once again to be resurrected. Learned men have descended on us from the academic world and threaten to destroy all that we hold sacred. As Christian, God-fearing folk, we have a duty to remind these ill-informed people of their duty to the one true God and his only Son, our savior Jesus Christ. We must stop them. They cannot be allowed to continue."

"And how do you propose to do that, Dad?"

All heads turned, Olivia's included. At the back of the church, standing in the aisle, Grant Ford stood, his face red with rage.

"Go on, tell us. I'm sure we are all dying to know. Are you going to call the hand of God down to strike them dead with a thunderbolt? Or perhaps you would prefer St. Michael and his angels came along and smote them in some holy war."

"*Grant.*" Almost as one, the congregation turned back to the rector. His face had blanched and he seemed to have aged ten years in the past few moments.

As Olivia watched, the rector's expression changed from a mix of anger and despair to one of horror. He pointed to Grant. "The devil is behind you, and she is a woman."

The rector collapsed and half a dozen parishioners raced to his aid. Others pushed and shoved their fellow worshipers aside in a scramble to get out of the church. Several knocked straight into Grant who continued to stand, rigid. Olivia struggled to his side and took his arm. It was like trying to move a statue.

"Come over here and sit," she said, tugging at him.

"Leave that boy alone," her mother said. Olivia ignored her. "Olivia. I said leave him alone."

"No, Mother, I will not. He is clearly not well. Don't you remember the parable of the Good Samaritan?"

Her mother made a harrumphing sound and strode out of the church – the last to leave apart from Olivia, Grant and the small throng trying to rouse the rector.

Suddenly, Grant snapped out of his fugue. "What happened?"

"You challenged your father in the middle of his sermon and he said there was a she-devil standing behind you."

Grant looked from Olivia to the front of the church. They had managed to get his father back up on his feet. The two exchanged perplexed looks.

"What do you remember?" Olivia asked.

"Dad denouncing the dig. Everything else is a blank. Like a black shadow descended on me. I suppose I must have passed out."

"But you were on your feet the whole time. Like…. As if something was controlling you."

Grant stared at her for a second and then slowly nodded. "That actually makes sense," he said.

Two sidesmen helped the rector down the aisle. The three of them stopped next to Olivia and Grant.

Grant shook his head. "I don't know what came over me, Dad. I don't even know what just happened."

"It was the devil, my son. I saw her clear as I can see you now. She was dressed in scarlet and gold. Scarlet and gold…." He slumped forward and the two men caught him. The other who had come to assist also stepped in.

Grant stood up and took a step forward. "I'll help—"

The older of the two sidesmen pushed him away. "Don't you think you've done enough damage for one day?"

Grant sat down again, his bewildered expression a testimony to the torment he must be feeling.

In a few moments, the church was empty save for Olivia and Grant. She put her arm around him and he leaned into her shoulder, sobbing.

And then they were no longer there.

CHAPTER TWELVE

The mist descended, shrouding them in a blanket of white. Olivia could see nothing more than the shape of Grant, although he was, she knew, only a couple of feet from her. A cold, damp chill on her face told her they were no longer in the church, but how had they got here? And where were they anyway?

In the distance, the stomping sound of thousands of people on the move, on foot, not marching in time, but with some sense of purpose. She should feel fear or at least trepidation, but otherwise her senses had grown numb. She was waiting but she had no idea what was to come. She tried to call out to Grant, but her voice was absorbed by the mist. How could she even breathe through this cloying atmosphere? It felt dank, airless.

And then it was gone.

Grant held her in a close embrace.

"Where are we?" Olivia asked.

The field stretched out before them. No, not a field. This was a landscape, pristine and undisturbed by humans. As if someone was painting it, other figures began to emerge. Animals. Massive cattle with enormous horns. Nothing like the domestic herds of Herefords and Guernseys she was used to.

"Look." Grant pointed behind them.

Olivia turned to see a large, apparently complete circle of massive standing stones. "That wasn't there a moment ago."

"I'm so glad you said that because I didn't see it either and I was facing in that direction when the mist disappeared."

"I suppose the next question is not where, but *when* are we?" Olivia caught her breath. "Oh heavens. I think I can understand why she asked that question."

"Who? What question?"

"That girl. The one we both saw. Remember, I told you, when I saw her on my own, she asked that same question, 'When am I?' Just like that."

"But she has the ability to disappear into the stone. We don't."

"Don't we? Think about it, Grant. We both had the same dream. She led us into the surgeon's stone. She's part of this. Maybe we are too. Do you remember how we got here?"

Grant shook his head. "Haven't a clue."

"Neither have I. Maybe we're dreaming now, but these aren't like normal dreams. Can you smell that?"

Grant sniffed. "Salt. Like being at the seaside."

Olivia looked around. "It's being carried on the breeze I suppose, but it's coming an awfully long way."

"And that's only just started up. Did you hear the sounds in the mist?"

"Like thousands of people on the move?"

Grant nodded. "I've heard those before."

"Listen, Grant. The birds have returned." Blackbirds, thrushes, others she couldn't make out trilled happily in the growing sunshine. In the distance the rapid-fire knocking of a woodpecker echoed from a small grove of trees a little way across the plain.

"Let's go into the circle," Grant said. "I don't understand what's happening here, but maybe the circle will give us some...I don't know...protection. Right now, I think we need it."

Olivia sensed the same feeling of increasing unease. In the distance, a vague but insistent thumping and rumbling seemed to ripple over the grass. From all around her, the breeze carried indeterminate whispers that collected and swirled around them. She clung to Grant's arm as he steered her into the circle and to a position directly in front of the surgeon's stone.

The ground trembled beneath their feet.

"Touch the stone, Olivia!" Grant pulled her toward it, let go of her and placed his hand on the weatherworn surface. As soon as he made contact with it, he flew back as if electrocuted, his eyes wide. Olivia put her hand out to him. "No, don't touch me, Olivia. Touch the stone. You must...touch it...yourself."

The rumbling became a roar. All around the outside of the circle the landscape began to undulate, but the stones stood firm.

Despite her brain screaming at her not to, Olivia laid her hand on the stone. There was no electric shock but its coldness swam into her body, momentarily chilling her before settling into waves of calm, stilling her fears. For a moment it seemed the stone became porous. She could see her hand through it and then she saw someone looking out at her, reaching for her hand. The girl.

"Do you see her, Grant?"

"Yes."

Olivia could barely hear him over the noise of the unquiet earth.

"She wants us to go to her." Once again, Grant set his hand flat against the stone. "And I *must* go to her."

"*Grant!*"

This time, Olivia was thrown back to the ground. Momentarily stunned by the force that threw her, she blinked rapidly.

* * *

"My dear Olivia, whatever's happened?" The professor helped her to her feet.

"I don't know, I...." She was back, as if she had never left. Here she was, at the dig. There was the surgeon's stone and, next to it, the one they would be raising in a few days' time. "Where's Grant?"

"I was about to ask you the same question. We missed both of you yesterday, but now at least you're back. Still no sign of Grant though. Do you know if he's at home?"

Her brain felt like thick porridge. Yesterday? But there was no dig yesterday. Yesterday was Sunday. She had been in church. The rector...Grant. And then they had been in the stone circle, although how they had arrived there was another matter. The stone...that strange girl.... None of it seemed real now. She looked wildly around. Where was Grant? He had been taken into the stone. That couldn't have happened.

"I don't know what's the matter with me," she said, rubbing her forehead. "I can't seem to remember anything that makes any sense. I'm not even sure.... Professor, it *is* Monday, isn't it?"

The professor shook his head. "No, my dear. It's Tuesday."

"But.... That's not possible. It means I've lost an entire day."

The professor frowned. "I don't think you're very well, my dear. Maybe I've been overworking you."

"Oh no, Professor. You haven't been overworking me. It's just that.... It's.... Some odd things have been happening around here and I think both Grant and I have been affected by them in some way. I don't understand it, but it's the only thing that makes any sense."

"Nevertheless, I shall walk you home and then go and check on Grant at the rectory."

There was no point in arguing. She was too tired for one thing. The thought of lying in her comfortable bed with its crisp cotton sheets was almost irresistible. Olivia suddenly felt as if she hadn't slept in days. "Could you let me know whether he's there?"

"Of course, my dear. Now, come along, let's get you back home. A good rest will do you the world of good."

"Thank you, Professor."

Her mother was leaving when they arrived at Olivia's home. She immediately took over, thanking the professor and ushering Olivia into the house.

"But where have you been, Olivia? Your father and I have been so worried."

"I can't answer that, Mama. I simply don't know what happened to... yesterday."

"You were with that boy, weren't you? I should never have walked out of church like that—"

"I wasn't *with* Grant. I...." It was no good, Olivia couldn't explain it with any words her mother would understand. A lie would have to suffice, even if it was a weak one. She swallowed. "I wasn't feeling very well and went for a walk into the woods. I must have lost track of time and sat down to have a little rest as my feet were hurting. Then I couldn't remember which way I'd come so I kept on walking until I came to this farm. It was getting dark and the farmer and his wife kindly let me in. They suggested I stay the night and start out again in the morning. By now it was too dark to see anything. I took them up on their kind offer and I was so tired, I must have slept the whole day through. They set me on the right path back to Landane and I'm perfectly all right. Maybe I've had a little too much sun. It's quite a walk. Some water and a rest and I shall be back to normal again."

Her mother didn't look convinced but she was clearly in a hurry and for that Olivia was more grateful than she could say.

"Well, it sounds quite ridiculous to me, but then how you spend your time these days is beyond me anyway. You know my views on all that scrubbing about in that field."

"Yes, Mama. But I'm not scrubbing about as you put it. I take notes and I sketch artifacts. That's all."

Her mother wore her disapproving expression, consisting of pursed lips and a frown that deeply etched itself into her forehead.

"I would stay but I am expected at Lady Cawston's 'At Home' in twenty minutes and I mustn't be late."

Olivia breathed an inward sigh of relief.

"Daisy will look after you. I should be back at about six. Rest at least until then."

"I will, Mama. I promise."

She waved her mother off and waited in the drawing room. Sure enough, five minutes later the doorbell rang. Daisy answered and announced the professor.

He bustled in, a worried expression on his face. "It's a bit of a mystery, I'm afraid. Poor Mrs. Ford is beside herself. Grant didn't return home after church on Sunday, and she has no idea where he is. That coupled with what I understand to have been quite a scene at Holy Communion is quite the talk of the village. The rector has mounted a search for his son and the police have been informed. Grant is officially a missing person."

Olivia sat down heavily. "I know where he is."

"You do? Well, that's excellent news. All we have to do is let everyone know and go and fetch the chap."

Olivia shook her head. "The problem is no one will believe me. I can barely believe it myself and I saw it happen."

"So where is he?"

Olivia took a deep breath. "In the stone. The surgeon's stone."

CHAPTER THIRTEEN

Shelly

1967

"Everyone's going to be there, Shelly. You can't miss it. It's the Summer of Love festival and it's right here on our doorstep." Vicki tossed her mane of chestnut curls over her shoulder. "Mick's going to be there. I know you fancy him. *Everyone* knows you fancy him."

Shelly's heart lurched. Mick Foster. The most gorgeous guy in Landane, with the deepest, most divine brown eyes. 'Come-to-bed eyes', Vicki called them. Not that she had ever...neither had Shelly. They were both seventeen years old and had been instructed by their mothers to 'save themselves', although how long that resolution would last with hunks like Mick around, long hot summer evenings and hormones raging all over the place, was anybody's guess. Of course, there was the new contraceptive pill, but Shelly Sullivan, as an unmarried girl, was barred from getting it. Still, at least there was a proposal to change that in the coming months. Until then.... Well, she could dream, couldn't she? Not for one moment did she believe Mick was a virgin. Another student in her English class had boasted of having 'gone all the way' with him, much to the disgust of some of the more prim and proper Catholic girls.

Shelly twisted a skein of her blonde hair around her fingers, barely aware she was doing it. Meanwhile, her best friend Vicki Donald flicked through the pages of an American fan magazine.

"There's an article here about that series they have called *Dark Shadows*. It looks great. Why don't we have anything like that over here? It's on in the late afternoon there. All we get at that time is bloody *Sooty* and *Pinky and Perky*. There's nothing for anyone our age."

"There's *Ready, Steady, Go* and *Top of the Pops, Batman, The Addams Family*—"

"I know, but *Dark Shadows* is proper spooky. Jonathan Frid plays a vampire and all sorts of creepy stuff goes on. The trouble is all the TV bosses over here are old, stuck-up posh blokes without a grain of imagination. They don't realize their time is over. It's our turn now. The world belongs to us. The young generation. Oh, look at him. He's *gorgeous*."

"Who? Jonathan Frid?"

"No, look. Mark Lindsay." She thrust her copy of *16* magazine with a glossy, full-page color portrait of a man with dark brown eyes, not unlike Mick's, and long hair, tied in a ponytail which had flicked over his shoulder. He was smiling.

"I mean, honestly, Shelly. Would you give up your virginity to him? I know I would, given half the chance."

"*Vicki!*" Shelly laughed.

"Well...." Vicki laughed too. "And that's another thing. He's the lead singer of Paul Revere and the Raiders. They're massive in America, but have you ever seen them on *Top of the Pops*? No. Have you heard them on the radio? No. Not even Radio Caroline or Luxembourg."

"Perhaps their music doesn't travel well."

"I tried the HMV store in Charnford. They said they didn't stock anything by them but could order it. But how can you order something when you've never heard it?"

"I'll go halves with you on their latest album if you like. That way, if we both don't like it we're only down sixteen and threepence each."

Vicki's eyes lit up. "That's a great idea. Let's see if it tells us...." She flicked pages back and forth until she found what she was looking for. "Here it is. It's called *Revolution*. Oh, it's not out until August, but it's got 'Him or Me (What's It Going to Be)' on it. That's a big hit right now over there."

"Let's go into Charnford tomorrow and order it then."

"Fab." Vicki tossed the magazine aside and curled her long, mini-skirted legs underneath her as she sat on Shelly's bed. "Now that's sorted out, what about the Summer of Love festival? Are you coming or aren't you? You've been 'umming' and 'erring' about it for weeks."

Shelly sighed. "My parents won't approve and if I go behind their backs they're bound to find out. Landane is such a small place."

"But the festival's going to be huge. The whole village will be taken over for the weekend. No one's ever seen anything like it in this country. There could be, I don't know, maybe five hundred people there."

"And that's precisely why my father's on that village committee to have it banned."

"But he can't, can he?"

"They're claiming it's a public nuisance. The noise and mess. The village can't sustain it."

"But the organizers have that covered, haven't they? There will be strictly enforced parking and no one from the festival is allowed out once they're in. There'll be security everywhere. Numbers strictly limited. No drugs. No alcohol. Music kept away from the houses. They've ticked all the boxes. It'll go through. After all, the mayor of Charnford owns the land, doesn't he? And his brother's the local MP."

"He's certainly well connected. Is there honestly going to be a no alcohol rule?"

Vicki winked. "It won't be on sale but...."

"Oh, right. Bring your own. I suppose that applies to drugs as well."

"Probably. There'll be a bit of acid and cannabis floating about I dare say."

"Have you tried any?"

"No. Have you?"

Shelly shook her head. Her dentist father and housewife mother were typical of their generation. Church on Sundays, mother in the Women's Institute baking cakes and making jam for charity sales raising money for worthy causes. Father busy at his practice in Charnford

Monday to Friday, with golf on Saturdays and a good long read of the Sunday paper to round off the weekend. Shelly was the only one left at home since her elder brother, Gordon, had decided to stay down in Canterbury after successfully completing his degree in English. Shelly was expected to perform well in her A-level examinations the following year, and then it would be university for her too. Her father believed she would make an excellent lawyer, although Shelly much preferred the idea of trying out for the Royal Academy of Dramatic Arts – an idea strongly dismissed by Daddy and greeted with something two rungs below enthusiasm by her mother.

"Very few people in acting make a decent living, dear. You have to make your own way in this world so you must train for a proper job."

This was also an argument dragged out when she ventured to suggest she might attend the festival.

"Out of the question," her father had said, his newspaper rustling ominously. If he carried on like that much longer, he would rip it. Yes, there we go.... A tear rent the broadsheet paper from top to bottom. Despite his vehement rebuttal of her request, Shelly still had to bite her lip to stop her from cracking up. His surprised reaction as he held the two halves of the newspaper in either hand only added to her dilemma and resulted in her leaving the room only to collapse into fits of giggles in her bedroom.

But that still left her with the problem. If she didn't go to the festival, she would lose face with her friends, and if she did, she would fly in defiance of her parents. She couldn't win. Of course, if her parents didn't actually *know* she had gone to the festival....

Vicki had picked up her magazine again and was gazing dreamily at a picture of Mike Nesmith of The Monkees. "If only he wasn't married..." she said, sighing.

"Vic, I'm going to need your help."

"Mmm?"

"Vic. Please. I'm serious."

Vicki reluctantly set aside the magazine. "What do you need my help with?"

"My parents have flatly refused to allow me to go to the festival. The only way I can go is to sneak out, but they like you. If you were to call round on some pretext that you need me to come with you somewhere, I'm sure they'd let me go with you."

"What pretext?"

"I don't know. I need your help with that as well."

"It would have to be something that meant you were away for a couple of days."

"No, they'd never buy that, but most of one day maybe. At least I would have gone."

"I suppose they do sell one-day tickets. But, even if they do, I can't think of any reason I would suddenly need you to come with me."

"Or what if it wasn't last minute? What if we were going to stay with your aunt in Salisbury?"

"I don't have an aunt in Salisbury."

"We'll invent one. She's invited you and a friend to stay for the weekend. That could work. And I can't see my parents refusing. In fact, they would probably be glad to hear I was going to be away from Landane when the festival was on."

"What if they talk to my parents?"

"They don't really know each other, do they? I think they've only met once in all the time we've been friends." For once, Shelly was glad of her parents' snobbishness. When they had found out that Vicki's mother worked in a factory and her father was a compositor for the local newspaper, any thoughts that the Donalds might be invited to the Sullivans for sherry and canapés were put firmly off the agenda.

"What will you tell your parents?" Shelly asked.

"I'll tell them the truth. They trust me to be sensible." She laughed. "They'll be happier knowing I'm going with you though."

"Do you have to mention that?"

"Yep. It'll only slip out anyway. I'm a terrible liar and even worse at keeping secrets. Good job I don't talk to your mum very often, isn't it?"

"As long as you don't say anything when you call round for me, that's all that matters."

"And it means we can go for the full weekend."

A rush of excitement flooded Shelly's veins. "Who's playing anyway? Anyone we've heard of?"

"I think Petra's Magic Garden will be there. They had that psychedelic, trippy song. A bit like Jefferson Airplane."

"*Soul Love.*"

"That's the one. And there's Luna's Silver Ray, Orlando, Quixotic Love Triangle, all sorts of people."

"No Monkees or Paul Revere and the Raiders though." Shelly giggled.

"Sadly, no. I shall just have to worship from afar." Vicki winked and giggled. "Anyway, you'll have your own drooling to do. Mick Foster. In the flesh. Be still my beating heart." Vicki performed an exaggerated fanning motion.

"I shall say the wrong things, stumble over my words, blush. Oh God, please don't let me blush."

"Get a couple of drinks down you and you'll be fine."

"My parents would slaughter me."

"Good job they're not going to be there, then, isn't it? Have you seriously never had a proper drink?"

"Oh yes. Wine at birthday dinners and Christmas. I had champagne at a wedding once. Had a terrible head the next day."

"We'll take cider. It's cheaper and goes further. It's only fizzy apple juice anyway."

"I had a glass of Woodpecker last summer. It was very refreshing."

"There you are."

"We'll need to look the part. You're so good at needlework. Could you run us up some stuff? We can get some material in Charnford tomorrow. There's that remnant shop in the market."

"Yeah, no problem. We'll go all floaty chiffon in bright colors. I'll tie-dye the material."

"Groovy. We'll get the tickets too. Do HMV have them?"

"I think so. This is so exciting. A real adventure."

"Do we need to take a tent? I haven't got one and anyway, why would I need to take a tent to your aunt's in Salisbury?"

"I'd forgotten that. We've got a tent. Hangover from my childhood when Dad thought it would be good for us to get into the whole outdoors thing. It didn't last long. That summer we went to the Lake District and it rained every day. We got flooded out. Ended up spending four days in a B&B in Grange Over Sands. The tent's been in the attic ever since."

They both laughed.

Vicki wiped tears from her eyes. "As for my fictitious aunt in Salisbury. I do have a real aunt in Andover. Aunt Sally."

"That'll do and it's easy to remember. Sally from Salisbury." That set them off again.

By the time Vicki left, her precious copy of *16* magazine clutched in her hand, Shelly's sides were aching from all the laughter.

★   ★   ★

As predicted, when Shelly told her parents about Vicki's 'invitation', there were no objections.

"I think that would be an excellent idea, Michelle." Daddy always used her given name. He hated the more familiar 'Shelly', as did her mother. "Salisbury's a beautiful city. You must visit the cathedral while you're there."

"We will, Daddy." Shelly made a mental note to look up Salisbury and its cathedral in the library. She would need to make some notes and commit them to memory.

★   ★   ★

"How do I look?" Shelly twirled. The sheer voile dress billowed around her, a haze of bright colors tie-dyed into a swirling random pattern of purple, orange, red, yellow, pink, green and blue.

"You look fab, Shelly. Good job you put that petticoat on though. That stuff is almost totally transparent."

"I'm keeping my bra on too. I know loads of girls will be ditching theirs, but that's something I don't feel comfortable with."

"Well, I don't have as much up top as you do so mine's coming off."

"You look great, Vic."

"Thanks. I'm pleased with it. I decided on the velvet pants in the end. That was a stroke of genius finding them in the charity shop. I couldn't believe it when they fit me."

"That top is so groovy, and all those beads."

"Mostly Mum's. The two strings of love beads came from Woolworth's."

"I've got that glitter we bought yesterday. We can sprinkle it on our cheeks and foreheads. I thought I'd do my eyes like Julie Driscoll. You know, really dark eyelids and heavy eyeliner, with a few swirls highlighted with glitter."

"Very dramatic. It'll suit you too. You're so slim and blonde, the contrast will make you look like a ghost."

"A psychedelic ghost, I hope."

"Naturally."

They were quiet for the next ten minutes while each of them concentrated on creating their own look. When she had finished, Shelly moved back from the mirror she had been using in Vicki's bedroom.

"What do you think?"

Vicki paused in the act of applying a soft pink lipstick. "Wow. That's amazing. I hardly recognize you. What make is that eyeshadow?"

"Mary Quant. I finally spent my birthday voucher. Couldn't afford the false eyelashes though."

"That would have been too much. Now, a little touch of patchouli and we're ready to go." She fished out a small black bottle from her copious tote bag and dabbed a little on their wrists and behind their ears. "Can you carry the sleeping bags while I carry the tent?"

"This is where a man would come in handy," Shelly said, heaving the rucksack onto her back.

"Maybe we'll get lucky and have help packing up." Vicki winked.

Her mother was waiting for them downstairs. She did a double take when she saw them. "Good Lord, Vicki, I never thought I'd see the day when a daughter of mine went out looking like that. Good job your dad's not here. He'd have a fit."

"Don't tell him then." Vicki gave her mother a peck on her proffered cheek.

"Have a nice time, girls, and behave yourselves."

Shelly smiled at the older woman. "'Bye, Mrs. Donald."

Outside, they lumbered their way the half mile or so to the festival entrance. From every direction, throngs of young people their age and older joined the swelling crowd. Some had bells, tambourines, guitars and a variety of other instruments. Shelly and Vicki made sure they were hidden among the crowd just in case some eagle-eyed villager should notice Shelly and blab to her parents. Hanging in the still, warm air, the sweetly nauseating aroma of cannabis cloaked them all. Shelly felt her mind relax. She wanted to dance, only the heavy rucksack held her back. It didn't matter. Soon they would pitch their tent and be able to relieve themselves of the weighty baggage.

There were plenty of stewards to ensure everyone was processed. Tickets were checked. Wrists stamped. Shelly hadn't anticipated this. "My parents don't know I'm here," she said, hoping her fluttering eyelashes might work some sort of magic on the steward who stared down at her from his lanky six feet plus, while he chewed gum as if he really meant it.

He gave the gum an extra vigorous mastication. "No exceptions. You don't get stamped, you don't come in. Your choice."

Shelly hoped the ink would wash off before she would have to explain to her parents why Salisbury Cathedral insisted on stamping visitors with a two-day pass. Once in the field, she forgot all about that as she and Vicki made for a shady spot under a chestnut tree.

"I just hope I can remember how to erect this thing," Vicki said. All around them, fellow festival goers were doing the same. Some were clearly expert. Others, like them, were having mixed results.

"Damn. I really thought I had it that time," Vicki said as the tent sagged and finally collapsed in a messy heap, for the third time.

A male voice behind her made Shelly jump. "Need some help?"

The hairs raised on the back of Shelly's neck. She swallowed and steeled herself before she spun round.

"He…hello, Mick. We're n…not used to tents."

She felt his eyes undress her and immediately gave thanks for her resolve to wear both petticoat and bra.

Vicki smiled at him. "Any help you could give us would be gratefully received."

Shelly nodded. Why couldn't *she* have said that? Because she was too preoccupied by the sight of Mick's lean body, legs encased in tight, dark red bell-bottoms, no shirt. His was the sort of skin that tanned easily and quickly. Right now, he looked as if he had stepped off a boat after a couple of weeks of Greek island hopping. She felt her face burn and knew it was nothing to do with the sunshine.

He smiled at her, revealing his even teeth, white against his tan. His hair had grown in the month since she had last seen him. Now it rested on his shoulders, healthy, lush, gleaming…. What would it be like to run her fingers through it?

Stop behaving like an infatuated schoolgirl. Even if you are one.

He had already started assembling the poles of their tent. Vicki nudged Shelly's elbow. "I enjoy watching a good-looking man at work," she said, and Shelly knew by the smile that played around Mick's lips that he had heard her. She blushed even harder. Her cheeks were flaming now.

"You two staying for the whole weekend?" Mick asked.

"Yes," Vicki replied while Shelly tried to form the word and failed.

"I'll see you around then. We're camped just a few yards away." He pointed in the direction of a cluster of tents the same size as theirs. Half a dozen people were smoking and drinking. Two of them were performing an undulating dance while three others played a tambourine, guitar and flute between them. "Come and join us. We've brought plenty of weed and cider, whatever's your preference."

"Thanks, Mick," Vicki said. "We'll do that."

"Well, you're all fixed now. Don't see that coming down in a hurry." He gave the tent pegs one last good wallop with his sledgehammer. "You'll see I moved you from under the tree. Bad idea to pitch there. And you forgot to lay your tarp first, but that's sorted now. You don't want to sleep on damp grass, do you?"

"You've done a great job, hasn't he, Shelly?"

Shelly nodded. "Thanks, Mick. It's great." Finally, she had managed an entire sentence without tripping over her words.

"All it takes is practice," he said. "And I've had plenty of that."

"I'll bet you have," Vicki said, giggling.

Shelly could have cheerfully strangled her. She watched Mick stride back to his companions and realized for the first time that he was barefoot. But then she hadn't been concentrating on his feet. She didn't want to keep watching but she couldn't help it. Which tent would he make for? Which girl? There were nine in his party now. Five men and four women. That meant that they weren't evenly balanced into male/female pairs – unless one couple was gay perhaps. Or maybe they weren't actual couples. Men and women could be friends without sex complicating things, after all.

"Earth calling Shelly." Vicki snapped her fingers.

"What? Oh yes. Unpacking."

It only took a few minutes to sort out their stuff and grab a large bottle of cider.

"I'm afraid it's not really cold anymore," Shelly said.

"It'll be fine. I doubt anyone will really notice. When's the first band on?"

"About six, I think. Doublet. I've not heard of them. Apparently, they're from Buckinghamshire. They play folky stuff and they're supposed to be the next big thing."

"Are we ready to go?" The urge to get started on their weekend was almost overwhelming. Shelly's spirits surged as she thought of freedom for the first time in her life. Here, in this field, she might only be less than a mile from her parents' house, but it could as easily have been half a world away. Maybe it was the effect of all that cannabis wafting through the air, but it was a lightness of her soul she had never experienced before and it was addictive.

"Come on," Vicki said, brandishing the lukewarm cider. "Let's go and grab him before one of those other girls gets her claws into him."

"If they haven't already. Anyway, less of the 'us'."

"Have you seen the one with the long blond hair and the beard?" Shelly shook her head as the two strolled over to Mick's encampment. "Can't say I noticed."

"Well, I don't suppose you would. Anyway, I intend to get to know him while you busy yourself with Mick."

"Hey, come and join us." Mick waved a spliff in their direction and exhaled a long stream of aromatic smoke. He proceeded to introduce his friends, but their names sailed over Shelly's head, all except for Davy, the object of Vicki's lust. As he was introduced, her friend made straight for him, causing the girl sitting next to him to make way. She didn't seem to mind. Probably too stoned to notice.

"Come and sit beside me, Shelly," Mick said, and she needed no further prompting. His invitation seemed to dispel her earlier shyness – at least enough to overcome her previous fits of blushing. She sat on the ground between Mick and a slightly older guy with short, tidy black hair.

"I'm Raj," he said, extending his hand. "Pleased to meet you, Shelly."

Shelly returned the handshake. "Pleased to meet you too, Raj."

Mick's arm encircled her shoulders. "Try this," he said, thrusting the spliff at her. "It's good stuff. Raj got it. You wouldn't think he was a stuffy accountant by day, would you? Except for the haircut of course."

Mick laughed and Shelly loved the way his eyes crinkled. She took the spliff and placed it between her lips. "Inhale. Draw the smoke right in and hold it," Mick said.

A fit of coughing ruined the effect, as her throat burned. The others started to laugh. She felt she was choking.

"Quiet, you unruly lot," Mick said, holding her close. "Don't you remember your first time?"

The laughs subsided and someone started to strum a guitar. One of the girls began to sing 'Chelsea Morning'. Shelly loved Joni Mitchell's song and, right at that moment, hearing it sung by a girl with such a pretty voice that held more than a hint of Joni's own, while being held close to the bare chest of Mick Foster, was all the heaven she needed. He smelled of sun, patchouli and a slightly salty aroma like sea air. The light dusting of dark hair on his chest felt soft under her cheek, beneath which his heart beat steadily, rhythmically, lulling her to sleep. She drifted off. Somewhere in the background the first band started up. 'Chelsea Morning' faded out, along with the chatter of hundreds of happy people. Now there was only Mick and her. And it felt right. She had only properly met him that day, but it could have been a lifetime ago. He gently lifted her head and took her hand. Her eyes heavy with sleep, she let him help her stand. In her dreamlike state, he drew her to him so she could lean on him while he led her away from the group.

"Let your eyes close and trust me. I'll look after you, Shelly." His voice was hypnotic, magical. Her feet moved one after the other seemingly of their own accord. She didn't stumble. At one point a male voice spoke. "Is she the one?"

"Yes," Mick said.

"Then we must go there."

Shelly tried to open her eyes but they were too heavy. She should have been scared but there was no trace of fear within her. Then they stopped. Mick spoke softly. "Lay your hands flat against the stone. In front of you, Shelly. That's it."

The stone felt cold, hard, uneven but somehow welcoming. Mick was pressed up against her back. He parted her hair and kissed the back of her neck. "You're almost there, Shelly. I'll be with you. You have nothing to fear."

The stone melted under her hands. Suddenly she could move into it, through it. Now her eyes opened. Mick was close behind her. She felt his warm breath on her neck. "Come with me," he said. "Learn what I know."

The ice crystal hall shimmered as she took her first uncertain steps along its glassy surface.

"Don't worry. You won't fall."

He was at her side now. He took her hand and squeezed it. "Let me show you."

Together they moved toward the end of the hall or, it seemed more as if the hall moved closer to them. Although she was moving one foot in front of the other, Shelly had the strange sensation of not moving at all.

At the end of the magnificent chamber, a pathway of lustrous black flecked with gold lay ahead leading to another hall, but where the first one had been brilliant white and silver, this one was black. Like jet but sprinkled with flakes of purest gold.

At the entrance, seemingly waiting for them, stood a woman dressed in a sweeping gown of scarlet and gold. Her eyes bridged the divide between them.

Mick positioned himself in front of Shelly, took her chin between his fingers and raised her face. He lowered his head and their lips met. He held her close and a hundred nights of dreams became reality. His kiss transported her, his hands explored her body, hungry for more. She entwined her fingers in his hair and found it as silky and sensuous as she had hoped.

He lifted her up and she realized they were both naked. He carried her across the path and up to the woman who was now bathed in a golden light.

"My lady Trenorjia. We are here."

★　★　★

"Shelly. Hey. Wake up."

Shelly opened her eyes and looked straight up into Mick's eyes. The band sounded louder now. Maybe they had just turned the amps up.

Mick smiled down at her. "You must have been really tired. You've been asleep at least an hour. We're all going up closer to the stage. Coming?" He held out his hand and she took it, allowing him to help her to her feet.

"I had the strangest dream," she said as they followed the others. Vicki was firmly latched onto Davy. She turned and gave Shelly a massive wink. Shelly smiled back.

"What was it about?"

"You took me into one of the stones and there was this woman there. She was like a goddess or a queen or something. You called her Lady Trenorj...something like that."

"Trenorjia?"

"Yes, that's right. Who is she?"

Mick shook his head. "You know, I haven't the slightest idea. It just came into my head. I've never heard that name in my life before."

CHAPTER FOURTEEN

"You don't need your own weed with all the stuff floating in the air," Vicki said.

Shelly's sense of unreality was becoming so acute she was glad Vicki had said that. It must be the still-warm air and the cannabis. Doublet had come off stage and Petra's Magic Garden would be on as soon as their equipment was ready. Meanwhile, Davy and Mick were chatting and passing a spliff around. This time Shelly declined, although Vicki took a hefty drag with no apparent ill effect.

She exhaled. "How are you two getting along?" she asked.

"Great. How about you and Davy?"

"He's a brilliant kisser. I think things may go a lot further tonight."

"Seriously? Are you...prepared?"

Vicki poked about in her tote bag and fished out a small packet. "There's five little rubber johnnies in there. Want one in case you get lucky with Mick?"

Shelly hesitated. But only for a second. She was so drawn to Mick that if he started something, she wasn't at all sure she wouldn't let him finish. "Go on then. Best to be safe."

She accepted the little packet and stuffed it in her shoulder purse. She almost told her friend about the weird dream, but then Petra stepped up to the microphone. The crowd fell quiet.

"Greetings, Landane!" Petra yelled and the audience yelled and whooped back. "Thank you all for being here...." The next words were so slurred, Shelly couldn't make them out. She wasn't alone. Shouts of, "Speak up!" chorused around the audience. Petra shook herself in an obvious attempt to sort herself out. "Sorreeee. Our first song...gonna be...be nest single. Never played before...." Petra was overcome with a paroxysm of coughing. Murmurs of frustration and discontent circulated.

Petra swayed as she hung on to the microphone. To Shelly it looked as if it was the only thing keeping her on her feet. The coughing stopped. Petra croaked, "Hope you'll like it. It's called 'Trenorjia and the Magical Stone'."

Shelly felt her face blanch and the hairs on her neck stand up. She glanced over at Mick. He appeared as surprised as she felt. He excused himself from Davy and was back with her in time for the opening, discordant chords. Vicki reconnected with Davy and the couple embraced and kissed.

"Come with me," Mick said, grabbing Shelly's hand.

She had to run to keep up with his long strides as he weaved them through the throngs of half-stoned revelers and neared the stage. They stopped a few feet short of a solid band of security guards, while the song meandered on. The performance was ragged. Petra clutched the microphone with both hands, her eyes half closed as her voice soared into areas it was ill-equipped to handle, cracking, breaking, falling flat. However much Shelly tried to make out what she was singing, the lyrics came over as little more than gibberish and the sound system didn't help, rendering everything garbled and indistinct. The accompaniment of acoustic guitars, keyboard, drums and an enthusiastic flute didn't gel and the whole thing ground to a halt rather than mounted to a crescendo. Its end was greeted with a mix of polite applause, insults and derision. Through it all, Petra seemed unaware of her surroundings or of anything that was going on. She gazed wildly around her and had to be pried away from the microphone by a burly stagehand who bodily lifted her, to the amusement of those nearest the stage. Shelly could only feel pity for the lost girl.

Mick squeezed Shelly's hand. "Come on. We'll catch her backstage."

Security had other ideas. "Where's your pass?" The questioner stood a good head taller than Mick. Shelly had to crane her head to look at him.

"Is Terry with you?" Mick asked calmly.

"Terry who?"

"Venning. He'll vouch for me."

The incredible hulk lumbered away, returning momentarily with a slight man in his twenties with bottle-glass spectacles and a worried expression that transformed into a wide grin as soon as he set eyes on Mick.

"Mick, my man. It's been too long."

"Terry, my old mucker, how've you been?"

"Great, Mick. Great. It's okay, Merv, he's with me." Terry caught sight of Shelly. "*They're* with me."

Merv nodded and moved off to intimidate someone else, no doubt.

"He's harmless," Terry said, mainly to Shelly. "So, tell me what's been happening with you and introduce me to your lady."

"This is Shelly and she's not my lady. Not yet anyway." Mick grinned. "We'll catch up over the weekend, but right now she and I need to speak to Petra. Can you arrange that for us?"

"Of course. Nothing simpler. Although how much sense you'll get out of her is another thing. I can't vouch for that. They all started on the cheap cider this morning and they've been taking every pill known to science, plus a few more that haven't been discovered yet. They're having a lousy set and they don't even know it."

A particularly violent clash of notes assaulted Shelly's ears so that she grimaced. "Are they always like that?" she asked.

Terry's face was contorted as if in pain. "Only when they're live. I'll have to get them off. I don't even think they realize Petra's not on stage. It's crazy though, because if you listen to their studio work, they're amazing. Could even be the next big thing, but promoters don't like them. They fight, they argue and sometimes they don't bother to turn up at all. Shame really because they really can write great songs and Petra has a sweet voice, when she's sober. She's been particularly odd since they arrived here yesterday night. She insisted on taking a walk around the stone circle and when she came back, she had some story about being in one of the stones. I mean actually inside it. She hadn't been drinking then or, as far as I know, taking anything.

She certainly sounded fine. But she insisted there was some strange ghostly woman in the stone who called to her by name and then all of a sudden, she was back, sprawled out on the grass."

"Had you heard that song they…*performed* probably isn't the right word," Mick said.

"Not as such. I heard extracts when they were doing a sound check first thing. It sounded much better then. I told Petra to stand a few inches back from the mic. And she did. Not when it counted though. All of a sudden, the fucking mic's a cross between a crutch and a lollipop. Excuse me a minute, I've got to stop this. I'll get the next band on. They're sober."

Petra's Magic Garden were suddenly unplugged and apparently unaware of the fact. The crowd began to boo. Members of Terry's crew ushered the band off and someone announced the next act. The boos transformed into cheers as a popular local group ran onto the stage.

Terry reappeared, with Petra in tow. She wasn't happy, although she was at least making sense and not swaying quite as much as she had been a few minutes earlier. "That wasn't cool, man. We were just getting into our stride there. We've still got half our set to play."

"Well, be a good girl, sober up, get clean and tell your band to do the same. If you can stand without falling over and if you can at least all finish the song at the same time, we'll look at getting you back on Sunday afternoon. Okay? Now these good people want to chat with you. Try and be civil and stay awake, will you?"

Petra gave a wide toothy grin. "Only if you fuck me afterward, Mr. Stage Manager."

Terry made a dismissive gesture as he dashed off.

"I'm sitting down," Petra said and squatted on the grass. Mick and Shelly sat down with her.

"You got any stuff?" she asked Mick.

"No. I need you to tell me about Trenorjia."

She ignored him and looked at Shelly. Her eyes were bloodshot, unfocused. "You got any stuff, Barbie?"

Shelly's hackles raised. "I'm not Barbie. My name's—"

"I'll take that as a 'no' then."

"What do you know about Trenorjia?" Shelly asked. "You wrote a song about her."

Petra swayed and ran a hand through her tangled hair. "Then you know as much as me. Listen to the lyrics, man. Listen to the words."

"I couldn't make them out," Shelly said. "You were slurring too much."

Petra glared at her and twisted her body so that she could face Mick directly. "Your girlfriend doesn't like me. Do *you* like me? We could fuck. Right here if you like." She patted the grass next to her.

"Not right now, thanks," Mick said. "Please, Petra, this is important. What do you know about Trenorjia? We both know the name and we don't know why."

Petra swayed some more. She rubbed her eyes with nicotine-stained fingers. "These stones. It's all in the stones."

Mick grabbed her hand. This seemed to pierce the fog of drugs and alcohol. "Petra. You told Terry you were in one of the stones and you saw a figure. A woman. She called your name."

"Trenorjia. Of the ancients. Like Ligvyr. The dark side of Ligvyr." Petra's head lolled to one side. "You're very pretty, Mr. Tall Man. I really want to fuck you." She keeled over and collapsed on the grass, unconscious.

Mick leaned over her. "She's breathing. That's something. Best leave her here to sleep it off. There's plenty of security around. Ah, there's Merv. I'll let him know."

Shelly's eyes filled with tears as she looked at the unconscious singer. The girl couldn't be more than a couple of years older than her, maybe not even that, but her skin had an unhealthy grayish tinge to it and she seemed unkempt, dirty, as if she had no hope and no self-respect. Her dress was cotton, full length with a hem so filthy it couldn't have been washed in weeks if not longer. A spreading stain spoke of a bladder which had taken upon itself to release its contents at that moment. The acrid stench of urine quickly followed.

Shelly stood as Mick returned. He followed her gaze. "Tragedy. You know how old she is? Sixteen."

"What?"

"Her father threw her out when he caught her smoking weed. Merv just told me. He's promised to look after her." A shadow blotted out the sun. Merv had arrived.

As gently as if she were a newborn kitten, he lifted Petra and balanced her over his shoulder. "There's a medical tent. I'll take her over there. They'll get her cleaned up."

"Until the next time," Mick said.

Merv nodded and took Petra away.

"Hey, Mick!" Terry darted over. "I see Merv got his girl in the end."

"Does he have a thing for her, then?" Mick asked.

"In the biggest way. He's always there for her. When she's sober she won't give him the time of day, but when she's like this…. Frankly she doesn't know how lucky she is. It can get pretty gross. My heart sank when I knew they were on the bill. It's almost like a competition as to which of them can behave the worst. Right now, the guitarists have both vomited, the drummer is having sex with two groupies and the keyboard player has been found unconscious in one of the portaloos. As to the whereabouts of the flautist, he was last seen wandering around stark bollock naked and humming to himself. You can never accuse Petra's Magic Garden of being professional. Give me Jefferson Airplane anytime. At least they turn up, give a great show and leave the punters satisfied. *Then* they go and get high. Professional, see? Get the job done first. Catch you later, I hope. Must have that drink. Right now, I gotta go. If you want to come backstage again, just see Merv. He'll let you in."

Terry dashed off again before they could thank him.

Mick put his arm around Shelly. "Come on, let's listen to some music. And find the others."

Vicki collared Shelly when Mick went to talk to Davy. "So where did you two sidle off to, then?"

"It wasn't like that. I…we…." How could she explain? She couldn't. "Mick knows the stage manager. We got to meet Petra backstage."

"What was she like? She looked pretty much out of it from over here."

"She was. Totally out of it. She's only sixteen as well."

Vicki's eyes opened wide. "Really? I thought she was about thirty. She looks so much older."

"It's the drugs, I think. She's a real mess. Anyway, what have you two been up to, then?"

"Making out."

"Not all the way?"

"Not yet. But he knows how to kiss and he knows what to do with his hands too."

"I suppose that's me kicked out of the tent tonight."

"Oh, I don't think we'll be waiting until nighttime."

Davy arrived with Mick and smiled at Shelly. "I think I'll be borrowing this young lady for a while, if you'll excuse us," he said.

Vicki smiled and put her arm around Davy's waist. He returned the gesture and the two of them moved away in the direction of their tents.

Mick turned Shelly to face him. "You're beautiful, Shelly. I want to be with you."

She felt his lips on hers, gently at first, then more urgent. Raining kisses on her lips, face and neck. His tongue probed her mouth and she parted her teeth, met his tongue with hers, tasting the tang of tobacco and whatever else he had been smoking, along with a faint taste of salt as if he had been swimming in the sea. But they were in the middle of England, miles from any coast. Maybe it was all the stuff people were inhaling, making her feel high. Or was she just caught up with her desire for him?

"My tent's free," he said as they paused for breath.

She nodded and they half-ran. Once inside the two-person tent, he helped her with her dress as she lifted it over her head. Now she wished she hadn't worn as much underwear. The petticoat and bra seemed so redundant, but he seemed to take pleasure in unhooking her, and even more pleasure in what he discovered underneath.

"I knew you would be everything I wanted," he said. She lay down and he came to her.

"First time?" he asked.

"Yes," she whispered.

"Don't worry."

"My purse. I need...."

He put his fingers over her lips. "All taken care of."

By then she was too far gone to care as he lifted her hips....

★　★　★

Shelly wasn't aware of falling asleep but there she was back in that strange dream. She wasn't alone as she stood at the threshold of the black and gold chamber. Mick stood close to her, his face transfixed.

The woman in scarlet and gold towered above them.

"My lady Trenorjia," Mick said, and his voice echoed around the crystal walls.

In that moment, Shelly realized this wasn't a dream.

And Mick wasn't who she thought he was.

CHAPTER FIFTEEN

"Shelly. *Shelly!*"

Vicki's voice dragged her out of her befuddled state. Shelly stopped in her tracks. Around her, the trees and bushes rustled, swayed and creaked in the stiffening breeze. The music drifted over from the field. She struggled to remember how she had managed to get here. The last thing she recalled was somehow being in the stone, but this was some distance away from the circle.

Vicki touched her arm. "Hey, we saw you wandering off down here on your own. Where's Mick?"

Shelly shrugged. "I…I don't know, Vic. It's all so strange."

Davy put his arm around her. "Come on, let's get you back to our camp."

Shelly's knees buckled and she fell against Davy, who caught her before she hit the ground. Between them, Vicki and he half-carried her.

"Man!" Davy exclaimed, whistling through his teeth. "Looks like someone slipped you something in your drink. That's not cool. What's the last thing you remember?"

"You wouldn't believe me if I told you."

"Try me."

"Let's get back first. I really need some water and to sit down. I feel so weird."

"You will do. Some people think it's hilarious spiking people's drinks. I could never see the joke."

"That's a terrible thing to do," Vicki said. "Did you put your drink down somewhere and leave it for a minute?"

"I don't even remember having a drink."

"Maybe that's the problem," Davy said. "We've got plenty of

water. Probably won't be too cold but at least it's fresh. We're nearly there now."

Vicki and Davy settled Shelly down on top of her sleeping bag, propped up against a pillow wedged against a tent pole. Davy fetched a large bottle of water and he and Vicki sat down beside her while she drank it.

Shelly found she was far thirstier than she had thought, and the water refreshed her as well as settled her mind a little. She took a deep breath and embarked on her account of everything she could remember, ignoring Vicki's ever-widening eyes. Her friend must believe she had lost her mind. Davy, on the other hand, seemed far more receptive.

When she finally ended with them finding her at the bottom of the field, Vicki stared at her as if she had grown an extra head, while Davy simply took a deep breath and steepled his fingers before speaking.

"You don't sound crazy at all, Shelly. And Mick's involvement doesn't surprise me. He believes in all that pagan religion stuff. Man, does he ever. I mean, I thought I knew a lot about it. I've studied it since I was a kid when my older sister got me into it. She's a white witch now and some of her spells really work too. With Mick though, there's something different. Even Laura – that's my sister – said so. She said he has a strange quality about him, as if he's lived a previous life, or lives, and carries the memories of all those past lives with him. That's not supposed to happen, by the way. It breaks all kinds of psychic rules and laws of nature."

As she listened, Davy's words served to remind Shelly that she had only just met Mick and knew nothing about him, despite her strong attraction to him. Yes, a lot of that was sexual, but there was something else. An attraction of another kind that transcended pure animal lust. Right now, instead of thrilling her, it left her feeling scared and vulnerable.

"You're talking about the druids and all that stuff, I suppose," Vicki said, apparently recovering the power of speech once more.

"Oh no, all this tradition goes way back before their time. Landane was constructed by people in Neolithic times to worship their gods. They wrote nothing down so we know very little about them, but there are traditions which have persisted and some are thought to have their origins back with those distant megalith builders. Have you ever heard of Ligvyr?"

Vicki looked blank. Shelly nodded. "I've heard the name. Petra mentioned him."

"How about Trenorjia? I mean apart from the song Petra's Magic Garden mangled today."

Shelly nodded. "When I thought I was in the stone, Mick greeted her. She was the being at the entrance to the black and gold chamber."

"She would be. According to legend, she's a goddess from the other side. The dark side, if you like. To oversimplify, Ligvyr is the force of good, the total antithesis of Trenorjia."

"So where does that leave Mick?" Shelly asked, fearing the answer.

"The only place he could be, I guess. With the forces of darkness."

Shelly wished she could stop the tears pricking her eyes, but they trickled over onto her cheeks.

Vicki squeezed her hand. "Oh, Shell, don't worry. I'm sure it's all a load of twaddle and Mick will turn up soon."

"I wouldn't be so sure of that," Davy said. "Look, Shell. I've known Mick a long time, but I've never really *known* him. I don't know where he comes from originally. He's never told me. I have no idea if he has brothers or sisters. I know he's been a road manager for a number of well-known bands and solo artists, which is presumably how he knew the guy that gave you backstage access. I'm not even sure how old he is, only that he must be somewhere in his late twenties or maybe early thirties at least, simply because of some of the musicians he knows. To me they're vague memories from my early childhood but to him – on the few occasions he has even slightly opened up to me – they're adult friends he's known for years. I was really surprised when he told me he was going to study Sociology as a mature student. I asked him whatever had made him choose to do that, but I never got a straight answer. That's typical though. He's always evasive about anything to do with himself. He changes the subject and turns your question about him into a question about you. The thing is, he does it with such subtlety you don't realize until he's gone how much you've told him and how little he's shared with you in return. All I really know for sure is his unshakeable belief in the power of these stone circles, and his knowledge of where they're all located is quite extensive. He seems to have visited pretty much all of them, from the Ring of Brodgar in Orkney, down to The Merry Maidens in Cornwall and everything in between and offshore. But Landane is the place he says he feels happiest in. That much he told me only this morning. That's why he decided to settle here. He also seemed very taken with you. He said, 'She belongs here.' When I asked him to elaborate, he changed the subject."

Fear wrapped itself around Shelly's spine. "He said I belong here? What did he mean by that? I mean I live here, so in that sense I belong here but...."

"I don't think he meant that, Shelly. I think he meant something more than that, something far more."

Vicki looked bewildered as her gaze switched from one to the other. "I haven't a clue what you're talking about."

Davy squeezed her hand. "Don't worry, Vicki. Neither of us know anything either. Not for certain."

Shelly felt suddenly exhausted. She had to strain to keep her eyes open.

Vicki touched her shoulder. "Why don't you get some sleep, Shell? We'll ask around and see if anyone's seen Mick. Maybe that stage manager might know. Perhaps he went back to try and talk to Petra again. You lie down and we'll drop by later."

Shelly lay down, grateful to rest her head on the pillow. They had barely left the tent before she fell into a deep sleep.

* * *

She awoke to Vicki smiling down at her. In her hands she held red flower blossoms. Only the blossoms though. No stems.

Shelly leaned up on one elbow. "Where did you get those?"

"Courtesy of Petra's Magic Garden. That stage manager, Terry, gave them to us. Apparently, Petra was supposed to toss them into the audience at the end of their set. Pretty red flowers. A sign of peace, only they're not. Not really anyway."

"I don't follow."

Vicki sat cross-legged, leaning against her rolled-up sleeping bag. "You know each flower has a special meaning?"

"I've heard of that. Yes."

"Well, begonias actually symbolize a warning. If you give begonias to someone, you're warning them of danger ahead. Rhododendrons mean the same, but begonias, or so I've just learned, are a bit more complicated. Red ones like this can symbolize passion, eternal love and so on but, when given away can also be a warning of danger, a need to be cautious or aware."

"Who told you all this?"

"Terry. He got it from Petra. She's gone, by the way. They rushed her to hospital. Her blood pressure had dropped dangerously low, so that's the last we'll see of her and her Magic Garden this weekend. These flowers were only going to waste, so I said I'd have them. I didn't realize there would be so many though. I thought I'd spread them about, share the love and peace."

"But not the warning?"

"Maybe a little of that as well." A shadow crossed her face. Nothing Shelly could pin down but, for a second, her friend looked worried. Before she could question it, the look was gone and a smile creased Vicki's face. "How are you feeling?"

"Better. I'm hungry actually."

"That's good because Davy and the others have gone in search of hot dogs, burgers and whatever else they can find. They'll be back soon so we'll have a feast and then catch some more music."

"Vicki, are you enjoying yourself? I mean with Davy and this weekend generally."

"Yes. Davy's great. And don't worry, we're not kicking you out tonight. Now Mick's not here, we'll use their tent. Davy was sharing with him. Oh, I'm sorry, Shell. That was thoughtless of me."

Shelly waved her hand dismissively, but it did hurt. Not knowing where Mick had gone, or what had really happened when she believed herself to be in the stone with him. She kept telling herself he was a few years older than her, a grown man, whose own friend hardly knew anything about him. Of course he was free to wander off on his own. Maybe he was with another girl. That thought hurt the most. It also had to be said that if she had drunk a spiked drink, he was the prime candidate for having slipped the acid or whatever it was into the glass. She ought to be mad at him but she couldn't bring herself to be. She had really hoped they might have something. Not merely sex, but a real relationship. How stupid and naïve she was – a silly little girl falling for the oldest trick in the book. He'd had his kicks and now he'd moved on. So why couldn't she bring herself to believe it? She needed to hear it from his own lips. One thing was certain though: he was unlikely to come for her here. If she was to find him, she must get up and go back out there.

She scrambled to her feet and straightened her dress. "Is my face all right?"

"A bit smudged in places. I've got some tissues."

"I'll get my makeup out of my bag."

Ten minutes later, faces repaired, Shelly and Vicki emerged into the late afternoon sun.

"How long was I asleep?" Shelly asked.

"About two hours, I think. You look much better. You've got the color back in your cheeks."

"That's courtesy of Mr. Rimmel and his company."

"He does have his uses."

They met Davy and the others coming back from the hamburger stand. Some of the group were stuffing food into their mouths as fast as they could.

"They've got the munchies," Vicki said.

"What have you got there, Davy?" Shelly asked, the mingling

aromas of grilled burgers and chicken making her stomach rumble. He handed her a burger, with onions and melted cheese in a bun.

She took a bite and the flavor set her taste buds tingling.

"There's plenty of chips if you want them," Davy said. "Better grab them quick though, before this bunch of gannets have them all."

Vicki and Shelly each grabbed handfuls of hot, golden chips. Shelly winced as they burned her fingers, but they tasted fabulous.

"Who's got the Cokes?"

A clanking of bottles resulted in one being thrust into Shelly's hand, complete with straw. Her appetite now sated, the Coke quenched her salt-enhanced thirst.

"Delicious," she said.

Back at their camp, Vicki said, "Hey, why don't I get those begonias now and we can start spreading the love?"

"Yeah, man. Let's do it." The voice belonged to a tall, skinny boy of around Shelly's age called Stu. Right now, he was drawing on an untidy spliff which he passed to an older girl with red hair, who was doing her best to entangle herself in him. It seemed only Shelly, Davy and Vicki weren't stoned. Shelly wanted to keep it that way. She guessed Vicki did too. As for Davy, he hesitated when the spliff came to him, then shrugged and took a deep drag.

He passed it to Vicki, who shook her head. "I'll be back in a sec," she said and disappeared into their tent.

"How about you, Shell?" Davy asked, exhaling clouds of aromatic smoke. His eyes were already slightly glazed. "It's good stuff. The best."

"Not right now, thanks," Shelly said. She kept her hand firmly around the neck of the Coke bottle. If she had been caught out once, it would be the last time if she had anything to do with it.

Vicki emerged. She had acquired a basket from somewhere and the blooms filled it. "Let's each take an armful. Shelly, you too."

Reluctantly, Shelly set down her now-empty bottle and allowed Vicki to fill her arms with crimson blooms.

"Let's dance around the stones, man," Stu said as he started skipping toward them, closely followed by the redhead. The rest of the little group followed. Some carried instruments and began to play them, oblivious to the latest band warming up for their performance.

Davy joined them and Vicki nodded at Shelly. It was obvious she didn't want to be separated from her new boyfriend and Shelly didn't want to be left alone as darkness fell. She caught up with Vicki as the others reached one of the upright megaliths and began to circle it, accompanied by the sound of guitars, a flute and tambourine.

The dance grew wilder, more erratic. They circled the stone, once, twice, three times…spinning faster and faster. Colors melted into one another as if they were spinning in some giant centrifuge. Voices. Laughter. Music. Fused together. Blurred. Indistinct. In the distance, cheering. A band began to play. Their noise clamored for attention above all the others. Shelly's mind whirled, nausea shot up from her stomach.

Everything and everyone stopped as if frozen in time. People stood like statues, as Shelly herself was standing, unable to move.

A short distance away, stood a man. Not one of them, but he looked familiar.

With a start, Shelly realized why. It was Mick. But it wasn't Mick. It *couldn't* be Mick. This man was older, but he looked so much like him. The others, even Vicki, seemed oblivious to what had happened. They stared ahead, their eyes apparently unseeing.

Shelly felt a twinge in both arms, as if fresh warm blood flowed through them. She found she could move her fingers, then her hands. She took a tentative, faltering step forward. Davy's expression was unchanging but, of all the others, he was the only one who seemed to be able to blink. He did so now. Only she and the older man seemed able to move. Shelly didn't know what made her do it, but she thrust a handful of the red begonias that had fallen at her feet at the stranger who wasn't a stranger. He took them. And then he wasn't there anymore.

Shelly's head felt as if it was clogged up with cottonwool. She shook it. Sounds gradually returned and the world around her began once again to move naturally. There they all were, dancing around the stones, retrieving scattered blossoms, throwing them lightheartedly in the air. Everything surreal. She had heard of acid flashbacks. If her drink had been spiked earlier, then this is what she must have been experiencing. It hadn't been real. There had been no stranger who looked like Mick – and Mick himself was still missing. That was reality and she must focus on that. If only her brain would work properly.

CHAPTER SIXTEEN

Shelly woke with a start. It took her a second or two to remember where she was. A few feet away, Vicki was snoring gently. It sounded more like the purr of a contented kitten, but then she had a lot to be contented about. She had staggered back at some ungodly hour, replete with the effects of drink, aromatic substances and the multiple attentions of Davy.

Shelly sat up, unzipped her sleeping bag, scrambled out and slipped her dress over her head. Careful not to wake Vicki, she unzipped the front flaps of the tent and emerged into the open air. The chill of pre-dawn clung all around. On the eastern horizon the sun was showing signs of life with a pale golden glow bathing the clouds.

Shelly hugged herself and took a few steps forward. Few people were around. Some wandered aimlessly, the effects of whatever they had imbibed still much in evidence. Any conversation was muted. No one wanted to disturb the peace that was punctured only by the sounds of nature. Led by a particularly vociferous blackbird, the dawn chorus filled the air as if it were an auditorium.

Into her brain, a name floated, unbidden. *Jonathan....*

Where had she heard that name before? As she approached the portaloos, their wafting aroma reminded her that it would be a good idea to take a deep breath and try to hold it for the duration of her necessary visit. Yesterday's evening trip there hadn't been the most pleasant experience and this morning was likely to be far worse.

Jonathan....

That name should mean something to her. She racked her brain to try to remember. All she came up with was the memory of that man who looked so much like an older version of Mick.

For once there was no queue for the row of portaloos and, mercifully, a couple of hardy souls who surely couldn't have possessed any sense of smell were hard at work, cleaning and replenishing. They nodded at her as she passed them. A welcome strong smell of chemicals greeted her as she opened a door. She dared to let out her breath.

Afterward, she made her way back to the tent, passing near the stage as she did so. She caught sight of Terry and he waved at her. Maybe he had some news? She dashed over to him.

"Any sign of Mick yet?" he asked, sending her hopes crashing to the ground again.

"No, I was hoping you might have seen him."

"Sorry. No. I had some sad news about Petra, though."

"Oh no…. She isn't…."

"'Fraid so. She slipped into a coma and passed away during the night. The doctors did all they could, but she had so much stuff in her system, her body couldn't handle it and her heart simply stopped. They tried to resuscitate but I suppose it was simply her time to go."

"She was so young."

"I know. She never really lived, did she? Merv was with her at the end. He's in pieces as you can imagine."

"Where is he now?"

"Back here. He won't go home. I don't really think he has a proper home anyway. He wanted to tell the rest of the band himself. I think most of them had sobered up enough to take it in. The crazy thing is, this will probably mean their new album goes gold and that single they premiered will probably go straight to number one. Ironic, isn't it?"

"Can I see him? Merv, I mean."

"Yeah, sure, come through."

The intimidating giant looked like a deflated zeppelin. He sat hunched over a chair that was half the size it needed to be. At her approach, he raised bloodshot, teary eyes.

"Oh Merv, I'm so sorry, Terry just told me."

He nodded before blowing his nose into a handkerchief that needed replacing. It looked sodden.

"Have you any tissues, Terry?" Shelly asked.

"Someone will have. I'll go and get some."

Shelly touched Merv's hand. It was bunched into a fist.

"She spoke to me, you know," he said, at last. "She said she was sorry for being a bitch to me. I told her I didn't care. All I wanted was for her to get better." He gave a strangled sob. "I could kill the bastards that did this to her. *Kill* them." He smashed his fist into his other palm.

Shelly jumped.

"She tried to get clean. I helped her. All through last winter. She went through hell, but I fought with her, all through the hallucinations, the screaming when she said her bones were breaking. Her muscles kept going into spasms, and the pain she was in…. But she kept right at it. We were so close. So close. She hadn't taken anything in months. Then we came here. An hour later…. I let her out of my sight for a few minutes. I had to. There was some trouble. A gang of guys on motorbikes, thinking they're some kind of Californian Hells Angels, trying to muscle in. I knew something was wrong when I got back and she wasn't here. As soon as I saw her, I knew she'd scored. Her eyes. It was all in her eyes. She said it was the stones. She'd been in the stones and seen Trenorjia." He shook his head.

Terry returned with a box of tissues. "Are you okay if I leave you here?" he asked Shelly.

She nodded. Terry squeezed her shoulder and left.

Merv took a handful of tissues out of the box Shelly offered to him.

"She'd been clean so long her body wasn't used to it…." The tears flowed again and the man's huge shoulders heaved. "They asked me who was her next of kin and I didn't know. Her parents threw her out when she was fourteen. I don't even know where they live. She mentioned Cornwall once, but she also said she'd lived in Darlington." He shook his head.

"Best leave it to the police then," Shelly said. "They can find people, put out appeals nationwide. Someone will pick it up. Have they got photos?"

"I lent them one of mine. I told them I want it back. They promised but…I fucking hate the cops. I wasn't going to call them but the hospital said they had a duty to. Illegal drugs involved. It made her a criminal when she died. Not those bastards that sold her the stuff though. They get off scot-free. If I ever find out who they are…."

He didn't need to finish his sentence. Shelly could only too well imagine the fate that would await them. A part of her half-hoped he would find them. Petra didn't deserve to die like that.

One thing kept niggling at her and this would be the only opportunity she had to raise it. "Merv, when Petra said she had been in the stones, did she describe what she saw there?"

"She said she was in this huge kind of temple made of glass. Then she said something about a bridge or a pathway or something and another room further along where some woman – Trenorjia – like the song she wrote…. She was waiting." He shook his head. "It didn't make any sense."

"What was Trenorjia wearing? Did she tell you?"

"She was dressed like some goddess or high priestess. Scarlet and gold robes."

"Is that mentioned in the song?"

"Yes. Petra wrote it back when she was tripping on acid but she hadn't a clue what it meant then. Now, she told me she had finally lived. That she now knew, for the first time, what it was all about. That's when I really knew she was stoned. That and her eyes. They were unfocused, tiny pupils…and that look in them. I'll never forget it. As if she was seeing something far away in the distance, that no one but she could see. Like some door had been opened but only to her." Something seemed to click in his brain. "Hey, you sound as if you believe her."

"I suppose I do. I've had the same experience and seen the same things."

Merv stared at her. She knew he was searching her eyes for any trace of what had killed his beloved Petra but Shelly knew he wouldn't find anything. He wanted answers and she didn't have any.

"But it can't be true. All that stuff. It's mumbo jumbo. Folklore. You can't walk through stone."

"Not *through* it. *Into* it. I believe Petra somehow penetrated the stone in the same way I have and so has Mick. He's my...." What could she call him? Boyfriend? Hardly. "He's my...friend and now he's missing. The last time I saw him, I would swear on all things holy that we were in the stone over there." She pointed to the surgeon's stone. "And we were on that bridge Petra told you about, in the presence of Trenorjia. That's all I know."

"I didn't believe her."

"Don't blame yourself, Merv. From what you've told me, I've no doubt you were right, and she had taken something. For all I know, that might have been how she was able to enter the stone in the first place. I have no idea how Mick and I were there, assuming we really were. But if we weren't, it's one hell of a coincidence that we should independently have the same hallucination, even if someone did manage to slip me some acid."

"But I didn't believe her. She was telling the truth and I didn't believe her." Without warning he leapt to his feet and kicked the chair away as if it were a toy he had grown tired of. One look at the anger suffusing his face and Shelly was ready to leave. Inching her way to the exit, she made one last attempt. "Merv, I'm so sorry you're hurting like this, but there was nothing you could do. Nothing. You did everything possible to protect and save her. And we don't know that she really did have that experience. Or that I did."

Merv didn't seem to see her anymore. All he saw was rage. He let out an agonized roar like that of a wounded wild animal. In seconds, three burly security officials raced inside. One picked Shelly up and deposited her outside. "You're safer away from this, girl. We'll take care of Merv now."

His roars were loud enough to wake those sleeping nearest to the stage, and all around her, tent flaps opened and sleepy, tousled, half-naked revelers emerged, blinking in the early morning sunshine.

"Where were you?" Vicki was dressing when Shelly opened the tent flap. She brought her up to date.

"Oh, poor Petra. That's awful."

"You should see Merv. He's blaming himself and I've made it all ten times worse."

"I'm sure you haven't," Vicki said. "Look, wait here. I'm going to have a word with Davy. He seems to know about all this pagan stuff."

★　　★　　★

There was a movement and the tent flap opened. Davy and Vicki came in, carrying coffees. Vicki handed one to Shelly and she welcomed the fragrance even if it was only instant Nescafé. Vicki and Davy squatted on Vicki's sleeping bag.

"You wanted to know about the legend of Ligvyr and Trenorjia?" he asked.

Shelly nodded. "I'm sure somewhere in there is the answer to where Mick has gone. It has to be." She felt tears welling up in her eyes and fought them back.

Davy appeared not to notice, or maybe he was being tactful. He cleared his throat. "It's all tied up in the folklore of the area. I'm surprised you don't know about it, seeing as you live here."

"I've never taken much interest in that sort of thing," Shelly said.

"Me neither," Vicki said. "Although I'm beginning to find it fascinating."

"Okay then. The myths and legends about Ligvyr and Trenorjia go way back. Back to the oral tradition when no one could read and write, nights were long and people needed something to do, so they sat around their fires and told stories. Some were probably pure fantasy, but others persisted down the ages, passed from one generation to the other, and handed on as factual accounts of incredible events. Guess which category Ligvyr and Trenorjia fall into?"

"Factual accounts," Shelly said.

Davy slapped his knee. "Give that girl a gold star and a milk monitor's badge. So, here goes. The story says that in past times, before anyone had a language that could be transcribed into words, our ancestors lived on the land and off the land in small groups, each with a leader. But one group emerged as the strongest of all because their leader was different. He simply appeared one day. He wouldn't say where he had come from, only that he had a message for them all. He told the people that it wasn't sufficient to honor their dead as they did with their long barrows. They must also honor the living and those yet to be born. The spirits of those who had passed on would be reborn in those who were yet to come and *that* miracle would take place on top of a great hill which they were to build. He said they must join with all the people for miles around, and between them they were to build a mountain reaching up to the heavens; one that would tower above anything else in the landscape but would align with their greatest barrow – the one we call Moreton Landane – and another structure whose design and purpose he would save for future generations. The people were spellbound by this great being. Although he appeared human, he didn't look like them. He was much taller, with a fair complexion and blue eyes. He wore robes made of some fabric none of the villagers had ever seen before, and he never ate meat. Some said they had never seen him partake of food and drink at all. They pressed him for more information about himself but he refused to say anything other than his name was Ligvyr – in itself strange to their ears – and that he was sent to protect them, guide and teach them.

"Years went by, generation after generation. Soon there was no one who remembered a time when Ligvyr hadn't led them. The mighty hill grew, built to his exact specifications. It towered over the landscape, shining brilliant white and able to be seen for miles in any direction. As it was nearing completion, Ligvyr drew the people together again. This time he had a new project for them.

"They were to build a great stone circle. Although, by now, there were others around, this one would be the largest of any ever built and would draw people from miles around. In fact, so important would it become that everyone, the world over, would learn of its power and majesty and would come to worship. The construction of what we call Landane began. The stones were to be local in origin. Sarsen. Chosen for their properties both of stone and their ability to act as a catalyst for whatever power Ligvyr would command. Once again, the people heard Ligvyr and obeyed. For four hundred years, work on the hill and the circle continued side by side. People were born, lived their short lives and died, yet still Ligvyr remained, unceasing, unaging, unchanging. He never took a wife, or fathered children. It got to the stage where no one questioned him anymore. He was Ligvyr. That was enough." Davy lit a cigarette, inhaled deeply and puffed out a plume of smoke.

"And now, I need a drink."

Shelly handed him a bottle of water. Davy took a deep gulp.

"That's a brilliant story," Shelly said. "But where does Trenorjia fit in?"

"I'm coming to that. Okay. It seems that, according to the legend, Trenorjia was the antithesis of Ligvyr. It's typical of such legends really. You know, in the Bible, Eve was supposed to have had a sister – Lilith – who was as evil as they come. She was born of the earth, not of 'man'. No Adam's rib for her. Well, in this far more ancient legend, Trenorjia, like Ligvyr, was never actually born at all. She just *was*. She came into existence somehow. Ligvyr was the goodly one and she was the she-devil. Her aim seems to have been to undo everything Ligvyr created and replace it with worship of her by any and all immoral and corrupt methods. Oh yes, she was a real piece of work that one. When the stone circle was completed, she must have slipped through, but needed time to gather her forces and her strength, so she quietly left the scene until she was ready."

A sudden blast of cold air swept past Shelly's cheek and she shivered. Davy shot her a concerned glance. "Are you okay, Shelly? You know this is all folklore and myth, don't you?"

"Yes, of course." She hoped she sounded convincing. Davy's look wasn't encouraging. "What happened next? Did she gather her forces?"

Davy shrugged and took another drag of his cigarette, followed by a lengthy swig of his drink. Shelly felt her impatience swelling inside her. Time was pressing. Mick was out there somewhere. She swallowed hard. Finally, he continued.

"The legend says there ensued a mighty battle in which Trenorjia massacred all but a handful of Ligvyr's people. But the price she paid was hefty. Her forces also suffered massive losses. She then turned on Ligvyr herself and the two fought for control of the world. That's what the story states anyway, but they damaged each other so badly, there are two versions of how it all ended. One says that both had to go away to recuperate and each vanished into a stone. The other states they killed each other and the stones took their remains. In either event, neither was ever seen again. And that, ladies, is the legend of Ligvyr and Trenorjia. No happy ending, I'm afraid."

"Wow!" Vicki sighed. "And this has never been written down anywhere?"

"Oh, it has now. You can buy it. Probably not everywhere though. I had a copy but I lent it to someone. Usual story, never got it back. You're frowning, Shelly."

"It's just that…. You said no one has ever seen them since, but how do we know that? Do we know what they look like? I mean apart from Ligvyr being tall and having blue eyes and robes and stuff."

"I don't suppose we do. Trenorjia was described as being exceptionally tall, even taller than Ligvyr, although that might be a matter of perspective. I doubt that anyone actually put them side by side and measured them. She's also described as wearing magnificent robes that shimmered in bright and vivid colors."

"Scarlet and gold maybe?"

Davy nodded. "Maybe. Who knows? I don't think they went much on colors in those far-off days."

"We don't know that for sure though, do we? I mean they used to use colors to paint those cave paintings."

"Yes, but they were simply reproducing, or trying to reproduce, what they saw, including the colors of the animals."

Vicki gave a light laugh. "It's a shame they didn't have a go at painting Trenorjia and Ligvyr. Then at least we would know what they looked like in the flesh."

Shelly agreed with her. Davy's recounting of the legend had made her skin prickle. "The version that says they went into the stones to recuperate. Supposing that were true. They never aged.... Well, Ligvyr didn't, so I suppose we can assume the same applied to Trenorjia. What if they've recuperated and are now beginning to show themselves again?"

Davy lit another cigarette and blew the smoke out. "If you believe in that then I suppose it's possible."

"But you believe in it, don't you? For all you told me it was all myth and legend."

This time, Davy took his time inhaling and exhaling the smoke. "I believe our pagan ancestors knew things we've forgotten. They were much more in tune with the land. More than that I really don't know. As I said a few minutes ago, what I've recounted to you is firmly couched under the heading of myth and folklore. How much, if any, is true, I couldn't possibly venture a guess."

Shelly took a deep breath. "Neither could I. Let's face it, our knowledge of what's possible and what isn't is always changing. I mean, it's not all that long ago that people really believed the Earth was created in seven days and now scientists are saying it all started with a big bang. That would have been dismissed as total fiction a century ago. Less even. I don't know whether what you've told us is fact or fiction, or a combination of both, but I believe I've seen Trenorjia, and I believe Mick was with me at the time and now he isn't. So where is he?"

Vicki fiddled with the bottle of water during the long pause that followed. Finally, Davy spoke.

"You think she kept him with her. In the stone."

"Don't you?"

"You realize how this sounds, Shelly?" he said.

"Like I'm stark, staring mad. I know." She glanced at Vicki, but her friend's face was difficult to read. Maybe she didn't believe what she was hearing or was waiting for Shelly to suddenly burst out laughing. *Sorry, Vicki, you'll be waiting a long time for this punchline.*

"Okay," Davy said, stubbing the cigarette out on the ground, taking his time, grinding it to make sure it was fully extinguished. "Let's say for one minute you're right. How did he go into the stone? Or you, come to that?"

"I've no idea. Trenorjia must have had something to do with it. Maybe she made it happen. If she can do it herself, I'm sure she can make it possible for others."

"Fine. So why isn't Mick here now? She let *you* go. Why not him?"

"I don't know. He recognized her when I didn't so I'm guessing he's been aware of her existence longer. Perhaps she's already got to him in some way. Maybe he's one of her...what did you call them? Disciples, or acolytes?"

Davy uncrossed his legs and stood. "Come on."

Vicki sprang to her feet. "Where are we going?"

"To the circle. I want Shelly to tell us which stone she remembers entering. Can you do that, Shelly?"

Shelly stood. "I think so. There were two that looked quite distinctive. They're next to each other. One's called the surgeon's stone and the other one looks like a hooded monk if you look at it from a certain angle. I think I went into the surgeon's stone, but there was something odd about the other one too."

The first band of the day was warming up and, as the festival goers moved closer to the stage, Shelly, Vicki and Davy moved away in the opposite direction, across the field that seemed so much bigger than it had before. The music faded into the distance as they neared the first arc of standing stones. Shelly stopped in front of the surgeon's stone. "This is the one I entered."

Davy looked at it for a moment, but his attention was diverted. He moved to the next stone. "This one's exactly how you would imagine a monk to look. Or a witch."

Vicki giggled. "A bit of a difference between the two, isn't there?"

Davy smiled at her. "Maybe less than you think. This is the other one you spoke about, isn't it, Shelly? The one you described as looking like a hooded monk?"

Shelly nodded. "Only from this angle, but the resemblance is quite striking. I've always thought so. When we were kids we used to imagine some monk had misbehaved and got himself turned to stone. Remember, Vic?"

Vicki looked blank for a second until light dawned. "Oh yes, now I remember. We used to dance around it and chant some silly verse or other...." Her voice faded and her face clouded over.

"What is it?" Shelly asked. Davy was busy examining the stone.

"Nothing. I thought I remembered.... No. I'm sure it was nothing."

"It was obviously *something*, Vic. You've gone quite pale."

"No, really. We played some daft games all those years ago, didn't we?" She laughed, but it sounded hollow. Like she was covering up something she didn't want to share.

"Hey," Davy called from behind the monk-like stone. "Come and have a look at this."

Shelly and Vicki joined him. He had three fingers positioned in three perfectly circular indentations in the stone.

"That is a seriously weird feeling. Try it."

He removed his fingers and rubbed his hand. Shelly hesitated but then stuck a finger in each hole. Instantly, her head filled with flashing images. Like a film being run too fast. It sped through her head at such a rate she could barely make anything out. Only an impression. A man and a woman, but not anyone she knew or recognized.

She withdrew her fingers and the images stopped. "You try, Vic."

Vicki backed away. "I don't think so. No, I think I'll pass on this one thanks."

"Come on, you must. We need to compare notes. See if we all experience the same thing."

Vicki looked as if she would like to strangle Shelly, but Davy urged her on. He even took her hand and led her to the stone, where he placed her fingers over the holes. "Go on, see what happens. We're perfectly fine as you can see and Shelly's right. We need to compare our experiences."

Slowly, hesitantly, Vicki inserted first one, then two, then all three fingers in the holes. She gasped and jumped back, clasping her hand and staring at it as if it had just slapped her. "What just happened?"

"What do you think happened?" Davy asked.

"I don't know. Something weird went on in my head."

"You didn't give it enough time. Come on, try again and stay there for a few more seconds."

Shelly knew that if anyone other than Davy had asked, Vicki would have point-blank refused, but she would do as he suggested, even if it killed her.

At first she seemed to feel nothing. Then a frown creased her forehead. A minute later, it all changed. The color drained from her face. "It's like tiny worms wriggling…oh, God, I can't stand it." With a shriek, she withdrew her hand and stared at it, turning it over and over. "Tiny, burrowing…." Vicki turned her head and vomited a thin stream of bile. Her whole body trembled.

Davy grabbed hold of her, let out a cry of pain, and the two of them fell back onto the grass, panting. Davy got up first. Vicki stayed where she was, sprawled on the ground.

"What happened?" Shelly asked, bending down to tend to her friend.

"It was like an electric shock," Davy said. "As soon as I touched Vicki, I felt it surge through me. I've never felt anything like it since I touched a live electric cable once. That shot me across the room. This was similar but not as bad. Pretty scary though, when you're not expecting it."

"I never felt that when I put my fingers into those holes," Shelly said.

"Neither did I, but then neither of us held on as long as Vicki did. The effect must be cumulative."

Shelly didn't dare touch Vicki, but her friend's expression worried her. She didn't appear to know where she was or what was happening. She looked at Shelly as if she were a stranger and, perhaps most worrying, she didn't blink. Not once. "Vicki. Can you hear me?"

Vicki gave no response. Davy knelt down in front of her. He touched her hand. No shock this time, but no reaction from Vicki either.

He drew her to him and cradled her in his arms. She let him rock her until suddenly her whole body stiffened. Davy relaxed his hold and she stood up, moving awkwardly, as if someone else was working her body.

Shelly stood and put her hand on her arm. It felt like touching a block of ice. Or cold stone. Vicki stared straight ahead. Shelly followed her gaze. The half-diamond-shaped side of the surgeon's stone was directly in her eyeline, but Shelly couldn't see anything odd about it. Certainly nothing to command such attention.

Davy stood silently, watching, his expression somewhere between shock and horror.

Vicki's lips moved. The words came out a fraction after her mouth uttered them. The bizarre effect made Shelly's flesh creep. The words themselves did nothing to dispel her feeling of dread.

"The lady Trenorjia is come again. She has found the one she sought. This is her time now. The time of the other one is over."

Vicki slumped forward and Davy managed to get there in time to catch her. Had she fallen she would have hit her head on the surgeon's stone.

"Let's get her back to the tent," Davy said. Shelly nodded and between them they steered the half-conscious Vicki back up the field. The band was in full swing now. Psychedelic funk matched the stoned mood of the audience who performed their writhing dances, smoked pot, waved joss sticks and proclaimed peace and love to the already converted.

By the time they arrived back at their small camp, the others had dispersed to watch the show and Davy and Shelly helped Vicki back into her tent. She was starting to make sentences at last. "I'm sorry, Shell. I don't know what happened. I saw Mick."

"You *saw* Mick?" Shelly grabbed her hand. "Where? In the stone?"

"I'm not sure. I think so. He was.... There was.... A woman. Trenorjia. He.... They...."

"He's gone over to the dark side."

"Davy?" Shelly stared at him. He seemed to be in some sort of trance. "Are you all right?"

And then he snapped straight out of it. "Of course, I'm all right."

"What do you mean about Mick going over to the dark side?"

"Don't you see, Shell? He's one of them now. The legend I told you of Ligvyr and Trenorjia. I know now. It's all true. And Mick is part of it."

"No. It's a hallucination. It has to be."

"No, Shelly. It's no hallucination. You were there. You know it's true too. You know because you're caught up in it too."

Davy didn't sound like himself. What was happening? It seemed the world was half a beat out of step with itself. Like Vicki, Davy's lips formed words that didn't emerge until half a second later. Shelly looked all around her, at the people who were oblivious to her; people who had no idea they were dancing and moving out of sync to the music. It was like watching a film that had slipped slightly behind its audio track. It made her dizzy and nauseous. "I don't know what's true anymore. None of this makes sense. *You* don't make sense.... Mick is missing and we don't know where he is."

"But we do," Vicki said. "We know exactly where he is."

"He's where he wants to be," Davy said. "At the right hand of Trenorjia. Deep within the stone. The one you said looked like a hooded monk."

Vicki reached out to her. No longer stone cold, her hand was warm and comforting. "The chamber, Shelly. You remember the black and gold chamber. That is the entrance to her realm. You've seen it. You nearly went there."

"Mick is lost to us," Davy said. "But you don't have to be."

Shelly stared at the two people. One of them her best friend. Both of them like strangers to her.

The two of them took one of Shelly's hands each. "Come with us," Davy said. "We'll show you. Don't be frightened. It's your destiny."

CHAPTER SEVENTEEN

Olivia

1900

And in the Time Before

Olivia's consciousness let her drift far from herself, far from the world she knew and had spent her entire life amongst. A quick glance all around showed her she was alone on a windswept plain, but only for an instant. Slowly, shadowy shapes took form as humans from a much earlier time; a time before any records existed. At first amorphous, they grew solid. Men and women were both slightly stooped and shorter than her. Their children, with unkempt hair and dirty faces, mirrored their parents, although for them the grime that years of exposure to all the elements had ingrained irreversibly into the skin had yet to take such a hold. A good bath would sort most of those infants out in no time.

How strange she should have such Victorian thoughts of domestic hygiene in such a place and in the middle of such an experience. That what she was seeing was real, she had no doubt. There remained one overriding question: Why had she been brought here?

The scene around her had coalesced into its own version of normality. These people with their strange language – which she couldn't begin to comprehend – were going about their daily lives. The sexes dressed in similar fashion. They were clothed in roughly sewn animal skins which, judging by the overpowering, sickening stench, had been imperfectly cured. Round dwellings built of timber and roofed with moss and dung seemed to house entire families and must have been, at best, cramped. Smoke belched out of holes in the conical roofs. Outside, cooking fires burned. Women ripped meat from bones, their arms strong and sinewy from hard, manual labor. The children ran barefoot and, as Olivia became acclimatized to her new surroundings, she sensed the season was early spring. In the distance, clumps of trees were festooned with young, bright green leaves.

A man, carrying a primitive-looking bow and quiver of flint-headed arrows, approached her at speed. At the last moment she had to lurch to one side or he would have barreled straight into her. She dusted herself off, wrinkling her nose at the smell of never-washed human that had accompanied the animal hide he was dressed in. Did he not see her? Was he blind?

She approached one of the women who was squatting by the fire, stirring a pot filled with what appeared to be some kind of vegetable stew. There could be no language between them, but perhaps gestures might work. Olivia waved her hand in front of the woman's face. Not a flicker. She carried on stirring.

No one can see you here.

The male voice echoed through her head. Olivia looked back over her shoulder. No one there. She turned back and there was a man, dressed unlike anyone else. His long white gown matched his hair, his face seemed at once old and ageless but it was his eyes that captivated her with their sharpness and clarity of vision. Here was a man who could not only see what was there, but also what lay beyond what could be perceived.

"Who are you?" Olivia recognized her own voice but wasn't conscious of speaking. Surely she should be afraid, but she wasn't.

The man did not reply, but in her mind, one word – it had to be a name – formed.

Ligvyr.

★   ★   ★

Olivia opened her eyes, expecting to find herself back in bed at home. But there were no snowy white sheets covering her. Instead, she lay on a raised platform covered in soft furs. She recognized her surroundings. After all, she had been here before. Around her gleamed black walls glittering with specks of gold. Above her, a cathedral-like ceiling from which hung stalactites of brilliant white and crystal. Echoing sounds like breathing assailed her ears from every angle.

Olivia put her hands to the sides of her head. Why was this happening to her? Where was Grant? Too many questions. Tears sprang to her eyes. A desperate longing for the old and familiar swamped her and a deep sob wrenched itself from her body. *Dear God, what is happening to me?*

She closed her eyes and prayed harder than she could ever remember.

Then she smelled woodsmoke and felt a cool breeze on her cheek. She blinked and struggled to focus. All around her, people were moving upward and she realized she was partway up a chalk-white hill. The realization brought with it sharp pains in her knees. She was kneeling on some shards of chalk. Olivia struggled to her feet and joined the massive throng of chanting people making their way to the top. Once there, she recognized it. Landane Mound as it must have looked when first constructed. At its summit a massive fire burned and there, arms outstretched, stood the strange figure she had seen earlier. Ligvyr. Olivia moved closer, weaving in and out of the assembly until she could see clearly what he was doing. The heat from the fire burned her cheeks but she ignored the discomfort.

The people chanted in their strange language. In Ligvyr's hands, he held what looked like the sort of offal people fed to their pigs. One organ in particular she recognized. It still glistened with blood. A human heart, and its host couldn't have been dead long. Sacrificed? Her mind shrank from the prospect. Ligvyr locked his eyes on hers for an instant and she forced herself to watch as he raised the dripping heart higher, chanted some verses that elicited responses from the throng, and then threw the heart onto the fire which sizzled and cast red, yellow and orange flames higher.

Olivia shrank back from the increased conflagration.

Once again, Ligvyr chanted before flinging the other body parts – which looked like entrails to Olivia – into the flames. This time the fire did not burn higher. Instead, its fierce flames slowly died down until it settled to a gentle glow. Olivia stared into what remained of the flames and gave a cry.

Deep within it she could have sworn she saw a creature stir. A creature of fire and smoldering embers, but possessed of a face of pure evil. What was even more shocking – it was female.

But Ligvyr wasn't finished. The throng was on the move again. They spread outward and clustered together, leaving a clear pathway. This time Ligvyr held an ornate jug. It gleamed gold in the spring sunshine. But even Olivia's limited knowledge of ancient history told her such a thing was not possible in Neolithic times, yet here it was, in Ligvyr's hand, as he stood and waited.

He didn't have to wait long, as a steady procession of young women, some of whom looked to be barely eleven or twelve years old, made their way steadily toward him, each carrying a newborn baby at their breast. As the women and babies grouped themselves in front of Ligvyr, so the rest of the assembly began to disperse back down the hill. Only Olivia remained.

Ligvyr stared long and hard at her, saying nothing. He didn't need to. She knew her place was to remain there for whatever was to follow.

Minutes passed and became an hour. All stood still, the only sounds coming from the babies, some of whom whimpered, others grizzled, a few wailed and cried. Slowly, the sun began to sink lower on the horizon and the shadows lengthened. The fire continued to glow. Olivia's feet ached and she longed to sit but didn't dare move beyond occasionally redistributing her weight.

At dusk, the fire suddenly shifted. Sparks flew up as the structure collapsed. Ligvyr stirred into action. The young women tensed. Even the babies stopped crying.

The fire crackled again. Burning branches collapsed in a shower of sparks. Something was trying to escape its clutches. A clawed hand...

talons smoking...curls of black, noxious smoke spiraling up from a body of gleaming black and scarlet. Eyes, flaming coals in scaly sockets. Yet the face was unmistakably female and human. Or some form of it.

And it saw Olivia, registered her presence before choosing to ignore it. Olivia held her breath as the rest of the creature of fire and scales emerged from its blazing nascence.

Screams went up from the assembled girls as they clutched their now-wailing babies tighter to them. They huddled together for comfort as the demon paced around them. Ligvyr watched, unflinching, motionless.

One of the girls tried to break free. Others cried out after her, seeming to try and stop her. The creature moved in a flash and caught the girl up in a rough embrace. She squirmed, screamed and struggled. Mercifully her agony only lasted a few seconds. Less than a minute later she was cinders and ash, along with the tiny baby she had been carrying. By their reaction, the others had guessed this would happen. They were sobbing, tears streaming down their faces, but they bowed to what they must have known was inevitable.

The creature hissed and all was quiet. Even the babies stopped crying. Ligvyr blinked and Olivia realized it was the first time she had seen him do so since this – ceremony or whatever it was – had begun. He dipped his hand into the golden jug and withdrew it. It was dripping blood. As the creature watched, he motioned one of the girls forward. She did so and knelt, bowing as he anointed her head and then that of her baby. She stood and turned to face in Olivia's direction. Her face glowed with radiant joy. She had been saved and so had her baby.

Ligvyr repeated the action three more times before he summoned one girl and the creature hissed. Ligvyr appeared to ignore the gesture and made to dip his hand once more into the jug. The creature hissed again and its whole body glowed with angry red flame. Ligvyr withdrew his hand and it was clean.

The girl screamed. It would be the last sound she made as she and her baby joined her 'sister' in ashes on the ground.

There would be no more saved women and babies that day. Those who had received the anointing made their joyous way down the hill. For those who remained, weeping, terrified and mindful of their fate, the creature wrapped one after the other in its deathly infernal embrace.

Olivia closed her eyes and prayed for their souls. When she opened them again, she was alone. The landscape had changed. She stood in the field, facing the surgeon's stone. A full moon illuminated the landscape with a ghostly glow. Then, as she watched, a shimmering clouded her vision and she felt herself drifting....

CHAPTER EIGHTEEN

Jonathan

I moistened lips that had dried to the texture of parchment. The photograph almost taunted me with its secrets, but the truth was undeniable. Dress Nadia and me in Olivia and her companion's clothes and we would be dead ringers for them. What *couldn't* be true somehow *was*. Olivia Anstruther's name meant nothing to me other than a plaque I had seen at the cathedral that day. In the mausoleum somewhere her body lay, rotting in its elaborate marble sarcophagus. As for the mystery man, I hadn't a clue. Needless to say, I bought the book.

On the drive back to Landane, Nadia was silent, lost in thought, judging by her expression. She had said barely a word to me since we laid eyes on that picture, and when I had asked her if she had any idea as to the identity of the man, she merely shook her head.

As the sunbaked countryside sped by, I remembered the odd incident in the crypt. Through the wrought-iron gates of the Anstruther Mausoleum, I had witnessed something. It was the sort of thing you wished you had caught on camera so you could replay it at slow speed to capture every detail. As it stood, I had merely an impression to assist me. And it wasn't helping much at all.

Nadia seemed to snap out of it when we arrived back at The White Hart, and I parked the car.

"Fancy a drink?" I asked.

Again, a silent nod. Still, at least she had agreed. Maybe with a glass of wine inside her she might share whatever thoughts were troubling her.

We took our drinks outside. I had brought the book with me and once we had settled at a table, shaded under a large umbrella, I flicked back the cover. The book automatically fell open at the page with the photograph. Nadia saw it and shuddered.

"What is it?" I asked, keeping my voice gentle. I wanted to encourage her to share.

Her eyes met mine. "There's something wrong there. That photograph. I have no idea who that man is, but I can tell you his name. Grant Ford. And don't ask me how I know that because I haven't a clue. It came to me the instant you showed this to me. I can tell you a bit about the Anstruthers, but nothing about anyone called Ford."

"Do you think Ken might know? After all, his family has lived here forever."

"It could be worth a try, but Jonathan, I…." She lowered her eyes and I could sense an inner turmoil.

"Tell me, Nadia. I know you're worried."

Once more her eyes met mine. Tear-filled eyes. "It's so much more than that. For the first time I can remember in years, if ever, I'm absolutely terrified, and I haven't a clue why or what I'm terrified of. I have nothing to tell you, except I'm scared and it has something to do with that photograph. Or, more specifically, those two in the photograph."

Ken's entrance couldn't have been better timed. "How are you two doing this bright sunny day, then?"

"Come and join us if you have a minute," I said, pushing a chair in his direction.

"Well, I don't mind taking the weight off for a minute or two to be honest. It's been busy this afternoon. The sun brings them all out, but I think Jackie can cope for a short while."

Ken pulled his chair up to the table and sat down. He glanced at the book. "I see you've been shopping, then."

"We went to Charnford. Nadia showed me the cathedral and we visited the crypt, so we saw the Anstruther Mausoleum."

"Was it open?"

"No. Locked. Can you go in there, then?"

"Oh yes. If you ask the Dean, he'll let you in, under supervision of course. Best to contact the cathedral and book a time."

I made a mental note to do just that.

Ken peered a little closer. "She does look a lot like you, Nadia, and the bloke...." He looked back and forth between the photograph and me. "He could be your double, Jonathan."

"It's shaken us up a bit," I said.

"I'm not surprised. Wow! The likeness is remarkable. Are you related?"

Both Nadia and I shook our heads.

"Have you seen a picture of Olivia Anstruther before?" I asked.

Ken thought for a moment. "I couldn't be sure. She died long before I was born and, as far as I know, there aren't any memorials around. So, no, probably not."

"And do you have any idea who the man is with her?"

"I would have said it was you if I hadn't seen the date, so no. I'm sorry, I don't."

Nadia pushed a stray lock of hair behind her ear. "If I mentioned the name Grant Ford, would it mean anything to you?"

"Grant...Ford. No. Ah, wait a second. There was a rector here. Reverend Ford. His name's on the list in the church. You can't miss it. It's a board on the wall. There's one for the churchwardens as well."

"Do you know if he had any family?" I asked.

"I can't help you there I'm afraid, but I'll ask around. See if one of the older villagers knows. Maybe they hung around here after he retired or moved on." His attention was distracted by his wife waving at him from the doorway. "Sorry, I have to go now. Jackie's summoning me."

I smiled over at a scowling Jackie, who instantly turned on her sunniest expression for my benefit. Ken disappeared inside with her and I drained my pint. I noticed Nadia had finished as well.

"Shall we wander over to the church and have a look at this board, then?" I asked.

"Seems like a good idea." Nadia pushed her chair back. She seemed to be returning to her normal self. Well, as normal as she had been during this stay in Landane.

We found him immediately. He was one of the shorter-serving rectors of the parish of Landane. Joseph Henry Grant Ford's dates were given as 1898–1919. A shuffling behind us turned out to be an elderly lady, her back stooped, wielding some half-dead flowers. As we approached, she registered our presence with a sort of double take before pasting a friendly – if not totally convincing – smile on her face. I took her reaction for a natural reticence around strangers.

"Hello," she said. "Are you new to the village or just passing through?"

"We're staying for a few days at The White Hart," I replied. "I'm Jonathan and this is my girlfriend, Nadia."

The old lady looked more closely at Nadia. "Oh yes, I've seen you before, haven't I?" she asked, and her smile faded. Just a shade, and then it was back, full on as before.

"I'm quite a regular visitor," Nadia said.

"Yes, dear, I know." The woman switched her attention to me. "I'm Lilian Torrance by the way. You're looking at our rectors, I see."

"Pleased to meet you, Mrs. Torrance. In answer to your question, yes," I said. "We're particularly interested in Reverend Ford. Do you know anything about him? Did he have any sons for example?"

"Do call me Lilian. Mrs. Torrance makes me feel so old. But then, I suppose I am these days." She gave a wry smile which took years off her age. "Of course, I never knew Reverend Ford. He died twenty years before I was born, but my mother was baptized by him in 1913. Elspeth Mary Elizabeth Powell she was then. She used to talk about him, but he died in 1919 when she was only a small child. This was his last parish." She sighed. "He came to a tragic end, I'm afraid. All that business with his eldest son...." She shook her head sadly and then resumed. "He had two sons and one daughter. The daughter was called...let me see. Oh, heavens, I'll forget my own name next. Sylvia? No, that's not right. Goodness, now what was it?" She stroked her chin with a forefinger bent and twisted from arthritis. For some reason I was reminded of a picture I had seen supposedly depicting a hook-nosed Mother Shipton, the famed and legendary witch who lived in a cave in Knaresborough in the fifteenth and sixteenth centuries. The picture had shown an old woman, bent and leaning on a stick, pointing with just such a crooked finger.

"Was it Cynthia?" Nadia suggested.

"That's it. Cynthia! How clever of you to guess, my dear." If Lilian had smiled then, I would have believed her words, but there was almost a hint of sarcasm in her voice I found unnecessary and a little disturbing.

"Lucky guess," Nadia said. "Cynthia and Sylvia sound similar, don't they?"

They did. Sort of. But was it a lucky guess? I smothered my thoughts. I would be doubting myself soon.

"How about the sons?" I asked. "Did he have one called Grant by any chance?"

"Oh yes. That was his eldest. The one who disappeared. You know, I haven't heard his name in years. Handsome chap too, I believe. Oh." She clapped her hand over her mouth. Her eyes grew wide and her face drained of color as if she had seen something shocking.

"What is it, Lilian?" I asked.

Lilian's gaze switched from me to Nadia and back again. Gradually, she lowered her hand.

"I saw a photograph of him once. He was standing next to Olivia Anstruther, I think. Over in the stone circle. When I first set eyes on you, Jonathan, you looked familiar even though I knew I'd never met you before. Now I know why. The thing is, he looked like you. I remember that picture because my mother seemed quite smitten by it. She used to say she wondered what he would have been like if only he hadn't.... Are you related to him? To the Fords, I mean?"

I shook my head. "Not that I'm aware of, although I'm sure I know the photograph you mean. He's holding a spade and they're standing in front of the surgeon's stone."

Lilian shifted her weight from one foot to the other. "They'd just raised it, I think."

"Are you all right?" Nadia asked.

It seemed it was only with great difficulty that Lilian switched her attention from me to Nadia. "Oh yes," she said. "*I'm* all right, but something here isn't."

Her former affability had melted away. As she addressed Nadia, a hint of hostility cloaked her voice. "I've seen you many times but you're not her. You *look* like her but you're not her."

"Well, I couldn't be her, could I?" Nadia's tone, while not as combative, still grated on me. The atmosphere had turned heavy and awkward, even though we were in a place that was supposed to promote tranquility and well-being. "That's if you mean Olivia Anstruther, and I presume you do."

Lilian nodded slowly. The silence that followed saw the two women staring at each other, neither apparently prepared to give ground.

I decided to distract them. "Tell me about the other brother, Lilian. What was his name?"

Lilian diverted her attention back to me. Her brow furrowed. "I'm struggling to remember.... Something to do with a brand of coffee."

"Coffee? You mean Nescafé?" Why I said that, I have no idea. Stupid suggestion.

"Yes. That's it. Maxwell House."

"His name was Maxwell House?"

"Yes. No, not Maxwell *House*. Maxwell." Lilian laughed and the tension was broken. Nadia managed a smile and I heaved an inward sigh of relief. "Maxwell Ford," Lilian confirmed. "Oh, he was a naughty boy. Broke his father's heart. As if it hadn't been broken enough already." Lilian looked around her and lowered her voice. "Got some local girl in the family way. They had to get married. You've heard the term 'shotgun wedding'?"

I nodded.

"Well, it almost literally came to that. Maxwell kept on denying responsibility, but it had to be him, you see. I think that's what hurt his father the most. Not the fact that the girl was carrying his child, but the repeated lies. Anyway, her father came over to the rectory one night. He was a local farmer, and he brought his gun with him. Poor Reverend Ford had his first heart attack a few days later. Another vicar had to be brought in to perform the wedding ceremony."

"That must have set the tongues wagging," I said.

Lilian giggled. "I'm sure it did. It certainly must have taken their minds off the war – and all the other business with Grant – for a while. I think that was in about 1915 or 1916. Maxwell would have been in the army but I don't know in what capacity."

"So what did happen to Grant?" I asked.

Lilian frowned. "One day he was here and then he wasn't. He was never seen again."

"But people don't just disappear," I said.

"Yes, they do," Nadia said. "It happens all the time."

Lilian glared at her. "You may be right about some people, but Grant would never have done that and cause his family so much pain. Not to mention Miss Anstruther. She never got over it any more than his parents."

"But they must have searched for him," I said.

"Oh yes. The police, everyone. Searched high and low for weeks. They sent frogmen down into the river. But there was no trace of him." She stared straight at Nadia when she said that and Nadia returned the stare. I could feel the icy chill penetrating my bones.

Once again, I tried to move us onto slightly safer ground. "So Reverend Ford died in 1919. What happened to his family then? Do you know?"

Lilian shifted her weight again. "I know Maxwell, his wife and child moved away. Somewhere up north, I think. Sheffield, Leeds, Bradford or some such place. I think once they got married and Maxwell had been forced to face up to his responsibilities, he must have tried to make the best of it. A fresh start in a place no one knew them. Well, it would probably give them the best chance, wouldn't it? As for Cynthia...." She shot Nadia a quick glance and, only for an instant,

166 • CATHERINE CAVENDISH

I read fear in that look. A second later, she passed her hand over her forehead in the manner of someone trying, and failing, to recall some distant memory. "No, I don't think I know what happened to her."

The church clock struck. This seemed to fill Lilian with relief. "Oh goodness, I must get on. They've got a confirmation class here in an hour and I'm not nearly done with the flowers for tomorrow's services. Please stay as long as you want. It's been lovely chatting with you."

For a woman who clearly suffered with her joints, Lilian could move surprisingly quickly when she needed to.

I glanced at Nadia. Her head was down and her voice barely audible. "Can we go now, please?"

"What was going on there? Between the two of you, I mean."

"What do you mean? I don't know her."

"You've seen her a few times though and she certainly recognized you."

"She thought I looked a lot like Olivia Anstruther. That's all it was. It's not as if she ever knew the woman anyway. Olivia died years before she was born." Nadia had a strange look in her eyes and her words came from somewhere deep in her conscious or maybe her subconscious. An uncomfortable sensation of foreboding gripped me. And it scared the hell out of me.

CHAPTER NINETEEN

I have always been a great sleeper. I know women often accuse men of being able to fall asleep at a moment's notice, absolutely anywhere – even upside down hanging from a washing line as a previous girlfriend cited when I rose from a perfect night's slumber only to find she had spent a virtually sleepless night owing to the most severe storms since records began, complete with crashing thunder, blinding lightning and torrential rain beating on the windows.

Here on my first trip to Landane though, sleep had to be earned. I dropped off all right. Slept for half an hour or so and then woke up. No apparent reason for it either. Nadia, next to me, slept soundly and any snores she made were more like a kitten's. Certainly not enough to disturb even the lightest sleeper.

That night, it was even worse. It took ages for me to drop off and then when I did, probably through sheer exhaustion, my dreams turned into nightmares. I was falling, then I was being pursued through a strange forest of trees by an indeterminate foe I knew wanted to kill me. Eyes protruded from every branch. Finally, I woke just as the creature was about to crush me. I sat up, careful not to wake Nadia. I was sweating and urgently needed to empty my bladder.

The bathroom door was ajar as always, and I didn't switch on the main light. The small one above the mirror served well enough and didn't cast too much illumination into the bedroom. After that strange encounter a couple of nights previously, I avoided looking into the mirror itself, but ran a little tepid water into the sink and washed down my face, arms and torso to cool me down. Refreshed, I dried myself on the towel and returned to the bedroom.

I stopped at the doorway. Nadia's bedside light was on but she wasn't there. A quick glance around told me she wasn't anywhere in the room either. The window was as we had left it, slightly open to let some fresh air in. I crossed the room, pushed it open wider and leaned out.

Nadia, dressed in a long white gown, was in the process of opening the gate at the bottom of the garden, leading into the field of standing stones. It was the middle of the night, so I couldn't call out to her for fear of waking everyone up. Anyway, she was probably too far away to hear me.

I caught up with her at the surgeon's stone. She was gazing up at it, transfixed, unaware I was even there.

"Nadia."

No response.

"*Nadia.*" My voice sounded loud in the silent darkness. Then I realized. Although it was indeed dark – there was no visible moon that night – I could see her quite clearly. She was bathed in a soft luminescence emanating from somewhere deep inside her, giving her a ghostly glow.

Slowly she turned to face me. She was smiling but didn't appear to see me. Her unblinking eyes stared straight at me but there was no recognition in them. She didn't seem to see anyone at all. I tried clicking my fingers, hoping she would snap out of this trance or whatever fugue state she was in.

Then I heard them again. The pounding of hundreds of pairs of feet, much closer than before. I looked beyond her toward the horizon that glimmered with a pre-dawn glow. An undulating mass moved steadily toward us. As they approached, the sky grew lighter. Surely someone in the village would see this. I looked back over my shoulder at the darkened houses where their inhabitants slumbered, blissfully unaware of what was going on so close by.

But that was the point. They slumbered in almost total darkness. Not a single streetlamp or light of any kind relieved the unremitting gloom. Only when I looked forward again, was I able to make anything out. It seemed, from my perspective, that the illumination came from the east, but it traveled with the horde, moving at their pace. No, I was wrong. They, like Nadia, were *bathed* in soft light as if they had generated it themselves somehow.

As they approached, I began to make out shapes, figures, dressed much as I had seen from depictions of people in the Neolithic Age. Animal skins, furs, long hair and beards on the men. The women were dressed similarly but they trailed young children. Some carried babies. They came to a ragged halt some twenty yards away. Nadia slowly turned to face them. She raised her arms high. Those unencumbered by children copied her. They stayed mute for a few moments while I watched – a silent witness seemingly unobserved by any of them. Then, as the others stood perfectly still, a tall figure dressed in a long white robe came forward. As he approached, I was struck by the intense blue of his eyes.

He walked toward us and I could tell by the way he looked at me that he at least saw me.

He approached Nadia and I took a step forward, ready to protect her if he threatened any harm. He didn't speak, but words I knew were his filled my mind.

She will come to no harm with me, Jonathan.

"Who are you?" I asked.

No audible reply. Just one word, transmitted into my brain. *Ligvyr.*

He touched Nadia's forehead. I lunged at him, intending to push him back, but there was nothing there. He had vanished. I looked over toward the horde of people only to find they had disappeared too. Once again the field was plunged into darkness.

"What am I doing out here?" Nadia sounded scared. "What happened? I felt something." She put first one hand to her head and then the other. "It hurts, Jonathan. It feels like…I can't explain. I don't understand what's happening to me. I don't understand any of this."

I held her close, both arms tightly around her so she couldn't fall. "Let's get out of here."

A part of me wanted to *really* go. Home – not merely to The White Hart – but we could discuss that in the morning. Right now, Nadia needed to lie down. She leaned close to me as we made our unsteady way back.

As we neared the gate into the pub garden, she pulled up sharp. "It's gone," she said. "It's gone completely. My head feels normal again. No pain."

"Thank God for that," I said. "But you still need to rest. Right now."

She didn't protest and a few minutes later, I was tucking her up under a duvet she immediately thrust from her. "It's too hot for that," she said, her eyes already closed.

I climbed into bed next to her and switched off the lamp before lying down, facing her back.

"Jonathan?" she said, softly.

"Mmm?"

"I had a grandfather called Max. Like the Reverend's son. Not Maxwell, though. Just Max. Max Gale. He would have been around the same age."

"We'll talk about it in the morning," I said, already half asleep.

But after a night when my dreams were filled with images of Ligvyr, begonias and roses that withered and died the moment I picked them, and a shadowy man in World War I army uniform, I woke with a craving for coffee and a sense that I needed to learn more about Nadia's paternal grandfather. After all, there had to be some reason for her link to Landane.

★　　★　　★

Nadia and I enjoyed a delicious breakfast and took our coffees into the bar, which was fairly quiet. Merely a handful of guests who, like us, were lingering over their breakfast beverages.

"Granddad Gale died before I was born so I never knew all that much. He married my Grandma Florence and they had five children I think, but only two survived infancy and there was a huge age gap between them. Uncle Chris died in the Second World War. On D-Day. He's buried somewhere in Normandy. He was around twenty-eight I think, but my father was born in 1936 so there was around twenty years' age difference. Then he kind of repeated history. Mum is a good twenty years younger than Dad so maybe that's why I'm an only child. My father was in his fifties before he ever held a baby in his arms."

"Do you know your grandmother's maiden name?"

Nadia frowned. She shook her head. "I can't ever remember being told what it was. She was always Grandma Gale or Grandma Flo to me."

"Okay, so would it have been possible that your grandfather, having left here under a pretty dark cloud, might choose to change his name to his wife's?"

"I suppose that's possible, yes."

"That old lady, Lilian, when we were in the church, told us Maxwell Ford had married the pregnant girl and moved north somewhere. She mentioned Sheffield, Leeds and Bradford. You've lived in Halifax all your life, is that right?"

"Yes. Dad got a job there and moved from Leeds. It's only about fifteen miles away.... Oh, I see where you're coming from."

"Did he grow up in Leeds?"

"Yes. In Headingley. Nice area."

"And he left there before you were born?"

"Yes, I don't remember when, but it was before he met Mum because she was Halifax born and bred as well."

"Seems to me like we need a chat with your dad."

Nadia's face clouded over. Her eyes filled with tears.

"Oh no, I'm sorry. I thought your dad was still alive. I mean, I know you don't talk about him much...." I struggled to think of even one mention of him in the time I'd known her. I assumed it was a touchy subject and that her parents were separated or divorced. I just never felt I could raise the subject.

She wiped a tear away with her finger. "He is. Still alive I mean. If you can call advanced dementia living. He's been in a care home for the past two years."

My heart went out to her. "I'm so sorry, Nadia. I had no idea."

Nadia blew her nose. "I didn't tell you and it's hardly something you could guess at. We could always call Mum though. Dad may have told her things I don't know about his father."

I took a deep breath. "Nadia, I have to ask you something. Does the name Ligvyr mean anything to you?"

Nadia paused in the act of wiping her nose. Her eyes had widened. "Ligvyr? How do you know that name?"

"Last night. When I found you outside. I had some sort of vision, or dream.... I don't know what it was.... I saw a strange man, or entity of some kind and the name Ligvyr came into my head. I believe it's his name."

Nadia crumpled her tissue in her hand. "I know the name. I know he exists, and there is something...." She shook her head. "I can't tell you more than that."

Couldn't? Or *wouldn't*? Right now, I couldn't decide and was tempted to push a bit further, but she added, "I think I'd like to call Mum now."

My questions would have to keep.

★　★　★

Back in our room, Nadia put her phone on speaker and laid it on the bedside cabinet while we sat next to each other. After the usual greetings and pleasantries, Nadia asked what she knew about her grandfather.

Mrs. Gale's distinctive Halifax accent seemed accentuated by the phone, or maybe it was because we were 'down south' and surrounded by the richer southwestern dialect of the local people. Strange what a difference a few days could make. In more ways than one.

Mrs. Gale sighed. "I don't know if anything I can tell you will come as any surprise. Your Granddad Gale was notoriously tight-lipped about his early life. Same with your grandma. I did get an idea that there'd been some sort of scandal and when I saw your uncle

Chris's birth certificate, it was clear he'd been born a mere five months after they married. Of course, it wasn't anything all that unusual in those days. Plenty of girls ended up 'having to get married' as they used to say. I never thought too much of it. One thing was a little odd though. After your grandma died, we found your granddad's birth certificate among her papers and it stated that his father was a vicar. I can't remember the first name, but the surname was Ford, not Gale. I asked your father about it and he was as mystified as I was—"

Nadia interrupted. "Mum, I think we can fill in that piece of the jigsaw. His father was the Reverend Joseph Ford and he served as rector of the parish of Landane until his death here in 1919. Did you find Grandma's birth certificate?"

"No, that never turned up. Caused us some problems too, I remember. The bank was especially unhelpful. Well, I never. Fancy you discovering that. What a small world."

"Did Dad ever say anything else about his father?"

"What sort of things, love?"

"Anything really. Did he ever mention someone called Olivia Anstruther?"

"Olivia Anstruther? No, I don't think so."

"Or Grant Ford? Cynthia Ford?"

"Doesn't sound familiar. Why? Who are they?"

"They would have been his aunt and uncle. Grant was the oldest of three children. Maxwell was the middle child and Cynthia the youngest."

"Maxwell? I never heard him called that."

"He probably shortened it when he took Grandma's name as his own."

"Yes, I can see that would work. I can't think of anything else I'm afraid, but I'll have a rummage around and see if I can turn up anything. If I find or remember something, I'll call you."

"Thanks, Mum."

"It sounds as if you're having a fascinating time down there. I wish I was with you."

No, I thought, *you really don't. Not if you'd experienced what I have, and I suspect your daughter probably feels the same way.*

"'Bye Mum, talk to you soon."

"'Bye, love. You both have a lovely time."

"Thanks, Mrs. Gale," I said.

Nadia ended the call. "I want to go back up to the stones."

I knew she would. And when we arrived there, I knew she would make straight for the surgeon's stone, and that she would touch it, and stroke it in a way that made me uncomfortable. Her fingers caressed the ancient gnarls and indentations. There weren't many tourists around and an overcast sky contained rain clouds threatening to deposit their showers at any moment. The air held the distinctive smell of an impending spring rainstorm. Above us, a small flock of crows circled. I thought it strange at the time. It was the formation. An almost perfect circle directly above the stone. At first their flight seemed random but, as the seconds became minutes and Nadia continued to stroke the stone, moving around it while I stood to one side, the increasingly deliberate flight of those birds disturbed me more and more. They reminded me of old Westerns I had seen on television when I was growing up – the circling vultures indicating a dead or dying man or men on the ground below. Those crows behaved in similar fashion, and I had no idea why, only that it made the hairs on the back of my neck stand to attention.

"Nadia?"

She seemed not to hear me.

"Nadia. Let's go."

She must have heard, but she gave no sign. The birds kept circling, their grating caws providing an unholy, relentless, tuneless chorus. One swooped down, narrowly missing my head. Two more landed on the ground between me and Nadia. Again, she took no notice and continued her perambulations.

As if on cue, the crows flew away. The air was silent, the only sound provided by a few drops of rain that pattered onto the stone, ignored by Nadia.

"Come on, Nadia. It's going to start pouring soon."

The sky had turned from gray to an ominous charcoal in seconds. Nadia looked at me, a half-smile on her face.

"Look behind you," she said.

I glanced over my shoulder, realizing as I did so that the few tourists had disappeared, leaving Nadia and me alone. Alone except for....

"I brought you begonias...." The girl's eyes seemed huge in her pale, thin face. She had looked much more wholesome last time I had seen her. Now she looked haunted, ghost-like.

"Who are you?"

"Shelly. But you know that, Mick. You *are* Mick, aren't you? He's been lost for so long."

I turned to face her full on. "No, I'm not Mick. I'm sorry. I hope you find him."

The bearded hippy approached us from out of the corner of my eye. The girl spoke to him. "Davy, he says he's not Mick."

Davy looked me up and down. "Then maybe he isn't."

I swallowed. Who was this? A real person? A ghost from the past?

Davy stared behind me, where Nadia stood. He nodded toward her. "*She* knows. She's got the answers."

Nadia moved forward and stood beside me. "I don't know who you are," she said, but she sounded false, as if she was reciting someone else's words.

I touched her arm. "Nadia, who are these people?"

She looked me straight in the eyes and shook her head.

I glanced back at Davy and Shelly, only to find that once again I was staring at nothing but a green field and a circle of standing stones.

"You did see them, didn't you?" I asked Nadia.

"I'm as confused as you are. Where did they go?"

"Are you though?" I asked. "Confused, I mean. Because I'm not at all sure you are. You seem to know or guess something you're not sharing with me. What is it? We're in this together and I need to know what you know."

"Honestly, Jonathan, I wish I did. All I have are theories, unanswered questions and my suspicions. None of them make any sense and all of them have their roots in the past. Far, far back in the past. I don't even know whether I've dreamed some of it or whether it's real."

She sounded genuine enough and I inwardly berated myself for what I had just said. I needed to make it up to her. "Let's get out of this rain and you can tell me. I promise I won't ride roughshod over anything you say. After all, I've seen the impossible with my own eyes. Who am I to judge?"

★   ★   ★

Back at The White Hart, we weren't the only ones to be taking shelter from the rain. Guests and visitors alike had crowded into the bar, an array of wet Barbour jackets, coats and umbrellas littering the place. We managed to find an unoccupied snug corner next to the fireplace and Nadia sat while I ordered coffee at the bar.

We deposited our wet jackets behind the chairs and settled in. Coffee arrived shortly and I waited for Nadia to take a sip.

She did so and set her coffee mug down. "This is going to be a bit of a tale, but it's all I've got."

"Maybe in that tale lies the answer to why all this has been happening," I said.

She gave a sardonic smile. "Do you think I haven't gone over every morsel, every crumb, every single atom to try and reason it out? Well, anyway, here goes. I know you haven't met Dad, but you've met Mum, and would you say she was very fair? In coloring I mean. Fair-skinned, blonde hair?"

"Yes."

"Dad's similar. Mum has photos of him when he had blond hair. He has blue eyes. Mum has blue eyes. Think of that couple and what sort of child would you imagine they might produce?"

"One with fair skin, blonde hair and blue eyes I suppose, but that doesn't always follow."

"The laws of genetics state that two blue-eyed parents usually produce a blue-eyed child. Add to that the fact that my parents have such fair skin and there is no known history of anyone on either side of the family having dark hair and olive skin, and you can see why everyone has such a hard time believing that my parents are mine biologically. Technically, it's impossible for two people with blond hair to produce a child with dark hair because the gene that produces a brunette isn't there. Dad even took a DNA test. He grew certain I wasn't his but, according to the results, I am."

She let that sink in. "So you've proved the geneticists wrong? I'll bet they didn't like that."

Nadia shrugged. "You know scientists, they came up with a whole load of waffle that, roughly translated, meant they didn't believe it. There must be something wrong with the DNA results. The results got mixed up with someone else's. Three tests later, they walked away from it leaving me feeling like a freak of nature. Over the years, I put it out of my head, but when Dad got sick, he started to accuse me of being a thief and a robber, he also accused me of being a cuckoo in the nest. Whenever he would see me, he would make these 'cuckoo' calls. That's when I stopped going to see him. I couldn't stand it. It also upset Mum so much to see him behave like that to his own daughter, even though it wasn't his fault. The thing is, Jonathan, it's true. I *am* a freak of nature. By rights, I shouldn't exist. Where have I sprung from?

"Mum told me she had a perfectly natural birth in the maternity unit of the local hospital. Nothing untoward. No last-minute panics and, yes, she was tested too, just in case she wasn't my biological mother, although if that had turned out to be the case it would have meant there were two babies born at the same time with my father's genes flowing through them. He was tested first, you see. Needless to say, both Mum and Dad turned out to be my biological parents. So there's anomaly number one out there."

"What's anomaly number two?"

"All this." She waved her arm to encompass The White Hart but I knew she meant the whole of Landane itself. "From my earliest memories, I dreamed of this place, of the stone circle, and Landane

Mound. Occasionally I would find myself in a stone-walled chamber and when I first visited Moreton Landane, I knew I'd been there before, and then I remembered those childhood dreams."

"What brought you here the first time?"

"I read an article in a magazine about standing stones. I was probably around fourteen at the time. I'd heard of Stonehenge, of course. Who hasn't? But I didn't know anything about the other stone circles. The Ring of Brodgar looked impressive, Callanish too, but then I turned the page and saw a picture of the surgeon's stone and that was it, I knew it. In my mind, an image of the entire stone circle flashed up. Not as it is today, but as it must have been when it was first built all those thousands of years ago. I knew then I had to come here. But it was another five years before I did. My parents weren't interested, you see, and, given my childhood experiences, those tests, the uncertainty and doubt.... I never felt I wanted to push anything that would highlight my feelings of being different. I waited until I left school and found a job and my own place to live. I was free to do what I wanted then so I saved up and booked my first stay down here. Initially it was at one of the B&Bs on the edge of the village. I started staying here at The White Hart around seven years ago, maybe longer. Each time I've come, I've done the same things and each time it's brought me a little closer to the answer. Funnily enough, this time, I've found out more about real people who lived here than on any single visit. I never knew much about Olivia Anstruther, apart from the little bit of history I told you, and the mausoleum. I'd never seen that photograph of her and Grant Ford and now I even know that my own grandfather led a double life."

"He didn't. Not really. Merely a change of name."

"But it *does* mean I had a link to Landane from before birth. That could explain so much."

I couldn't deny that.

"So, anomaly number two is your link to Maxwell Gale né Ford."

"No, that's anomaly number three. Anomaly two was all those childhood dreams of Landane."

"Unless you'd seen a picture of Landane when you were a small child and had forgotten it consciously, but it stayed with you in your unconscious mind."

Nadia considered this for a moment. "Okay, I'll agree that's a possibility, although where I would have seen it is a mystery. My parents didn't go in for standing stones, ley lines or anything like that."

"But it could have turned up in a holiday brochure, or a newspaper. Maybe some archeological find. Anywhere really. As a young child, you see it, but it doesn't register. It's not something your young mind can compute at the time so you store it up for future reference. Then, one day, years later, bingo!"

Nadia smiled. "You're right, of course. Okay, let's say that did happen. We still have the other two anomalies and it doesn't stop there."

I took a gulp of coffee. I was tempted to add that name into the mix – Ligvyr – but I needed to let her tell me at her own pace. "Go on," I said.

"The things that happen at the surgeon's stone. That all started the first time I went there. I was drawn to it, more than any of the others. When I walked round the circle, the one next to it – the one that looks like a hooded monk – it seemed to…. Look, to say it pointed towards it sounds too silly for words. Obviously, it didn't produce a finger and…. It, sort of, commanded my eyes to look at it, and my feet to approach it. Oh, now I sound like one of those stupid zombies in those crap films, being propelled along, eyes staring wildly and bits of bloody skin dropping off."

We laughed and it broke a tension I could sense mounting inside her.

"I really can't explain it properly," she said, recovering herself. "But I *had* to go right up to the surgeon's stone and touch it. The stone itself felt quite warm and tactile, everything a sarsen shouldn't feel like. I remember it was a cold, foggy day in November. There had been no sun and the frost was only now melting, so that the grass still crunched a bit when you walked. I smelled salt, as if I was at the seaside even though we're in the middle of the country here, with no sea for miles. It was around then I had my first vision. I saw Ligvyr. I didn't know his name then – not until much later – but I saw him. He connected with me psychically somehow and then stood at the side of the stone and beckoned me to him. I felt protected. I never hesitated. I felt perfectly safe and at home there. I took a step closer to him, my hand still touching the stone. He extended his hand toward me and made a connection, not by holding my hand but through the juxtaposition of himself with me and the stone. The next thing I remember was waking up in bed at the B&B in the middle of the night, with no recollection of how I'd got back or what had happened in those lost hours.

"The following day I had an irresistible urge to go to Landane Mound. The odd thing is I don't remember driving there that time. It seemed that one minute I was at the B&B and the next I was standing at the foot of the mound itself. A man called to me. He was slithering down the hill, although there were copious signs warning of heavy fines for climbing it. That was the first time I met Ken. He told me they had only put up the signs a few months earlier because of the erosion caused by thousands of tramping feet and excavations over the centuries. He said he had taken a trip up there for old times' sake but had found something he'd never seen before. I don't know why, but he took me into his confidence and that's when he showed me the secret way into and up the mound. He made me promise I would never tell a living soul where to find it and I haven't."

"You showed me the way, though."

"Could you find it now? You were blindfolded."

I shook my head. "You didn't break your promise to him."

"I haven't told you everything yet, Jonathan. You see, the next time I came down here, I went to Moreton Landane first, even before the circle. I stopped off there on the way here. I had briefly been before and didn't really connect with the place, but that time. Oh, that time...." Her voice trailed off. She seemed to have gone off into a dreamworld where she was reliving her experience.

"What happened?"

She snapped back and blinked rapidly. "I met the other one. The female entity. Ligvyr's equivalent, except she is the exact opposite of Ligvyr as much as black is to white. Her name is Trenorjia and her origins are as ancient and mysterious as Ligvyr's. I was alone at the barrow. Not a soul around on a calm, still day. There was barely a breeze to flutter the leaves. It was springtime but there was no birdsong. Inside the barrow, the air was cold, so cold that I could see my breath misting in front of me, yet outside was a pleasant, warm afternoon. I peered into the recesses and the further back I progressed, the more anxious I became. I told myself it was just my imagination, but I didn't imagine what I saw. She was real and terrifying.

"Darkness seemed to shroud the back of the barrow. As I scanned the walls, they shimmered and somehow melted, forming themselves into an entrance. I couldn't help it, I had to see what was there, so I forced myself to move forward until I came to where the barrow should have ended. Without leaning forward, I peered in. In a flash, a woman, at least a foot taller than me, maybe more, filled the entrance. She wore a robe of scarlet and gold and held her hand out to me. I recoiled from the long fingers that tried to claw at me. I knew she wanted to take me through that entrance. I stumbled backwards and almost fell. She leaned out, bending to get under the roof of the entrance. Her mouth opened and there was blackness there – a cavern of total emptiness. I let out a shriek and the woman...creature... entity.... Trenorjia was gone. I was staring once more at a perfectly constructed Neolithic wall of stone. I ran out of there, vowing never to return. But I did, of course. Time after time. I can't help myself. But I've never seen her there again."

"She's the one you've seen in the stone."

Nadia nodded.

Ken interrupted us. "You two look serious," he said. "May I join you?"

I half-wished he wouldn't, but Nadia had already indicated a chair for him to take. He sat down.

"We've been talking about phenomena," Nadia said. "The strange things I've seen in Landane during my visits. The thing is, Ken, we've discovered that I have a family link to this village. My grandfather was Maxwell Ford, the son of the rector here in the early nineteen hundreds."

Ken's eyes widened. "Really? That's a coincidence. Explains a lot though."

"That's what we think," Nadia said. "He was the Reverend Ford's son, but everything points to him changing his last name to his wife's and becoming a Gale. It was a shotgun wedding and I suppose he wanted a fresh start, new identity. I gather there was some trouble over it all."

"I can imagine. Getting a girl in the family way. Mind you, there are a lot of folk around here who could tell a similar tale. My own family had its fair share of skeletons in closets. My grandfather was allegedly his sister's son by a wandering laborer who just happened to be on the run from the police following a murder in Cheltenham. The gossip has it that he stayed long enough to get poor Elsie knocked up and then disappeared never to be seen again. Meanwhile, her parents rallied round and Elsie's mother started wearing padding and talking about having a late baby. Apparently, she was nearing fifty at the time and hadn't produced a child for nigh on fifteen years, so the local busybodies had a field day. Elsie went away for a lengthy holiday to some trusted family friend or relative miles away and returned just after her new baby 'brother' was born. Of course, her arrival just happened to be in the middle of the night and the baby was first seen the day after, possessed of a full head of hair and not a newborn wrinkle in sight. Quite an achievement for a day old." Ken looked thoughtful. "You spoke to Lilian Torrance, didn't you?"

"At the church," I said. "She was the one that put us on to Reverend Ford. She filled in the details of his children."

"Did she mention Cynthia?"

"Yes. She said she didn't know what became of her."

"The thing is, I was talking to my mother about that photograph of yours and how the people in it looked like you two. As soon as I mentioned Olivia Anstruther, she gave a little gasp. I asked her what the matter was and she said, 'You do know she went mad, don't you? Stark staring mad.' She told me Olivia and Cynthia Ford became fast friends after Grant Ford disappeared. It was all news to me because up to when you told me what Lilian had said, I knew nothing about these people." He glanced away. Jackie was beckoning to him. "Sorry, I have to go. Customers to serve."

He left us and Nadia stood. "Let's go back to the stones," she said. "There's something I need to do."

There were significantly more people milling around than had been there earlier. On the horizon, the sky was darkening with storm clouds. A couple stood in front of the surgeon's stone. One glance at Nadia, though, and they moved on. I couldn't see her expression from my angle but, judging by their reaction, it couldn't have been too friendly. But why? Did I know this woman at all?

I stood to one side as Nadia circled the stone, her hand trailing its surface, her eyes half closed. Her lips moved as if she was uttering some chant. The sound of people chattering and laughing faded into the distance. A chill wind blew up from nowhere and I had a sense of something unnatural. Then I saw it.

Moving ever closer, the dark cloud enveloped the figures I had seen before. Then it had been darkness, nighttime. Now it was broad daylight. Except, as I looked around, I saw a strange and empty landscape, devoid of the buildings that should have been there. The thumping feet made the ground rumble as I had heard before. I prayed that at any moment it would all stop and I would wake up in our room at The White Hart, except this time it didn't stop. They kept coming, closer and closer, until I could smell them. A pervading sour animal smell of unwashed bodies. As before, they stopped, but closer to me than on the previous occasion. Surely Ligvyr would appear now.

But it wasn't Ligvyr. And Nadia had gone.

CHAPTER TWENTY

Four people stood in front of me. I recognized Olivia Anstruther and Grant Ford, and the girl I knew as Shelly. A short distance away stood a man who, like Grant, bore a remarkable resemblance to me. Maybe he was the missing hippy boyfriend Shelly called Mick. Everyone, the horde of men, the people from the past and I, stood in perfect silence. No one looked at anyone else, except for me. They didn't seem aware of each other either, as if each existed in their own personal bubble. I kept glancing from one to another of them before it dawned on me that I was the only one who could see the complete picture. I looked beyond the people standing closest to me and realized that each member of the hundreds of people who had assembled there was entirely alone. Could they see me? There was only one way to find out.

"I'm Jonathan," I said. "Who are you?"

No one spoke. No one registered that I had spoken.

"Why are you here?"

Again, nothing. A distant sound of cruel and raucous female laughter was my only acknowledgment, and it hadn't come from any of the assembled.

I addressed the stone. "Who are you and what do you want?"

Nadia emerged from behind the hooded stone, taking me by surprise. But she was not herself. This Nadia spoke with a hollow voice and seemed to be trying to keep up with the words she was speaking, as if someone was using her like a ventriloquist's dummy.

"The time is coming," 'Nadia' said. "The time when all things must be reckoned, and the spirits of the lost must be saved. They cannot be suppressed forever. The time of Ligvyr is ending and the time of Trenorjia will begin as she emerges victorious from the long night of imprisonment."

Nadia crumpled to the ground like a discarded rag doll. Everyone else vanished. I rushed to her. A couple of tourists came to see if they could help, and I realized that, apart from Nadia lying collapsed on the ground, everything was back to normal in Landane. The landscape, houses, stone circle. I thanked the couple as they helped me get Nadia to her feet. She was stirring as consciousness returned.

Her eyelids fluttered and she opened her eyes. "What happened?" Her expression was one of panic as she shrugged my hand off, along with the one from the kindly stranger. He looked startled by the rebuff.

"Thank you so much," I said to him. "I'll get her back to the hotel now. You've been very kind."

The couple exchanged looks and nodded at me. "She doesn't look well," the woman said. "Perhaps she needs to go to hospital."

"I think she'll be all right when she's had a rest," I said, mentally crossing my fingers and wishing Nadia didn't look as if she was seeing things for the first time in her life.

The couple moved off, muttering to each other. I couldn't concern myself with what they must be thinking. Right now, I had Nadia to take care of. "Let's get you back. You can have a rest and then we'll have dinner. When you feel up to it, we can talk about what just happened."

Nadia looked blankly. "What do you mean? What happened? No, nothing happened. We were having a walk. I tripped and fell over. That's all."

She shook her head and set off back across the field, leaving me in her wake, confused and determined that we would go back home. Tomorrow – it might be a couple of days ahead of schedule, but no way was this place good for her.

Ken stopped me as we entered The White Hart. Nadia carried on walking, blithely ignoring him when he greeted her.

"Is she all right?" he asked me.

I shook my head. "I wish to God I knew, Ken. So much has gone on here since we arrived, I don't know what's real and what's fantasy. I don't know if there are strange forces at work here or I'm going mad. Or maybe she is. Perhaps we all are. Maybe this place has become infected with some sort of weird virus. I have no idea. All I know for sure is that each day that passes takes her further and further away from me. She's in some kind of trance half the time. I can't explain what just happened up at the stones. I can't explain what she told me before we went up to the stones. What is it about this place I'm not getting?"

Maybe it was the desperation I felt that transmitted itself to Ken. Maybe he was simply a kind bloke who wanted to help someone who was obviously suffering. Whatever the reason, that's when everything changed.

"Okay, enough's enough. It's about time I told you. You're going to have to come with me. Oh, don't worry about Nadia. I'm sure she'll have a rest and be back to her old self by the time we get back. In any case, I'll get Jackie to look in on her in a while. I'll be back in a minute."

He was as good as his word. "Come on, I'll drive us."

"Where are we going?" I asked.

"To Moreton Landane. Where it all began."

CHAPTER TWENTY-ONE

Ken's Land Rover had seen better days. Much better. Its lack of suspension clattered, bumped, groaned and protested its way up to the lay-by where we parked prior to the one-mile walk up to Moreton Landane.

"It's good there's no one here. It would ruin the atmosphere, and we need to be able to concentrate," Ken said.

The pathway was barely wide enough for the two of us to walk abreast, but alongside Ken, I matched his long strides with my own, relieved that, while I had spent my life in a town, it was one where almost every road inclined steeply. It made for strong leg muscles to compensate for any lack of stamina on my part. "What's this all about then, Ken? You've brought me here for a reason."

"I have indeed. You needed to witness things for yourself. Without seeing and hearing what you strongly believe couldn't be happening, you would never be receptive to the incredible truth of Landane itself. Of all the hundreds and thousands of ancient and sacred sites in this country and elsewhere, Landane is special."

"And how does Nadia fit into all of this?"

"That's why we're here and why I'll also be taking you to the mound and back to the stone circle. You need to get the complete picture if you're ever going to understand."

The entrance stones of Moreton Landane loomed ahead of us as we neared them. A dark cloud enveloped the sun and I shivered. The temperature must have dropped a good few degrees in only a few seconds.

Ken must have noticed my reaction. "It does that here. It's another peculiarity of the place. It seems to generate its own microclimate, but only occasionally. Look back there."

I turned my head. A few yards behind us, the sun cast its rays over the fields of barley. I took a few steps back and it was as if someone had switched on a heater. I retraced my steps and once again the drop in temperature was palpable. "Incredible."

"Now try walking back there again but a little further this time, then look up into the sky and straight ahead."

I did as he suggested. When I had walked back maybe twenty yards or so, I looked into the cloudless blue sky and then straight ahead at the barrow. I called ahead to Ken. "The cloud's gone."

He grinned. "Now come back here. Keep looking."

I did so, keeping my gaze firmly straight ahead, but I was able to see the sky which suddenly blackened as the cloud came into view. "That's not possible. The cloud has to come from somewhere. It can't just appear from nowhere."

Ken laughed. "You tell the cloud that. As I said, it's a phenomenon of this place. It applies to the mound and to the stone circle. Things happen which defy the laws of nature and, so I'm told, physics. The trouble is it doesn't happen all the time. Only when something significant is about to take place. It doesn't necessarily have anything directly to do with the event either. Or at least I don't think so. Whenever someone has come down from some university or other to make a study, the phenomena stop. One scientist spent the whole summer staying at The White Hart. He brought goodness knows what kinds of measuring devices and so on, spent entire nights and days at the three main sites, and nothing. Absolutely nothing unusual happened. Three days after he went back…. Let's just say that was an interesting day. Nadia had come to stay with us."

"Was she here at the same time as the scientist?"

"No, I don't believe so. Let's finish our walk."

Inside the long barrow, the chill was as intense as when I was last there. Ken led me to the back of the structure.

"Now we wait," he said.

"What for?" I asked, but he put his finger on his lips.

He raised his hands. "Ancient spirit, we come in peace. We come to learn your wisdom."

Maybe my imagination was running riot in the cold and gloom of Moreton Landane, but I would swear it seemed as if a crowd was pressing close up to me. It was almost suffocating, reminding me of the last football match I had ever attended when the officials had let in far too many spectators, leading to a crush. I was in amongst it, being hemmed in on all sides and swept along, despite trying to keep my feet firmly on the ground. Such was the momentum of the crowd, I could barely breathe. I was one of the lucky ones though. Many needed hospital attention and a handful died. It led to a major scandal and I vowed I would never set foot in a stadium again.

The fear I had felt then rushed back into my mind. Panic rose in my stomach while Ken stood calmly waiting for something to happen. I wanted to get the hell out of there. Only the thought that something here might help Nadia kept me where I was. I must trust this man. But I hardly knew him. What if he meant me harm? What if he was a complete lunatic who intended to perform some sort of human sacrifice and I was to be the victim? Every second that passed brought wilder ideas into my head.

Ken spoke. "Ancient spirit. This man, Jonathan, is not from this place but he fears for the life of Nadia Gale. He desires your help. He begs your counsel. He craves enlightenment that only you can bring, as you brought to me."

A shuffling at the entrance sent my nerves jangling. At first I didn't recognize the stooped old woman who limped toward us. As she came closer, I could make out her face. "Lilian. What are you doing here?"

The old woman pointed at Ken. "He knows. Don't you, Davy?"

"*Davy?*" He couldn't be. The hirsute hippy friend of Shelly's from 1967? He would surely have to be in his seventies by now, but Ken couldn't even be sixty.

Ken lowered his hands. "Now you're going to say I don't look my age, aren't you?"

I nodded dumbly.

"Thank you, that's most kind. It's what everyone says when they find out. Not that many do. We tend to keep such things within the village, with few exceptions. Nadia being one, of course, and now you."

"But why me?" I asked.

"Because of your relationship with Nadia," Ken said, "and also because you've been granted the vision to see some of what we see. Ligvyr reveals himself to very few. If he revealed himself to you, he's done that for a purpose."

"But I thought your name was Ken."

"It was and is, but I hated it when I was young so I called myself Davy. David is my middle name. Years later, I reverted to Ken." He smiled. "Davy seemed a name more suited to a young lad than a middle-aged man."

"But Lilian, how do you fit into all this? How did you know to come here?"

"My dear, there were nine of us in Davy's group at the festival that weekend when Mick disappeared. Shelly and her friend Vicki joined us, making eleven in total. I was one of the lithe, half-stoned ones. Old enough to know better, I should add. They were nearly all younger than me. I was twenty-seven at the time. Most of them were in their late teens and I attached myself, temporarily as it turned out, to a boy called Stu. That relationship lasted as long as the festival – maybe not even that long. Mick was older of course. Older than any of us...." Her eyes registered a faraway look as if she was drawn to a distant memory. "If you see the vision again, look for the girl with red hair decorated with daisy chains. I was slim in those days. People called me Lily. I always hated Lilian anyway because it sounded ancient and old-fashioned, but I've grown into it now of course." She gave that wry smile of hers and, just for a second, I could see the young woman she must have been. "I'm here because Ken called me as you two were leaving The White Hart and told me to come up here. It works better when there are a couple of us rather than just one on their own. Ken and I don't have a lot of power, you see. In fact, you probably have more than we do. When we see the images and visions, they're always a bit shadowy and often only in monochrome. I would guess you see them as clearly as you can see us and they're in full color."

I nodded.

"Has anything happened yet, Ken? I saw the cloud."

"Not yet, Lil, not yet, but I'm hopeful. Just as you arrived, the atmosphere was changing. You noticed it too, didn't you, Jonathan?"

"Yes, it spooked me if I'm honest."

"You'll get used to it," Lilian said. "We all had our first experiences during that festival. It seemed that something about the vibe of that event set up a chain reaction of some kind. Maybe it was all the various drugs working on everyone's subconscious and bringing us together in some way that created a communication link with the power of this place. In any case, we've all had over fifty years to get used to it. You're only starting out."

"And what about Nadia?"

I didn't like the way Ken and Lilian exchanged glances. "There's something you two aren't telling me. What is it?"

"You ask him, Ken." Lilian stepped aside, rubbing her forehead as if she had a pain there.

"The truth is, we don't really know. Has she mentioned another entity to you? Apart from Ligvyr?"

"Yes. Trenorjia."

Lilian gave a little gasp.

Ken raised his hand and lowered it in a calming gesture. "How did she speak of her?"

"She said she was the opposite of Ligvyr. Pretty evil."

Lilian made a tutting noise. "Pretty evil? Oh no, she's much more than that. She'll have your soul in an instant. She'll change you so that even your own mother wouldn't recognize you. Shelly—"

"Lil, don't. We can't be sure that ever happened."

"Oh, really? You explain it then. You tell me how a perfectly lovely, levelheaded girl like Vicki could end up like.... Well, you know."

"What do you mean? What happened to her?"

"Not in here, Lilian," Ken said. "Save it for later if you must. Right now we have more urgent things to do. I'm sorry, Jonathan, but your curiosity will have to wait. We need Ligvyr's protection if we're ever going to accomplish what I have set out to do today. Lil, please take my hand. Jonathan, stay where you are."

There was no point in arguing. Ken was determined. Lilian took his hand and I stayed put.

They raised their free arms upward. Ken spoke. "Ancient spirit, we beg your counsel. Help us, protect us, guide us."

The temperature dropped still further. A low hum like the sound of electricity passing through a pylon sounded all around us.

The rumble of the multitude of pounding feet I now recognized all too well penetrated the barrow and echoed off the stone walls. It grew darker all around us, as if night was falling.

"They're here." Lilian's voice was a mere whisper. "They're all here."

I could barely make out Ken in the gloom. "I hear them," he said. "Do you, Jonathan?"

"Yes," I said quietly. "But I don't know who they are."

"Come with us," Ken said. Lilian clasped my hand and patted it with her other hand. "They won't harm you. You'll see."

The reason for the darkness soon became clear. The hundreds, no thousands, of figures were pressed in tightly, leaving barely enough space for Ken, Lilian and me to get out of the barrow.

"Who are they?" I whispered.

Ken answered. "They're no longer living. Not in the sense you and I are, at any rate. They are, for want of a better word, ghosts, spirits if you prefer. All have lived their lives at some point in the last six thousand years. Each one represents an entire generation, although, naturally, some generations lived far shorter lives than others – especially those in what we would term prehistoric ages. Each of these people was taken early, chosen by Ligvyr and passed through into his stone. That's the one everyone calls the surgeon's stone."

"But what are they doing here? Is this part of some ritual? And why is it I can only see prehistoric people?"

"That's simply because the throng is so vast and the people are pressed so tightly together," Lilian said. "The later generations are further towards the back. The thing is, as you can probably see, none of these individuals is aware of any other. As far as they're concerned, they're all alone here. They have come on their own and will return on their own."

Ken cleared his throat. "I used to know only two versions of how the story of Ligvyr and Trenorjia ended. But there is a third. From what I now understand, Ligvyr and Trenorjia had a pact. After a disastrous battle between them where many souls were lost on both sides, they came to an understanding. They would alternate generations. Ligvyr would select someone from one generation and Trenorjia the next, and so it went on for millennia until a few hundred years ago when Trenorjia decided to change the rules and build up her numbers. Secretly she began to select from each generation so that now two would pass through the stones. One would go to Ligvyr's side and the other to Trenorjia's. There's a bridge that links the two sides. It lies deep within the surgeon's stone and links it to Trenorjia's world, which is accessed through the stone next to it."

"The one that looks like a hooded monk?"

"Exactly. Trenorjia was able to conceal her activities from Ligvyr because he's unable to see into her world. Likewise, she can't see into his. But there are other ways he can sense if something is wrong. What she was doing over generations increased the numbers on her side to such an extent that the whole balance was disrupted and out of kilter. That which they call the equilibrium was becoming distorted to a catastrophic degree. If it's allowed to continue, it won't be too long before people in our world of the living begin to notice. We're talking serious catastrophe here. If you thought climate change and global warming were bad enough, wait until you see what Trenorjia is capable of. Every story you ever read about, every demonic creature you have ever heard of, is personified by Trenorjia. She can be a beautiful, desirable woman one minute, and a raging fire demon the next."

"And what about these people here?" I indicated the silent mass.

"They're waiting," Lilian said. "They're Ligvyr's chosen and they await his command."

"And he represents the force of good?"

"It's never as simple as that with Ligvyr but that's a reasonable analogy," Ken said. "Look, I would love to be able to give you hard-and-fast answers. I simply can't because they don't exist. Not that I know of anyway. All we really have to go on is folklore, tradition and legend. Most cultures seem to have their version of Ligvyr and Trenorjia."

"God and Lucifer?" I asked.

"Not exactly," Lilian said. "Ligvyr is not a creator, but Trenorjia is certainly a destroyer. Some legends speak of them as coming from the sea, either of this world or another. That's how they account for the salty smell that seems to accompany their activities."

A ripple of movement spread through the crowd.

"What's happening?" I asked.

The sky grew lighter. As I watched, the mass of people in front of me began to melt away. It felt as if someone had erased them, starting with those at the front – those from the earliest times. The wave of disappearances sped up as more and more generations were wiped out. The clothing of those remaining began to be more familiar.

"What's happening to them?" I asked.

"I don't know," Ken said.

"Nor me," Lilian said. "I've never seen this before."

More and more figures disappeared and, as they did so, the ones remaining moved closer toward us, propelled by something and not by their own volition. They didn't walk. They just *became* closer. By now thousands of them had vanished.

And then merely a handful remained.

Finally, only Grant Ford and the girl I now knew as Shelly were left. Both remained silent and locked in their own space.

"What does this mean?" I asked.

Neither of my companions answered.

A couple of minutes passed. Were we to remain here forever?

Ken broke the silence. "I'm going to try again and see if I can enlist Ligvyr's help."

Once again, he took Lilian's hand and they raised their arms skyward.

"Oh, ancient spirit, we ask for clarification and for your guidance. What are we to do? How do we know the right path to take?"

"I don't think he'll answer you."

Her voice was so unexpected, I jumped. "*Nadia.*"

She ignored me and when she spoke, her words struck dread into every fiber of my body.

"Only Trenorjia is listening now."

Ken blinked rapidly. He staggered. I caught him.

"What the hell are you talking about, Nadia?" I asked.

She laughed; the sound more chilling than her words. "This is the best you can come up with? *You* are Ligvyr's army against Trenorjia?"

"You're not Nadia," I said.

"What are you babbling about?" Nadia's voice had changed, the tone harsher and almost raucous. I stared at her and a stranger stared back.

I took a punt. "Trenorjia."

The woman in front of me opened her mouth and let out a sound that reminded me of a murder of crows. Maybe it was her version of laughter. It sounded to me like the gates of hell had just been flung open.

She collapsed in a dead faint.

I knelt down beside her. "Who is she?" I asked. "What has she turned into?"

"She's under Trenorjia's control," Lilian said. "But inside her, Nadia remains and she needs you."

Nadia stirred. Her eyelids flickered and then she opened them. She put out her hand to me and I helped her to her feet. She clung to my arm and this was Nadia, but more scared and confused than I had ever seen her.

"Jonathan. I don't know what's happening to me. I keep seeing things. Things that can't be there, but they're so real."

"What do you see now?" Ken asked her.

"Now it seems normal. I see you, Lilian and Jonathan," she said.

"Anything else?"

Nadia looked around, her eyes wide and frightened. "Nothing except the barrow and the countryside. Why? Is there something else? What am I supposed to be seeing?"

I stroked her hair off her cheeks. "Nothing at all. That's what we can see, but do you remember getting here? Do you remember what you said before you fainted? Or seeing anyone else here?"

To each question she shook her head. "All I remember is a feeling that I had to come and then I was here with no idea how I arrived. Everything else is a blur. Like a bad dream where you know something's chasing you, or is waiting for you, or…I don't know. I simply don't know."

Lilian sighed. "I've seen all this before. Shelly was the same. She used to wander around Landane in a trance half the time, talking to herself. She was sectioned twice. Tried to slit her wrists, right by the surgeon's stone once, and then the second time, she threw herself off the church roof. How she survived the fall was a mystery but it seems she fell loosely, you know, like a kitten, and she landed on a deep pile of leaves, so that must have helped to break her fall. She suffered multiple fractures and could only walk with a stick after that. She was supposed to go to university and become some fancy high-paid lawyer. At least that's what her father always said. To his dying day. Of course, losing her mind and ending up in such a state put paid to that. Didn't stop her wandering though, lost in her own world, muttering all sorts to herself. No one could understand her. It seemed to all be in some language no one could make out. Then one day, she disappeared and, like Mick, we never saw her again."

"Except I think we can be fairly sure what happened to her," Ken said, his voice breaking with emotion.

"What?"

"She was murdered. Just like Vicki," Ken said with as much venom as I have ever heard attached to any exclamation.

"How can you be so sure?" I asked. "And what happened to Vicki?"

"Trenorjia had no further use for Vicki, and Shelly was Ligvyr's. You want to be careful...." He didn't complete his sentence. He didn't need to.

"Where is Ligvyr in all this?" I asked. "You've tried to contact him and there's no sign he's even listening." My anger was growing, fueled by Ken's outburst. He seemed to have calmed down because when he spoke, he was much more rational.

"Ligvyr is not there to come when he's called. He'll know we've asked for his help and guidance. When the time is right, he will be there."

"I wish I had your confidence. In the meantime, Nadia and I will be checking out. Today."

The look of horror on Ken's and Lilian's faces was uniform.

"It won't do any good," Lilian said.

"You're locked into this now," Ken said. "Just as she is. There's nothing you can do about it."

"Maybe not, but we're still going. Come on, Nadia. Let's go."

I had momentarily forgotten I didn't have my car. Luckily it didn't seem Ken was in the mood for an argument.

"Probably best to get back," he said. "Nothing more's going to happen here, but I really wish you wouldn't go so soon. I need to show you something at the mound and there's so much more you need to know about the stones."

"Save it," I said. "We won't be back."

"Oh, but you will," Lilian said. "Nadia can't help it. She *must* come back, and if you love her, you'll come with her. That's the way it's always been. Those who love the ones affected have to carry a heavy burden."

We had almost reached the end of the path. I stopped and turned back to Lilian, who was a few feet behind me. Nadia and Ken also stopped.

"You too?" I said to Lilian.

She nodded. "Before Shelly – that is, before the festival – I was Mick's girlfriend. I loved him with a passion I thought he returned.

Then he laid eyes on Shelly and ignored me. That's why I got stoned and latched on to Stu. He was so far out of it I doubt he even noticed. It numbed the pain of seeing them together. I thought once the festival was over things would return to normal but, as we know, they didn't." Tears flowed freely down Lilian's face. Nadia went to hug her but she backed away, almost tripping over a mound of grass in the process. "Don't," she said. "I'm sorry, but please don't touch me."

Nadia looked as if Lilian had just slapped her face. "I'm…I'm so… sorry for everything that happened to you."

Lilian gazed at her steadily, almost unblinking, as if she was trying to see deep into her mind. Finally, she seemed to find the words. "You can't help it. It's your destiny as much as it's mine to always wonder what might have been if Mick hadn't become entangled in Trenorjia's web. Petra tried to warn me.…" Another tear trickled down Lilian's cheek. She ignored it.

"Who's Petra?" I asked.

Ken sighed. "She was a singer. She died at the festival."

"A girl died there?"

Ken nodded. "Terrible shame. She was only sixteen and she was one of the acts. Well, her band was. Petra's Magic Garden. She was the lead singer. Lovely voice, except when they played live and got stoned beforehand. She took everything that was on offer and then collapsed. They took her to hospital but it was no good. I didn't know you'd ever spoken to her, Lil."

"She didn't make a lot of sense. I bumped into her wandering around, half out of her brain. She called me by name. She said I wouldn't find Mick. None of us would. Trenorjia had him. Petra had seen him enter the stone. Naturally I assumed she'd had a hallucination. But then I found out I couldn't have seen Petra at all because she had been rushed to the hospital. When I saw her, she was either dead or dying. It had to be her ghost, or else I imagined it all. God knows how much stuff we inhaled that weekend. The air was so still and that smoke clung to everything."

Beside me, Nadia seemed restless. I wanted to get our things, check out and get on the road back up north as fast as possible. "Can we leave now, please? It would be good to set off and get some miles under our belts before it gets dark."

"Of course. Let's go." Ken's effort to appear normal seemed to require a lot of concentration. I wondered what he would say to Lilian when we were out of earshot. I hoped he wouldn't be too hard on her.

★   ★   ★

"I wish you'd reconsider," Ken said as he handed me the bill. "Just a couple more days. Let me take you up to the mound and show you what you weren't permitted to see when Nadia took you there."

"You said no one was to know that," Nadia said, her voice tinged with reproach.

"And I meant it, but things have gone too far now. Jonathan is involved in this. Whether it's Ligvyr's will or Trenorjia's, there's no going back."

"I'll wait outside in the car," Nadia said. "Goodbye, Ken."

"See you soon, Nadia."

She didn't reply. Instead, she wheeled her suitcase out through the bar as we watched.

"Take care of her, Jonathan," Ken said. "Lilian's right, though. She will return here. She won't be able to stay away."

"But why? Why does she have to return?"

"That's why I wanted you to come to the mound with me. There's something you can only see inside it. On the walls."

I hesitated. Should we stay? But then I thought of Nadia and how disturbed she had been ever since we arrived. I couldn't risk any more of that. Who knew how much damage she had already suffered?

"Tell me what I'm missing."

Ken shook his head. "No, you have to see it for yourself."

"Then I shall have to remain in ignorance and keep Nadia away from here in future, won't I?"

"Good luck with that," Ken said. "I only hope you don't live to regret it."

He didn't see us off. Lilian had gone straight home after wishing us well, but I could tell she was also skeptical about what the future might hold for us. I started the engine and glanced across at Nadia. She managed a wavering half-smile but her hands were clasped tightly in her lap, so tightly the knuckles showed white.

As the mound came into view she took a sharp intake of breath. "Stop, please, Jonathan. I need to get out here."

"No, Nadia, no more of this. Please."

"*Jonathan*. I *have* to do this. And you must come with me."

CHAPTER TWENTY-TWO

If you didn't know it was there, you would never have found it. Maybe the scientists with their fancy techno gear could have penetrated the surface and found a hollow, but even they wouldn't have known where to look. For Nadia, it seemed to be some sort of homing signal that drew her to the exact spot. She beckoned me to copy her actions. She leaned against the grass of Landane Mound and then we were inside. The smell of damp earth tinged with salt once again assailed my nose.

It was dark, but light penetrated from some unknown source all around us. The passage was narrow, steep-sided, and the walls covered in designs. Some looked like dragons, others like mazes; there were concentric rings and yet more were pictures. I followed close behind Nadia. The silence was overpowering, as was the sense of being observed by something nearby, so close it almost touched me. It was behind me, next to me, above me, in front of me, yet I could see nothing except Nadia as she pressed on. Even though I could make out where I was going, I still had no impression of ascending. The passageway seemed perfectly flat, although I couldn't see far enough ahead of me to know whether that would change.

"Here." Nadia broke the silence so abruptly I jumped. She turned to face me. "Look at the wall, where I'm pointing."

I peered at the depiction of a woman in late Victorian or Edwardian dress. The artist was accomplished because the face was recognizable. "It's.... But it can't be. It's Olivia Anstruther, or someone who looks a lot like her."

"Oh, it's her all right. I wasn't sure myself when I saw that photograph in the book you bought. I didn't know it was her then, of course, but I knew I'd seen her face somewhere before.

And here she is. Now look next to her." Nadia took a couple of steps forward.

"This is crazy. It's Grant Ford."

"Right again. Now we move a little further along. Who's that?"

A group of young people had been caught dancing. Some faces were turned away. Others stared out at us, as clearly as if they had been photographed. "That's Shelly and Davy, or Ken. I'm guessing the other guy is Mick. I don't know for sure about the others."

"I think that's probably Vicki and Lilian, or Lily as she was known then. If you look closely, there's another girl, off in the distance a little."

I peered more closely. "I see her. She looks stoned. Don't tell me. Petra."

"It could be, couldn't it? It would fit...and it feels right. In here." She tapped her forehead.

"Who drew these? And why?"

"I could guess and I might be right, but one thing is for sure: they're not just here to make the walls look pretty. After all, very few people ever get to see this. It's a timeline and, when we first entered, we passed lots of other pictures. I didn't bother stopping for those because we wouldn't know anyone, but both Ken and I believe the timeline was started when Landane first came into existence. Each of these pictures is of someone from each generation. Someone who was selected by Ligvyr or Trenorjia or who was inextricably linked to them so that their fates entwined."

"They're here to commemorate them in some way?"

"Maybe." Nadia didn't sound too sure, though.

The walls seemed so much closer all of a sudden. Too close, as if someone had lowered me into a coffin and were now nailing down the lid. My breath came in shallow gasps.

Nadia put a steadying hand on my arm. "You're hyperventilating. Deep breaths, Jonathan. Copy me."

I forced myself to concentrate on breathing as deeply as my lungs would allow, holding it in, then breathing out gently and fully through my open mouth. We repeated the action half a dozen times before Nadia was satisfied I had recovered.

"The best is yet to come," she said as she backed up a couple of feet and pointed at the wall.

I knew what I was going to see. It had become obvious. It didn't mean it wasn't a shock though.

Nadia and I were depicted holding hands. That in itself was strange because in all the other illustrations, even the one with the group of hippies at the festival, no one was holding hands or even touching another person.

"What does it mean?" I asked. "The fact we are holding hands and no one else is."

"I don't know, but it must mean something. Nothing here is by chance. And this depiction has only appeared since you and I first came here together."

Silence, like a heavy, damp shroud, penetrated my bones and twisted my nerve endings into a frenzy. "Can you feel that?" I asked.

Nadia looked blankly at me. "Feel what?"

"There's something in here with us. I'm sure of it."

She gave a light laugh. "But Jonathan, there's always something in here. Landane Mound is real. It's a living, sentient life force."

"That makes no sense."

"Does any of this?" She indicated the walls, the floor and ceiling. "We are moving vertically but we walk on even ground without a hint of an incline. The pictures shouldn't be here, but they are. The entrance we came through doesn't exist, but clearly it does or we wouldn't be here. Nothing makes sense in our perception of the natural world because we know so little."

"Okay, so what is this life force? Where did it come from? What's it called?"

For the first time since we had entered the mound, Nadia's expression turned to fear. "We must go. Come on. Turn around and go back. *Now*, Jonathan. Don't hang about. Get moving."

My questions would have to wait. The atmosphere of the place had turned much darker, the smell more acrid. The salt tang had grown sulfurous. I picked up the pace and half-ran down the passageway. We had walked in a straight line so there was no possibility of a wrong turn but when we came to the end, we faced a sheer wall of tightly packed chalk.

"Let me get in front. I know what to do." Nadia pushed me behind her and leaned up against the chalk. "Hold my hand. Tightly."

And then we were out. Never had fresh air smelled as sweet. Nadia tugged my hand. "Come on, let's get back to the car." She had been reluctant to leave Landane but now she seemed to have a burning desire to get out of there as fast as possible.

The tires screeched as I pulled out of the car park and onto the main road. In my rearview mirror I saw the hill recede into the distance. A large truck pulled out of a side road behind me and blocked my view of it. I wasn't sorry.

"What happened in there?" I asked eventually. "I mean apart from the impossibility of ever being in there in the first place. Something changed. The atmosphere. The smell of sulfur. And you...you couldn't get away fast enough. I've never seen you so scared."

"I was. Jonathan, you were disrespectful."

"Who to?"

"Whatever the life force is that inhabits Landane Mound. I felt danger. And, like you, I could even smell it."

"You know how this sounds?"

"Of course. But you know as well as I do that, however crazy it is, this is what we have to deal with. Ligvyr is real. Trenorjia is real. The stones have the power to transform. They're portals. Well, some of them at least. Our ancestors understood all this. They worked with it, lived with it, respected it and died with it. We must too. To fail has consequences. People have died, Jonathan. Shelly you've heard about, and then there's Vicki."

"Was she murdered?"

Nadia nodded. "She refused to believe the legends and she paid the price. Her death was ruled to be accidental, but Ken and I – and I suppose Lilian as well – know it was down to the ancient ones."

"They found her body?"

"What was left of it. Yes."

"That sounds gruesome."

"It was." Nadia sighed. "Ken told me. Her father had to identify her. The mere sight of her contorted face was enough to send him over the edge. He spent his last years in a mental institution, heavily sedated. If they tried to lower the dose of his medication he began raving again."

"I assume he died."

"Yes, and her mother passed away a few weeks later. She was an emotional wreck."

"Poor woman."

"It could have been avoided. If Vicki had obeyed the rules…if she could only have believed, like the rest of us, she would probably be alive today and her father would never have had to see his dismembered daughter."

"Dismembered? Surely the police didn't make him see all of that."

"They didn't," Nadia said. "He had to see her face though. They had reconstructed the rest of her body from the parts they found at the scene. That was all covered by a tightly fitted sheet. As the poor man was standing there, distraught and being comforted by a young police officer, the sheet somehow became unwound and fell to the floor."

"Oh my God."

"There was hell to pay, of course, but the damage was done. The thing is, that sheet was so tightly wound. No one tugged at it. No one even touched it, so how did it become loose? How did it fall off?"

"I'm guessing no one ever solved that particular riddle."

"Some of us have our theories. When Trenorjia punishes, she does a thorough job of it. I haven't told you where Vicki was found, have I?"

"No."

"It was at dawn one morning, scattered around the base of the surgeon's stone."

"But I thought that was Ligvyr's stone? Surely, he's the good guy, isn't he?"

"You wouldn't leave a dead body in your own backyard if you could implicate someone else, would you?"

"Seriously? That's human reasoning. I thought these ancient ones were above all that."

"Maybe. Needless to say, all sorts of satanic rites, black magic, sacrifice and so on were cited. The surgeon's stone is pretty significant and well known anyway thanks to that poor itinerant who was buried under it. I think they even made a film about it. Not a very good one and certainly not accurate."

"Poor Vicki."

Nadia nodded. "And poor you too."

There was a catch in her voice; a desperation that struck me like a hammer blow. "What do you mean? Poor me?"

"Don't you get it, Jonathan? Because of me, you're mixed up in this. Because of Mick, because of Shelly, because of Grant, Olivia…. There are always casualties. I expect if we searched back in time through the generations we would find countless others – people who, through no fault of their own, have been impacted by an eternal battle they haven't a hope in hell of winning."

CHAPTER TWENTY-THREE

Back in Halifax, we made decisions. Within a couple of days of getting home, to me at least, Landane and the incredible things that happened there seemed unreal, as if experienced in a bad dream. I didn't even want to raise the subject because as the days became weeks, Nadia returned to normal. Our relationship took on a new closeness, and we were ready for the next step. Landane was off the radar.

Nadia put her house up for sale and, much to our amazement, it sold within weeks. It needed plenty of work to modernize it and drag it kicking and screaming into the twenty-first century, but a young couple were keen to get started, so the offer was generous, contracts were exchanged and Nadia moved in with me. We redecorated, refurbished. She gained a promotion to manager of her own store. Life was sweet. Landane? What Landane? I dared to hope again. To look forward to our life together.

But the following spring she started to mention Landane again. I managed to put her off. I succeeded for a year but it became increasingly difficult. My job changed so that I was now working from home and that gave me increased flexibility. I distracted her with holidays abroad. A fortnight in Barbados, romantic city breaks to Rome, Venice, Paris. Eventually we even went months without one mention of the accursed Landane.

But a part of me knew it wouldn't last forever. It was once again summer, three years after we had made our last trip, and the mentioning had gone up more than a notch. Now a note of desperation had crept into her voice.

"I must go back, Jonathan. It'll be different this time. I promise."

"How?"

"Because I know more now. Lilian has been so helpful."

Over the ensuing years, Lilian's infrequent letters had been chatty, friendly. She had been conducting some research I'd rather she hadn't undertaken and had included what she had discovered of Olivia Anstruther's later life – details Nadia had lapped up with increasing relish and couldn't wait to share with me.

Every instinct told me to resist Nadia's pressure to return. Until the morning an email dropped into my inbox.

It was sent from The White Hart's account and a quick glance at who had sent it showed Ken's name. Normally I waited until the end of my working day before dealing with personal stuff but I was having trouble concentrating anyway. A particularly fussy client wanted some ideas from me to promote his jewelry business on social media, and my head simply wouldn't focus on diamonds and gold. Besides, Ken never emailed me. I had to know why he had made an exception this time.

Hi Jonathan. I trust you and Nadia are keeping well. I'm afraid I have some sad news. I have to tell you that Lilian Torrance has not been at all well and she keeps asking for Nadia. Is there any way you could come down in the next few days? I could put you up here. I wouldn't ask because I know how you were when you left last time, but we really don't hold out too much hope for Lilian and she seems to desperately want to see Nadia. She had a bad dose of 'flu in the winter and has never really recovered. At present she's at home, with carers coming in a few times a day and the district nurse visiting almost daily. But her breathing is really bad and she needs oxygen all the time now. Let me know if you can come. It would mean a lot to her as she seems quite agitated about it. Warm regards, Ken.

I considered it for a few moments but there was nothing for it. I rang Nadia at work.

"I must go to her," she said, her voice breaking. "It's my day off tomorrow and I'll add some holiday onto that. Compassionate leave. If they don't pay me, then fuck them. I have to go. You do understand, don't you, Jonathan?"

"Yes," I said, my heart heavy. "I understand, and I'm going with you. I'll tell Ken we'll see him tomorrow."

"No, tonight, Jonathan. Please."

I would have to come up with some excuse for the jeweler, but hopefully I could claw a little time back while we were down in Landane. He was a valuable client and I didn't want to lose him. The trouble was, he knew he was valuable. I rang him.

"I'm disappointed, Jonathan. I had you down for being the consummate pro. You came highly recommended and I like your work for me so far, but if you're going to be unreliable—"

"Gordon, this is the first time in ten years I have ever had to ask a client to give me a few days' grace. My partner has been summoned away owing to the terminal illness of a close relative and she needs my support." In the circumstances, I thought a little white lie was acceptable.

"Maybe she does, but *I* need those ideas from you as we agreed. Who's paying your salary? Me or her?"

A red veil came down in my mind. If the man had been standing in front of me, I would probably have lunged for him. Luckily for him – and no doubt for me as well – he wasn't. "You know what, Gordon? Go fuck yourself."

I slammed down the phone. A rush of adrenaline made me feel good and bad in equal measure. So what if I'd lost him? There were other Gordon Leinsters in the world. The trouble was, he knew most of them.

By contrast, Nadia's boss was both concerned and reasonable. "I've definitely got the rest of the week and more if I need it," she said. "How did you get on?"

"No problems," I lied. "It's a quiet time of the year for me anyway." Even quieter now I had lost one of my biggest clients.

We threw clothes and other essentials into a suitcase and locked up the house. By half past six we were well on our way back to Landane.

"I'll drive from Sarsden Services," Nadia said. I nodded. Sarsden was the halfway point. I wasn't going to argue. The implications of my altercation with Gordon Leinster were beginning to hit me. He was well known for his vindictiveness. I hardly thought he was going to take my instruction to go and fuck himself lightly.

★　　★　　★

I slept most of the way after Sarsden, waking only when Landane Mound lay ahead of us. My stomach gave a lurch but I couldn't inflict my misgivings on Nadia right now. "This looks familiar," I said, wishing I didn't feel such a strong sense of foreboding. I closed my eyes again and drifted off for a few minutes.

Ken greeted us at the bar. He looked serious and sad as he embraced Nadia and shook my hand.

"How is she?" I asked.

Ken shook his head. "I'm glad you could come so promptly," he said. "Lilian was asking for you again today, Nadia. She seemed even more agitated than usual. I don't think she has long and I believe she knows it."

"I need to go to her. Now."

"Wouldn't it be better to wait until morning?" I said. "It's half past nine now. She may be asleep."

"And she could die in her sleep tonight," Nadia said. "I'm right, aren't I, Ken?"

"I'm sorry, but, yes, the doctor said it could happen at any time."

"And there's no one with her?" I asked.

Ken shook his head. "Not overnight. The care assistants come again at around seven in the morning."

"I'm going round there," Nadia said and started out of the door.

"I'll come with you," I said. "The bags can wait."

Ken handed me a front door key. "You'll need that. To get in."

I took it. "Thanks."

I followed Nadia as she half-ran down the main street and round the corner. "Her cottage is in Rectory Close. This one." She turned down a leafy, quiet cul-de-sac of immaculately maintained thatched cottages, each with its own perfectly manicured front garden where sunflowers, roses, red-hot pokers and lupins proliferated. It was like stepping back in time to the world of Miss Marple and St. Mary Mead.

Inside Lilian's home brought us forward in time, but not by much. The furniture was teak G Plan. I recognized it from my family home growing up. All the rage in the sixties and seventies. Downstairs, the hallway and living room were immaculate. Whoever did Lilian's housework made a superb job of it.

We mounted the carpeted stairs and Nadia called out her name. The noise of a machine whirring came from one of the rooms and we followed the sound.

Lilian was propped up on pillows. A mask covering her nose and mouth was linked to a large oxygen tank which stood to one side. When she saw us, she raised her hand slightly, fluttering it in a feeble wave.

Nadia went over to her and sat on a chair next to the bed. She clasped a thin hand in hers. "Lilian?"

The old woman made a gesture to her mask. Nadia lifted it. I moved closer.

"Thank you…dear. I…." Every breath was an effort. She would need that mask back on in seconds rather than minutes.

"You wanted to tell me something," Nadia said.

"Olivia…." Again, the gasp for breath.

Nadia replaced the mask and Lilian took some shallow breaths before once more waving it away.

Nadia lifted it away from her mouth.

"Olivia. You must go to Olivia. She's waiting. Needs to tell you. Danger…all around…danger…." Lilian's eyes fluttered shut and Nadia quickly replaced the mask.

I was relieved to see Lilian take a breath, then another and another. Her eyes opened. I stood behind Nadia so she could see us both and she registered my presence with a slight smile.

She took another breath and her eyes closed.

And then there were no more breaths.

★   ★   ★

"She wasn't alone," Ken said, brushing away tears. The atmosphere in the busy bar was hushed. Respectful. Most of the customers were locals. "She wanted to see you and you were there, Nadia. And you, Jonathan. Did she say anything to you before she passed?"

Nadia blew her nose. "She told us we had to go to Olivia because she was waiting for us. But did she mean the mausoleum?"

I had forgotten, but when she said that I remembered. That fleeting impression of movement in the cathedral crypt. In the Anstruther Mausoleum. Could that have been Olivia?

"We'll go there tomorrow," I said. "Who's making the funeral arrangements?"

"That's all taken care of," Ken said. "In cases like this, the whole village rallies round. You'd be surprised how many people die alone with no living relatives, even in a small place like Landane."

I didn't say that nothing that happened in Landane would ever surprise me.

Ken handed us two glasses of white wine and rang the bell.

"Ladies and gentlemen. Please raise your glasses in a toast to Lilian Torrance, who passed away this evening. May she rest in peace."

Glasses were raised, a chorus of "To Lilian" echoed around the room and sips were taken. I let my gaze wander. Everyone was behaving as you would expect when an old and much-liked member of the community passed on. Memories were being shared by some. Others were chatting quietly.

Nadia stared into her glass. She had barely exchanged a word since we left Lilian's bedside. Her tears hadn't stopped flowing either. Maybe she really had come to think of Lilian as a surrogate relation, so my lie to Gordon Leinster hadn't been far off the mark.

And then there were Lilian's final words. At first when she had said Olivia's name I wondered if she had been confusing the two women who looked so much alike, but then she had said we must go to Olivia. It had to be the mausoleum, and I dreaded what we would find when we got there.

*   *   *

My breath misted in front of me and I was glad I had chosen to wear a jacket after all. "It's freezing down here," I said, my teeth chattering. Outside, the summer sun blazed, but the cathedral provided a cool, calm place of solace and reflection. The crypt was another case entirely. Here it was as if winter had suddenly descended. I almost expected to see icicles hanging off the gargoyles.

Our footsteps echoed on the stone flags as we made our way to the Anstruther Mausoleum. The Dean had unlocked it earlier for us but had then been called away, so we had the place to ourselves until he returned.

As Nadia pushed it open, the wrought-iron gate creaked, its hinges crying out for a dab of oil. We entered the dark room, the only light emanating from a couple of small windows high up in the far wall. I took out my phone and switched on the flashlight. Nadia did the same.

We passed the tombs of the Anstruthers who, judging by the lack of ornate and flowery epitaphs, had been a fairly unromantic lot. Then, we were faced with the one tomb that stood apart from the rest. This one was in a rose-colored marble while all the rest were white. Once again, the epitaph was simple. I read it out loud. "'Olivia Anstruther, March 8th 1880–October 23rd 1928.' I wonder who paid for this. It must have cost a packet."

Nadia shone her flashlight over the tomb, so that almost all of it was revealed. "They weren't short of money." She sighed. "So, what are we supposed to do now? Call out to her?"

The hairs on the back of my neck prickled and I soon saw why. Directly behind the tomb, a shadow moved. Nadia saw it at the same time I did. She gripped my hand. We shone our flashlights to the back of the mausoleum. The shadows were there. Undulating blackness. Occasional glimpses of what looked like faces. We watched, mesmerized, as one face took precedence over the rest. In seconds, the ghostly form of Olivia Anstruther stood before us. She was holding something. A folded-up piece of paper. Our eyes met and I knew she recognized me, although whether she saw me as Grant or my real self I couldn't tell. Her lips moved but I heard nothing. Then she bent and seemed to shove the paper behind her tomb. She stood, stepped back, and became enveloped in the shadows once more. They faded and disappeared.

Nadia and I continued to stand there, pointing our flashlights at the back of the mausoleum. When it seemed clear that the vision was not going to reappear, I tapped Nadia on the shoulder. "Come on," I said.

Behind the tomb, I bent and reached around the marble, shining my flashlight as I did so. In a few seconds, my search was rewarded. My fingers touched paper and I tugged it out of its hiding place. It was old, yellowed with age and the damp of the crypt. I unfolded it. Nadia leaned over my shoulder.

It was a letter dated October 20th, 1928 and it was from Olivia.

My darling Grant,

I know I don't have much time left. Your sister has been a wonderful companion to me but even she won't believe what I know to be true. The girl – Shelly – came to me again tonight. She told me to prepare. Ligvyr is waiting and he will take me. So strange she should come from the future. It's something she doesn't understand either. But you would, Grant, my darling. You, more than anyone. You who live through the ages, never knowing your true destiny. I understand that now.

I have asked Cynthia to hide this note behind my tomb. It's all ready for me. Whether she will do me this small service I cannot know. If she doesn't, I can only hope that when the time is right, Ligvyr will show me how it can be delivered to the one who must receive it.

Trenorjia grows stronger with each generation. She must be stopped.

Until we meet again, within the stone.

Your loving,

Olivia

I stared at the note for a few more seconds before refolding it and tucking it in my inside jacket pocket. "What do you make of that?"

Nadia looked shaken. "I want to get out of here. Now." She was halfway out of the mausoleum before she finished her sentence. I certainly wasn't going to argue with her.

In our haste to get out, we almost knocked the Dean over. We both apologized and he smoothed down his cassock.

"It was so cold down there, we needed to get back out into the sunshine," I said. Nadia nodded.

"I hope you found what you were looking for?" he asked.

"Yes, we did. Thank you for letting us in," I said. What the man must have thought to see us scurrying out of there as if a demon was behind us, I really don't know. Frankly, I had other things on my mind.

Back in the car, I started the engine with shaking hands.

"Olivia and Cynthia Ford became friends after Grant disappeared, didn't they?" Nadia said. "But I think we can assume Cynthia didn't do as Olivia requested and put the note behind the tomb."

"Or maybe she did and that was simply Olivia's way of drawing our attention to it."

"It's strange she should mention Shelly. Assuming the note is authentic and there's no reason to assume otherwise, she seems to travel backward and forward through time whenever she chooses, or someone else chooses for her."

"But why pick now? Why is now the right time for that letter to be delivered and why should it be delivered to us?"

"Not us. You, Jonathan," Nadia said, as we pulled into the car park at The White Hart. "I saw Olivia, she was looking directly at you when she hid the note there. I saw her lips move and I heard one word. *Jonathan.* She spoke your name."

216 • CATHERINE CAVENDISH

CHAPTER TWENTY-FOUR

I was still reeling from this when we sat with cups of coffee in the bar. It was a quiet time and Ken came over to join us with his morning cup of tea.

"What have you two been up to this morning?" he asked.

"You're not going to believe this," Nadia said.

I took out the letter from my jacket pocket and unfolded it before handing it to Ken. His eyes grew wider as he read.

"She mentions Shelly. That means everything I believed about Landane is true. They can manifest through the stones at any point in time."

"Leaving that to one side," I said. "There's still the matter of timing. Olivia writes that Trenorjia is becoming too powerful and must be stopped. She says Ligvyr is coming for her, so she's an important piece of this infernal jigsaw."

Nadia nodded. "Grant Ford and Jonathan could have been twins. I know that what we saw in the mausoleum was Olivia's ghost. She put the note behind the tomb or maybe she simply directed us to it."

"You actually saw Olivia's ghost and she did that?" Ken's voice contained more than a note of awe.

"Yes," Nadia replied. "And as she was about to position the note, she looked directly at Jonathan and mouthed his name."

"You must have lip-read that because I heard nothing," I said.

"I heard it as clearly as I can hear you now," she said, her voice reproachful as if I had accused her of lying.

I let it drop.

Nadia continued, directing her comments solely at Ken. "It's possible she thought Jonathan was Grant, but what if she didn't?

What if she knew exactly who he was? I believe she did and that's why she used his name."

"So why didn't I hear it? I couldn't make out what she was saying. I know I don't lip-read, but it didn't look like 'Jonathan' to me."

"What did it look like?" The hostility in her voice was palpable and, to add insult to injury, Ken was looking at me strangely as well.

I replayed the moments back in my mind, but it was no good. "I don't know. It didn't seem like any exact word, or words."

"I know what I heard, and what I heard was your name. 'Jonathan', she said. The note was meant for you to find. If I had been there alone, I don't believe she would have manifested herself to me."

"Let's assume for a moment that you're correct. What am I supposed to draw from this? That I'm a reincarnation of Grant who, according to her, lives on from age to age?"

"Maybe," Nadia said, her eyes never leaving mine.

"Hold on now," Ken said. "Don't let's get too far off down that road. Grant living from age to age could also be like Shelly's ability to appear in the early nineteen hundreds, and Jonathan's physical resemblance could be a pure coincidence."

Nadia gave a half-laugh. "Where Landane is concerned, I'm not a fan of coincidences. It seems to me that here, of all places, nothing happens by chance. Everything is ordered, maybe even preordained. I think it's perfectly plausible that Jonathan is Grant reincarnated and that means he has a special purpose here. A link stronger than anything I have. Maybe the only reason I've been drawn to this place is simply because at some stage in time, I was meant to bring you here, Jonathan. Of course, if that's true, I've fulfilled my purpose."

Was that jealousy she was feeling? Or maybe genuine fear for her future. And then there was Ken again. It felt as if he was suddenly waking up to something. I wanted to question him on it but, if I was wrong, I would sound at worst confrontational and at best paranoid. I would start doubting my own shadow next.

As for Nadia, her expression was too closed for me to make anything out for certain. I plowed on regardless and covered her hand with mine in what I hoped was a reassuring gesture. "You're the one the magic happens to here. You're the one who can connect with the surgeon's stone."

She fixed me with a hard stare and pulled her hand from mine before folding her arms in a defensive gesture. "But once I had shown you how, you could do it yourself without any further help from me. It was the same at Landane Mound. I could pass through into it. Ken could pass through into it. No one else could. Maybe Lilian could, but I don't know if she ever did. Then you came along and I had a hunch. I blindfolded you to keep my promise but there was always a chance you wouldn't be permitted to enter the mound. As we know, you did. Now, if you wish, I know you can come and go at will. You can see the secrets of the barrow. Only a handful of us in any generation are permitted to do that. You saw beyond the back wall, into the realm of the past."

"I thought he might," Ken said.

My palms sweated. Seeing the two of them sitting there staring at me, I suddenly felt fear. Nadia wasn't concealing a glare of open antagonism. Ken wore a look almost of contempt. I read hatred in that look and in the curl of his lip. The previously affable 'mine host' had melted away. I wanted to get away from them both and from Landane as if my life depended on it. Maybe it did.

"It's no good, Jonathan," Ken said. "It's too late. You can't escape what is to come. It's your destiny."

★   ★   ★

Maybe Ken had slipped something into my coffee or perhaps it was the strange forces that were constantly at work in Landane, but I remember nothing until I came to in a dark place that smelled of damp earth and rot. Slivers of daylight penetrated through chinks in the stone walls. I was sitting, propped up against a cold, damp wall. I called out but no one answered except my own voice.

Where was I? Something about it made me think of the long barrow of Moreton Landane, or maybe this could be within a stone in the circle. Of the two, the former seemed the more likely. If I was there, I had to be at the back of the barrow, beyond the wall.

A sudden movement to my left told me I was not alone. The voice confirmed it.

"Good afternoon, Mr. Warner." The woman moved into view. I recognized her instantly and struggled to my feet.

"Miss Anstruther."

"Indeed. This is a strange place in which to finally meet. But these are strange circumstances."

I couldn't help staring at her. She was as real, as substantial as I was, yet she couldn't be. She had been dead for a hundred years.

"I can see you are as I was when I first realized what was happening to me."

"I don't think I'm at that point yet, Miss Anstruther. I'm still at the point of not understanding what the hell is going on here or who I can trust. As far as I'm concerned, and forgive me for being so blunt, you're a ghost." A sweet smell of gardenias wafted toward me as she moved closer. "I shouldn't be able to...smell your perfume."

She smiled. "First of all, please call me Olivia. Thrust together as we are, there is precious little need for formalities. You say I am a ghost and I have to take your word for that. You see, I know time must have passed. Quite a lot of time judging by your appearance and your words, but to me, my...experiences...took place mere days or perhaps weeks ago."

"I saw you...in Charnford Cathedral."

"Yes, and you took my note as you were meant to."

"You spoke to me but I couldn't hear you. Only my girlfriend, Nadia, heard you call my name."

Olivia gave a wry smile and cast her eyes upward. "I didn't call your name, Jonathan. She didn't hear me say anything. Haven't you worked that part out yet? No, I suppose it's too soon."

"How did Nadia get so mixed up in this? When we're at home she's the woman I fell in love with, but when we come here, it's as if she becomes someone else."

"That's because she does. The sad part is that she doesn't know it. Or I should probably say she didn't know it. I'm guessing she's fairly aware by now. I expect Ken will have seen to that. He is surely aware by now of his role."

"I thought he was her friend. Maybe even my friend as well, but just now, in the pub...."

"Just now? Are you sure it was just now?"

She was right. I couldn't be sure of anything, could I? Only that Olivia and I were trapped in this place together. "Why are we here? What's going to happen to us?"

"They have plans for us. Ken knows the legends and he knows now that they are, in part at least, accurate."

"Ligvyr and Trenorjia take souls. But what do they take them for?"

"They maintain their strength through the power of the human soul."

"Like some sort of cannibalism?"

"You can call it that if you wish but it's less barbaric than that. It's a spiritual symbiosis, but it does have its downside and that is because the relationship is something of a two-way transaction. Ligvyr imparts something of himself into his people and Trenorjia imparts something of herself into her people."

"Slavery, then. It sounds no better than that. These people have been taken against their will or without their knowledge or consent. I'd call that enslavement."

Olivia nodded. "I can see that as a valid argument. But you said 'these people'. Don't you realize you and I are among them?"

"What?" As my voice continued to echo, a subtle change to our surroundings began. Tendrils of light snaked their way up the far wall. Olivia took a few steps closer until we were standing side by side.

She took my hand and gave it a gentle squeeze. "Don't be scared, Jonathan." Her voice was soft and comforting. "It won't be long now. We're going to join the others."

CHAPTER TWENTY-FIVE

Nadia

Now – and Then

"Is it time, Ken?"

He nodded.

Two years had passed since we took Jonathan up to Moreton Landane. Two years when he had been left in limbo. My heart had been heavy. The feelings I had for Jonathan were strong and real; the only time in my life when I really fell in love, only to find that our relationship, as with everything else in my life, had been preordained. Olivia and Grant. Shelly and Mick. Nadia and Jonathan. It had taken all this time for us to piece that much together.

Except it wasn't even as simple as that.

It was a bitter January day, the wind howled over the plain as Ken and I made our stumbling way across the field to Moreton Landane. We had chosen that place away from the stone circle deliberately. Here at least, we were away from the two stones that held the greatest of Ligvyr and Trenorjia's power and from the circle that enhanced it. It wasn't a perfect solution and couldn't last much longer, but it was something until we were ready to move on and do what needed to be done. I had to keep Jonathan as safe as possible, and Olivia needed a place of sanctuary. The cathedral didn't hold enough of the old power to keep her safe from Trenorjia. If Trenorjia ensnared Jonathan, she would possess Grant and ultimately Olivia and would directly threaten me on a level I couldn't trust myself with. It would work the same if she got to Olivia first. I was too closely connected and my spirit entwined so tightly with theirs.

Avoiding the main entrance, Ken and I continued along the outside of the barrow, keeping close to the grassy mound that hugged the shape of the structure. At the far end we turned and faced it.

Ken took my hand and we pressed ourselves close to the grassy hump. A loud buzzing intensified as the natural forces combined to transform the solid bank into a transparent entrance that enveloped us and drew us in.

Olivia and Jonathan were there waiting as I knew they would be. Tears pricked my eyes at the sight of him. The sadness and incomprehension in his eyes tore at my being. I could never explain, and he would never understand. If only our lives could have been those of normal people, there would be no Landane. Only our life together in Yorkshire.

But we weren't normal people.

Our lives were irrevocably tied to the lives of the people of Landane – most of whom carried on their daily grind unaware of the real power that lay within their ancient monuments. Even I had only recently realized the extent of it and how it changed and formed me. I knew it was the same for Ken and for all of us, past and present, who had been caught up in the eternal battle between Ligvyr and Trenorjia.

"We must wait, Ken," I said.

He nodded. "But we can't stay here much longer. There's work to do."

As he spoke those words, someone else emerged from the shadowy recesses at the far end of the barrow. Grant stepped forward and stood next to Olivia. She was unaware of him until he touched her hand. She turned and her eyes glistened with tears. "Grant," she murmured. He held her close to him.

"Enough!"

I didn't think Ken needed to sound so harsh.

"We are all met. It is time," he said, less gruffly.

Moreton Landane melted away and we were in the circle, facing the surgeon's stone. Only Ken and I seemed aware of the extreme cold that penetrated our skin and clawed its way into our bones. I bit down hard to stop my teeth from chattering. Beside me, I sensed Ken doing the same.

One by one we stepped forward and the stone accepted us, until we were all assembled in Ligvyr's chamber. I led the way. Ken brought up the rear. Around us, the crystal glittered, its brittle glow doing nothing to warm me.

We stopped, facing the pathway that led to Trenorjia's realm deep within the hooded monk stone. She was standing a few feet back from the entrance. In front of her stood Mick and Shelly.

Slowly, Trenorjia advanced toward the edge of her domain. Her voice carried over to us as if she was standing right next to us and not some yards away.

"You want to trade souls, Nadia."

I took a deep breath. "I do."

"You know I have more than Ligvyr. I can do as I please. And where is he? Why is he not here begging for my cooperation?"

"You know that my soul is worth countless others. You know I was born of…. You know I was born of you and of Ligvyr."

I spoke those words. They issued from my mouth but my brain had not formulated them. At that moment I had no idea where that conclusion had come from, but suddenly it was as if the last pieces of the jigsaw fell into place. A veil lifted from me and I saw the whole picture clearly for the first time.

I let my mind open up and time flashed back in an instant. Millennia. Back and farther back until the time before time. The visions took me with them.

Under my bare feet, I felt tough, springy grass. In front of me, a tall man with silvery-white hair, wearing a white robe, stared at me with an unutterable sadness in his blue eyes. And, in that second, I knew. I realized what I had denied my entire life. And I knew it was true.

I wasn't spawned by the people I knew as my parents. My father had been right. A cuckoo had been planted in their nest. I belonged to Ligvyr and Trenorjia. I was indeed their offspring but I was more than that. Their blood flowed through my veins and created in me a synergy – a power greater than theirs.

They feared no one. But they feared me. Trenorjia had wanted to trade my soul, but this would never happen now. I had finally come of age – and their power had passed.

And in that moment, Ligvyr appeared. He stood silently next to me, facing Trenorjia. When I turned to look at him, he met my gaze and lowered his head and I sensed his ultimate mortality.

I had an important job to do. Trenorjia had taken too many souls. It was up to me to redress the balance. It would take time, but the biggest of all revelations showed me time was in my hands. I realized that Ken's soul had been trapped, Jonathan had barely escaped with his, while Grant and Mick had lingered, caught in the void between Ligvyr and Trenorjia. As for poor Petra…. I found her soul drifting, anchored to no one and nothing, and set her free. Instantly, she became enveloped in a golden light and I knew she was finally at peace.

In the corner of my eye, I saw Vicki, wide-eyed. Lost. Uncomprehending of what was happening or where she was. Alone, but staring at Ken with a mixture of recognition and a fear that bothered me. I couldn't let it distract me. For now, that would have to keep.

Of all of them, Grant's spirit had been the one to resist the dark side for the longest time. Now he could reunite with his spiritual twins, Mick and Jonathan. To give them back their souls and lives, I must reach back in time and take back all those earlier incarnations of them. Their past manifestations must all be integrated into one body, their souls joined to make one. Vicki had never lived her life. Now she would have a chance. I felt Shelly's spirit move within me and join with Olivia…and the Nadia I had been. Yes, even I was to be rejoined. Would there be a chance for me to live a life others took for granted?

Opposite Ligvyr, the now-shadowy figure of Trenorjia moved. She drew her robes around her and the scarlet faded, the gold tarnished. I raised my hand and met her still-defiant gaze with my own. She drew back graying lips, feral-like over her teeth. Her voice hissed like a box of angry snakes. "You think you know so much. The stones may be yours now, but you will discover, you are no match for what lies beyond. The power that created all this is far greater than you could ever aspire to be."

My heart soared. I didn't care what she said. She was beaten. Within me, a power I had been born for surged. It raced through my veins and filled my body with strength and passion. Ligvyr and Trenorjia faded before my eyes. In their place, two massive sarsens rose on the empty landscape. One shaped like a half-diamond and the other like a hooded monk. The past and the present of this timeless landscape merged and became one.

I closed my eyes.

I was the future now. Their time was done.

Fear her now, fear the queen,
As in her stone she reigns serene,
Trading souls is her life's work,
A fight for victory she'll never shirk,
Run from her if you value your life,
Hide if you can, the danger's rife,
And your soul you never more shall own,
It goes to Trenorjia and the Magical Stone.
'Trenorjia and the Magical Stone'
Petra's Magic Garden

AFTERWORD

Any resemblance between the fictional Landane depicted in this story and the actual Neolithic complex of Avebury in Wiltshire is purely intentional.

When most people think of ancient circles of standing stones, the familiar presence of Stonehenge immediately springs to mind, yet, some twenty-five miles to the north, the far larger and more significant concentric circles of Avebury weave their enigmatic spell. In fact, they set the scene for the entire landscape which also encompasses (among others) the somewhat surreal, man-made Silbury Hill (here rendered as Landane Mound) and West Kennet Long Barrow (Moreton Landane). This part of Wiltshire is a microcosm of life in those faraway prehistoric times of which we know so little. But once the magic grabs you, it hangs on relentlessly. At least, that's what happened to me.

Walking around the site of the Avebury circles, you will come across a couple of stones you will recognize from my story. The real-life Barber Stone has a distinctive half-diamond shape attributed in *The Stones of Landane* to the surgeon's stone, and stands right next to one that, viewed from a particular angle, resembles a hooded monk.

Many years ago (far more than I wish to admit to at this stage in my life), I read a book by eminent archeologist Aubrey Burl called *Prehistoric Avebury*. Once I had devoured that, I had to go there. I had already visited Stonehenge and been suitably impressed. Back in those days you could wander among the towering stones, which made you feel you were in a cathedral or temple of some kind. But once I set foot in Avebury, I was hooked. You need to use your imagination more in order to get a feel of how it must have looked before it was so vandalized by successive generations who believed the very existence of the stones should be erased from the face of the Earth as the devil's handiwork.

Dear old Aubrey Burl came to my rescue, recreating what life could have been like for our long-dead ancestors. One thing always eludes us though. Despite all our best and most informed guesswork, we still cannot say with any certainty why those ancient engineers, working with such primitive tools, took such time, labor and effort to construct such magnificent monuments. Not merely the stone circles, but all of them – including Silbury Hill. This was long thought to have contained the burial of the legendary King Zel, yet excavations have discovered no trace of any burial of any kind. We are still pretty much flummoxed, but no trip to Avebury is complete without a stop-off to view this magnificent, mysterious structure and not far away, West Kennet Long Barrow is worth the walk from the main road. If you're there on your own, it is suitably spooky with incredible acoustics.

No mention of the ancient history of this area is complete without including my favorite archeologist – Dr. Phil Harding of Wessex Archeology, who is a TV personality in his own right (*Time Team* in particular), best known for his old, battered field hat, rich West Country accent, phenomenal knowledge of archeology and ability to reach near-orgasmic enthusiasm over a well-knapped piece of flint. While I didn't model Professor Scott on him in any way, I am sure the two of them would have had much to discuss. You can catch Phil on YouTube and, if you're lucky, in person. He lives and works in Salisbury and regularly gives talks on aspects of local archeology.

The Stones of Landane is by no means the first time Avebury has inspired a work of fiction. There are many examples, but to cite one: *Children of the Stones*, a British TV series made in the mid-1970s, was filmed there and well worth a second watch (or first if you weren't around the first time it was shown).

All these years after my first visit there, Avebury still has the power to transport me back over the millennia to those far-off days when our ancestors lived in, and worked, the land around present-day Avebury. However many stone circles and prehistoric monuments I have visited since, none can exert quite the pull of that mystical place whose secrets it chooses firmly to keep to itself.

Catherine Cavendish
Southport, 2024

ACKNOWLEDGMENTS

Julia Kavan, my trusted friend and fellow writer, confirmed the error of my ways with an earlier ending to this story. This is why you have been spared the improbable and unnecessary 'sliding doors' chapter. Believe me, you should be as relieved as I am. Thank you, Julia. I don't know what I was thinking but I can always rely on you to cast a blanket of common sense over my wilder and more chaotic ramblings.

Don D'Auria – my wonderful editor – was spared that particular exercise in folly as I had already deleted the offending three thousand or more words before I sent the completed story to him. My continuing thanks and appreciation go to him. May we continue for many more years to come. Also on the editing front, huge thanks to Mike Valsted, who must be sick of typing the word 'echo' by now! I try to eliminate them before they get to you but the pesky little things keep reappearing. Rather like moles on your lawn.

Nick Wells and all the lovely people at Flame Tree Press are such a joy to work with, and a pleasure to meet, when our paths cross either in person or online, so please accept my sincere appreciation.

And, of course, massive thanks go to you. You're reading this book and I am grateful for your attention. I hope you enjoyed it and will spread the word that horror isn't all slash, gore, and flying body parts. It isn't just about vampires, werewolves (or 'were-anything-else' for that matter) or zombies, although, of course, there is nothing wrong with any of those. Horror is a rich tapestry and I am happy to be able to add my few stitches here and there.

I hope to see you again soon – where darkness lies and shadows move…

Catherine Cavendish
June 2024

ABOUT THE AUTHOR

Catherine Cavendish first started writing when someone thrust a pencil into her hand. Unfortunately, as she could neither read nor write properly at the time, none of her stories actually made much sense. As she grew up, however, they gradually began to take form and, at the tender age of nine or ten, she sold her dolls' house, and various other toys, to buy her first typewriter – an Empire Smith Corona. She hasn't stopped bashing away at the keys ever since, although her keyboard of choice now belongs to her laptop.

The need to earn a living led to a varied career in sales, advertising and career guidance, but Cat is now the full-time author of a number of supernatural, ghostly, haunted house and Gothic horror novels, novellas and short story collections, including: *Those Who Dwell in Mordenhyrst Hall, The After-Death of Caroline Rand; Dark Observation; In Darkness, Shadows Breathe; The Garden of Bewitchment; The Haunting of Henderson Close; The Darkest Veil;* and *The Crow Witch and Other Conjurings.*

Find out more on her website: catherinecavendish.com.